Valentine's Day
COLLECTION

A TIMELESS Romance ANTHOLOGY

Valentine's Day COLLECTION

Six Romance Novellas

Janette Rallison
Heather B. Moore
Jenny Proctor
Annette Lyon
Heather Tullis
Sarah M. Eden

Mirror Press

Copyright © 2017 by Mirror Press, LLC
Print edition
All rights reserved

No part of this book may be reproduced in any form whatsoever without prior written permission of the publisher, except in the case of brief passages embodied in critical reviews and articles. This is a work of fiction. The characters, names, incidents, places, and dialogue are products of the authors' imaginations and are not to be construed as real.

Interior Design by Cora Johnson
Edited by Anna DeStefano and Lisa Shepherd

Cover design by Mirror Press, LLC
Cover Photo Credit: Shutterstock #276925928
Cover Photo Copyright: Syda Productions

Published by Mirror Press, LLC
http://timelessromanceanthologies.blogspot.com

ISBN: 978-1-947152-58-8

MORE TIMELESS ROMANCE ANTHOLOGIES

Winter Collection
Spring Vacation Collection
Summer Wedding Collection
Autumn Collection
European Collection
Love Letter Collection
Old West Collection
Summer in New York Collection
Silver Bells Collection
All Regency Collection
Annette Lyon Collection
Sarah M. Eden British Isles Collection
Under the Mistletoe Collection
Mail Order Bride Collection
Road Trip Collection
Blind Date Collection
Happily Ever After Collection
A Yuletide Regency Collection
Kissing A Billionaire Collection

Table of Contents

A Brush with the Law
by Janette Rallison

Every Occasion
by Heather B. Moore

Hold Your Breath
by Jenny Proctor

The Ultimate Bachelor Challenge
by Annette Lyon

Deal Breakers
by Heather Tullis

Hey, Helen!
by Sarah M. Eden

A Brush with the Law

By Janette Rallison

One

It was going to be another great Valentine's Day—at least for someone else. For Bethany Daniels it was another work day—one where her shoulders ached and she was splattered in paint.

She took a step back from her mural, inspecting the work she'd done over the last week: violin-playing angels serenaded their music above Mr. and Mrs. Dupont's bed, while a sunrise hovered near the ceiling, sending pale golden rays across the wall. Beautiful. It was moments like this that Bethany was glad she'd become an artist, despite what her parents thought of that decision. She'd been able to match the picture of *Song of the Angels* so well that William-Adolphe Bouguereau himself would have been impressed. Or sued her for copyright infringement, if he'd still been alive and of a litigious mind. At any rate, Mr. Dupont was going to love it. Hopefully *Mrs.* Dupont would love it just as much. The mural was to be a post-Valentine's Day surprise for her when the couple got back from Paris next Monday.

Right now the Duponts were probably off at the Eiffel tower, snapping selfies—or doing whatever wealthy, jet-setting people did on Valentine's Day. Bethany wasn't likely to ever be one of those people. She was the sort whose friends set her up on pity dates so she wouldn't be completely alone on the one day a year dedicated to romance.

Technically, at the time her best friend, Hannah, had told Bethany about her matchmaking plans, Hannah hadn't called it a pity date; but that's clearly what it was. Now Hannah was celebrating her first anniversary—yes, she'd gotten married on Valentine's Day—by taking a Caribbean cruise. Two of their other friends had decided it was the perfect vacation to escape the cold, wet Seattle weather, so they'd signed up with their husbands, and the trip had turned into one big love excursion. But Bethany had needed to finish this mural, and more importantly, she didn't have anyone to go with.

Hannah had lectured Bethany about working too hard and told her that if she didn't put herself out there, she was never going to find the right man. Then Hannah said that her husband, Greg, had an awesome friend she should meet. James was pre-law and supposedly to-die-for gorgeous. Which was how Bethany had ended up with a blind date scheduled for tonight. Sometimes it was easier to give into Hannah than to fight her edicts.

Bethany took a few more steps backward, giving the mural another critical once-over. The angels had just the right amount of rosiness to their cheeks, the clouds were ethereal, and the lighting had the right mixture of illumination. She'd even managed to paint the Duponts' Siamese cat—obviously their surrogate child—into the scene, without the effect seeming too kitschy. Everything was perfect, except for the opposite wall. She'd run out of the sky-blue paint she'd used to transform the rest of the bedroom and had forgotten to stop by the store to buy some more on the way to the Duponts' townhouse.

Also, she really should paint over that pigeon she'd doodled near the window. She'd created it on a whim—a startled bird that had apparently wandered into the room and was now looking around in confusion. The Duponts probably wouldn't appreciate her humor. Few people did.

She wiped her hands on a rag and glanced at her phone to check the time. It was nearly three, and she still had an appointment with a client to discuss faux finishing a room to look like marble. Then she was meeting James at the Santorini Grill at six forty-five. Still, she'd told Mr. Dupont she would finish painting today. No one would be around to let her in tomorrow. Marta, the Duponts' housekeeper, was going away with her husband for the weekend. She'd already poked her head inside the room several times to check her progress.

Bethany would just have to hurry to the store and buy more paint so both of them could head off to their respective fates. She could be to the store and back in half an hour. Wrapping up the mural itself wouldn't take more than ten minutes. Then she could be done with her other appointment by five, which would give her plenty of time to go home and make herself presentable for Pre-law James.

She grabbed her purse, headed down the three-story staircase, and yelled over her shoulder that she'd be back in a few minutes.

Marta, in a less than happy voice, called out, "I need to leave by four." She was a heavy-set older woman with jowls that made her look like she was perpetually frowning.

"I'll hurry," Bethany promised.

That promise, as it turned out, was what doomed her.

The line for paint was three people long. Which in and of itself wouldn't have been so bad, if the second woman in line hadn't been certain that her paint was mixed wrong and made the guy redo her order. Then the cashier had some sort of problem ringing up Bethany's paint and had to call a manager. By the time Bethany got to her car, it was twenty minutes to four. She'd have to rush, or she'd be inconveniencing Marta by making her stay later.

Bethany sped out of the parking lot and down the street, going as fast as traffic would allow. When a light in front of her turned yellow, she decided yellow was close enough to green on the color wheel to justify flooring the gas instead of slowing down.

She was almost to the intersection before the light turned red. No car crashes ensued, so everything should have been fine. But no. A set of colored lights flicked on from one of the cars lined up across the street.

How had she not noticed that a police car was sitting there? She moaned, pulled over into a nearby gas station, and waited for her impending doom. The patrol car pulled in behind her. A few moments later, an officer exited and sauntered toward her car.

She rolled down her window, letting the cold air seep inside while she watched his approach. Did he look like the compassionate type? Probably not. He was in his late twenties. Tall and broad-shouldered. One of those guys who moved with power and confidence. He had short, blond hair and the kind of chiseled features that landed men in those Hot Cops Calendars. The guy was most likely perpetually Mr. October. He wasn't the sort who would be moved by a doe-eyed eyelash flutter.

And besides, even if he could be swayed by a pretty girl, she wasn't that girl right now. Bethany's gaze moved from his approaching figure to her own reflection. She was dressed in a splattered sweatshirt. Her long, strawberry blonde hair was pulled into a ponytail, and she wore only a hint of makeup. Blue flecks dotted her entire body, and white paint was streaked across her cheek. She rubbed at the spot, trying to remove it.

The police officer leaned toward her window. "Ma'am, do you realize you ran a red light back there?"

She sent him an apologetic smile. "Um . . . that depends. Will you go easier on me if I knew, or if I didn't?"

He looked at her patiently. "Ma'am, you endanger your life and others' when you disregard traffic lights. People die every day in car accidents."

He was being a bit dramatic about a light that had been

almost yellow—at worst, a pale shade of red. "The intersection was clear," she pointed out. "The Grim Reaper was nowhere in sight."

His blue eyes ran over her with an unspoken sigh as though he didn't think she was fully grasping his point. "Look, you're young, so I'm guessing you have a lot to live for, don't you?"

She tapped her fingers against the steering wheel. "Oh, I don't know. It's Valentine's Day, and all I've got going is a blind date. Seems like a good time to throw caution to the wind." Some people got quiet when they were nervous. Bethany wasn't one of them. She clamped her lips together, and then added, "I'm just kidding, officer. I'm sorry I ran the light."

He raised an eyebrow at her skeptically. "You're on your way to a blind date dressed like that?"

She shrugged. "If the guy is blind, it shouldn't matter what I wear." She blinked innocently. "That's what a blind date means, right? I don't know; I don't get set up a lot."

He smiled politely at her joke. "I bet. Can I see your license and registration?"

She handed both over. He nodded and returned to his car. She rolled up the window and slumped into her seat. *A good time to throw caution to the wind.* Honestly, what was wrong with her? She knew better than to joke around with police officers. They no doubt had their senses of humor surgically removed when they entered the police academy.

She glanced in the rearview mirror to see what he was doing. He sat in the car next to his partner. Would having another officer around make this process go faster?

Bethany impatiently watched the minutes tick by on her dashboard clock. *Three forty-five. Three fifty.* How long did it take to run her license? She didn't have much of a record. She'd only ever received one other speeding ticket, and that had been when she was eighteen. Did tickets from seven years ago stay on your record? *Three fifty-five.* Oh, and there had been that unfortunate brush with the law when she'd been in college and rushing a sorority. The freshmen had been sent to steal the opposing football team's mascot costume. That assignment really should have been Bethany's first clue that the sorority life wasn't all it was cracked up to be. The lot of them ended up down at the police station, and Bethany had her mugshot taken while wearing the cougar mascot outfit. The policewoman wouldn't let Bethany keep the head on for the photo, which was too bad since it would have been a much better picture that way.

Four o'clock clicked by on the dashboard clock. Had Marta left the Duponts' townhouse and locked up? Bethany had no way to contact her and tell her what was happening. Mr. Dupont's was the only phone number Bethany had, and she couldn't call him in France. It was midnight there.

Mr. Hot-Cop October strolled back to her car window. She rolled it down so he could hand her a piece of paper along with her license and insurance card.

"I'm letting you off with a warning this time." The corner of the guy's lips lifted in a suggestion of a smile. "But only because I'm no stranger to blind dates. I can't bring myself to add to your suffering today." His gaze went over her again. "Have fun painting the town. You're definitely dressed for the occasion."

She tucked her license into her wallet. "Thanks. Truly. I promise I'll be more careful."

His smile grew, blue eyes flashing. "And if the guy is blind . . . Well, it's a tough call, but don't let him do the driving."

Apparently, she'd been wrong about cops having no sense of humor. She'd gotten the one officer in town with comedic ambitions. "Yeah. Thanks again."

She didn't reach the townhouse until ten minutes after four. Marta had just walked down the front steps. The woman glared when she saw Bethany getting out of her car.

"Sorry I'm late," Bethany said. "I was hurrying back when a police officer pulled me over." She lifted the quart-sized can of paint. "It will only take me ten minutes to finish the job."

Marta pressed her lips together in a frown. "I already locked up. I told you I had to leave at four."

Bethany held up a hand, pleading. "I still have to finish one wall. The Duponts won't be happy if they come home and it's not done."

The woman's frown didn't change. "My husband won't be happy either. I'm already leaving ten minutes after I was supposed to because I was waiting for you."

"Sorry," Bethany said again. "I can come back tomorrow, if someone will let me in."

"It's Saturday tomorrow," the woman said, still unhappy. "No one will be here."

Bethany rubbed her forehead. "All right. I'll explain to Mr. Dupont that I could have finished, but you had to leave."

Marta let out a tormented sigh and headed up the stairs. "Fine. I'll let you in, but I can't stay." She unlocked the door with quick motions. "Don't tell the Duponts I did this."

"Not a word," Bethany said, following her inside. "Thanks so much."

The woman didn't acknowledge Bethany's thanks, just strode into the kitchen. "I'll reset the alarm to turn on when you leave. Once you go out the front door, it will lock behind you, so make sure you take all your stuff with you. I stacked your things in the mudroom."

Marta had taken the art supplies out of the master bedroom? Well, that would make finishing this job take longer because now Bethany had to haul everything back.

"Don't leave any trash behind." Marta emphasized this sentence, like she thought Bethany was likely to leave paint brushes lying around.

Granted, her painting supplies had been at the Duponts' all week, but only because she was using them. "The place will be spotless," Bethany promised.

Marta let out another sigh. "And don't get anything dirty. I put clean towels in all the bathrooms, and I don't want them messed up." Without waiting for a reply, she left, shutting the door with more force than the task required.

Lovely woman.

As Bethany set off to find the mudroom, she calculated how much time the job would take. She wouldn't get out of here until four-twenty, and she still had to stop by her other client's house. Getting home would take another half hour. Longer, if the traffic was bad. And at that time of night, yeah, it was going to be bad. Maybe it would be best to call the other client and see if Bethany could come tomorrow. She wanted to allow herself enough time to get ready for her date. If the guy was as hot as Hannah claimed, he deserved smoky eyeshadow and hair that fell in soft curls around Bethany's shoulders.

She called her client to reschedule, and then found the mud room on the other side of the Duponts' kitchen. Her clean brushes and the small paint bottles she'd used for the mural sat in a pristine sink. The drop cloths, paint roller, and pan were suspiciously absent. Had the housekeeper thrown them away? She wouldn't have, would she?

Bethany suspected she already knew the answer, even before she hiked up the three stories to the master bedroom. Yep, they were gone. Marta had probably shoved them in a trash can outside along with the empty tin of blue paint Bethany had used for the rest of the walls.

Bethany headed downstairs, saying a lot of things to Marta even though the woman was no longer around. And none of what she said was very nice. The missing equipment hadn't been expensive—cheap plastic drop cloths and a disposable paint roller, but still. Painting without a roller would take twice as long.

And how was Bethany supposed to finish the job without a drop cloth? Even if she had the time, she couldn't go to the store and buy new supplies. The door would lock behind her.

She picked up her biggest paint brush along with the hammer she used to open and close paint cans, then headed back up the stairs two at a time. She'd have to improvise. She only had a small area to paint, so she didn't need a big drop cloth; just something to catch any drips.

She seriously considered using one of the precious clean towels in the guest bathroom and leaving a note explaining she'd had no other choice because the housekeeper had thrown away her drop cloths. But she wasn't that vindictive. Her sweatshirt and jeans could do the job. Any paint that was already on them was long dry, and a few more spots wouldn't matter.

She would finish the job in her underwear and hope she didn't get paint on her bra and panties. She'd worn her red ones in honor of Valentine's Day. They were lacy, yes, but surprisingly comfortable.

She adjusted the window shutters, slanting them to hide her from outside view while still allowing in natural light. The French doors that led to the balcony had small windows in their top halves. Hopefully no one could see through those.

She kicked off her shoes and socks and then undressed, feeling oddly self-conscious about being half naked in someone else's bedroom. What if the Duponts came home early? People did that sometimes. Best to hurry. She laid her clothes in front of the wall, put the paint can in the middle of her sweatshirt, and started painting.

She made quick, wide strokes with the brush, working as fast as she could. The bare spot disappeared. So did the startled pigeon. She had just finished the wall when a noise sounded off to her side, startling her. She spun around, paint brush gripped like a weapon.

It took a moment for her to realize the noise was a bedside phone ringing, but by then it was too late. She'd accidentally knocked into the paint can, tipping it over. Paint spilled across her foot and onto her sweatshirt.

No. Oh no. This could not happen. Her sweatshirt had been sufficient to protect the carpet from paint splatters, but it wouldn't prevent half a can of paint from soaking through.

She needed to get the mess out of the bedroom before it leaked everywhere. She grabbed her jeans and used them to wipe off her foot, so she didn't leave blue footprints on the carpet. With every second that took, she was acutely aware that the paint puddle was spreading out and soaking through her sweatshirt.

She couldn't ruin the Duponts' carpet. That would be horrible.

The phone continued to ring, making it hard to think. She picked up her sweatshirt, paint can and all, cradling both in an attempt to keep the paint from spilling. Where to go? The bathroom was too far away. She'd drip before she got there. That left only one solution that she could see. She darted to the balcony, flung open the door, and stepped outside into the cold air.

Now what? She'd saved the carpet from paint, but the balcony had expensive-looking stonework and she doubted the Duponts would want a paint-soaked sweatshirt lying on the floor. Two wooden reclining chairs sat on the balcony along with a wrought iron coffee table. She couldn't put her sweatshirt on any of those without ruining them.

She didn't glance at the neighboring townhouses or the ones across the street. She didn't have time to worry if anyone had noticed her, although a silent prayer went through her mind: *Please don't let any leering teenage boys or easily shocked old ladies be nearby.* Really, anyone with a camera . . .

The paint was running down her hands. Below was the

street, the sidewalk, a small patch of grass, and a couple of bushes bordering the walkway that wound toward the front of the house. If she flung her shirt into the street, how long would the blue spot at the curb last? Months? Years? She could imagine the Duponts grimacing every time they pulled up to their townhouse and saw it. That left one option, the grass.

She hung over the balcony, aimed, and tossed her sweatshirt in the direction of the lawn. As soon as the bundle left her hands, she thought of all the things that could go wrong. She could have horribly bad aim and hit her own car, which was parked on the street. Worse, some random pedestrian could suddenly appear. How awful would that be—death by falling paint can? Fortunately, the sweatshirt hit the lawn with an uneventful thud. The can rolled off, leaving a blue smudge next to her shirt.

Crisis averted. She would clear away the mess she'd made on her way out, and she'd text Mr. Dupont tomorrow to explain what had happened to the lawn. Hopefully he wouldn't be too upset about his grass getting a coat of paint. She finally glanced at the neighboring townhouses to see if anyone had noticed her on the balcony in her underwear. No one seemed to be around. Good. Finally, one of her prayers had been answered.

She turned to go inside and saw that the French doors had shut. She wiped the paint from her hands so she wouldn't leave fingerprints anywhere and reached for the doorknob. Her mind was already working on the problem of driving home shirtless. The Duponts had to have something she could borrow. An old jacket. Or a roll of paper towels she could tape together in the shape of a shirt. Anything.

She twisted the doorknob. It didn't turn.

"No!" She knew what this meant, but couldn't accept it for several seconds. She kept turning the knob, all the while muttering the word, "No!" over and over again.

Apparently, the front door wasn't the only one that locked

automatically. The balcony doors did, too, and now she was locked out in her underwear.

Two

BETHANY STOOD ON the balcony, reviewing her options. She was three stories up, and even if she had been able to scale down the front of the Duponts' townhouse, her keys and phone were locked inside. She had no way to drive home, and no means to call anyone for help.

She started shivering, and it wasn't just from the cold. She wrapped her arms around herself and once more scanned the rows of townhouses surrounding her, looking for anyone who might have noticed her predicament. If a neighbor saw her, they could do something to help, like call the Duponts and have them send someone to let her inside. Or at the very least, contact the fire department to come with a ladder.

No one was around except for a Siamese cat that regarded her placidly from a chair on the balcony to her left. Bethany stood there, bouncing on the balls of her feet to try and keep warm. Her teeth began to chatter. "Okay, God, I need to take back that prayer you granted a couple of minutes ago. I'll take an easily shocked old lady, or even a leering teenage boy . . ."

No one decided to stroll out onto their balcony at this moment. Of course they didn't. Murphy's law.

The air was chilly and was going to get colder as the day shifted to night. She was probably in for rain, too. This was Seattle, after all. She pulled her hair from its ponytail holder in an effort to keep her neck warm. How long would it take before someone noticed her up here? Should she scream for help? Was there any other way to avoid complete humiliation?

The cat on the balcony to her left jumped from its perch, hurried to its door, and slipped inside.

Wait. The Duponts had a Siamese cat that looked just like that one. She'd painted it onto their bedroom wall, so she knew. Was the next balcony over actually one of the rooms in their townhouse? Had to be. What were the chances that the Duponts' neighbors had an identical Siamese cat?

The cat had gone through a balcony door that had been propped open. Marta had opened some windows and doors earlier, to air out the place so it didn't smell like paint. Had she forgotten to close one of them?

The balconies were close together—maybe four or five feet apart. Too far to jump from a standstill. Bethany would have to find another way to get over there. She couldn't be stuck out here in her underwear when an open door was so close.

The only items on her side were two chairs, a table, and a wind chime. The wooden reclining chairs were built like pool loungers. Long enough to use as a bridge? If she tried, would one of them hold her or would it fold?

She stood there for a few minutes waiting for another solution to present itself or for someone to come to their window and see her. Neither happened, even though she yelled out, "Hey! Is anyone around?" Twice. Sheesh, where were all the people in this neighborhood? Working late at their high-power jobs? Busy with Valentine's plans? Maybe they were so wealthy they had other homes and only used their townhouses in the summer. This wouldn't have surprised her. The Duponts were certainly loaded.

Bethany dragged the wooden chair over to the edge of the balcony, reclined it until it lay flat, and then flipped it over. To keep it from folding and collapsing, she took down the wind chime and wound it between the chair slats then tied it tight. With one of the chair's ends resting on the floor, she leaned the other end against the railing and pushed the middle to see if it would fold. It didn't. She put more pressure against it. Still held. Maybe it would work as a bridge.

She hefted the chair up and began sliding it across the space between the balconies. The thing was unwieldy, scraped her arms, and before she was done she had several sliver splinters in her fingers. But she held on, afraid the chair would slip from her grasp and fall to the ground before it reached the other balcony. Which perhaps wouldn't have been a bad thing, if the crash caused someone to come out of their townhouse and notice her.

Fortunately, or perhaps unfortunately, she didn't drop the chair. With a little bit of swinging and shoving, she managed to lay it across the balcony railings. Then she stared at her impromptu bridge and wondered if trying to go across it was really worth risking her life. She imagined news stories about a woman found dead in her underwear, mysteriously sprawled on a near stranger's lawn. Would people speculate whether Bethany had decided to end it all, rather than face another Valentine's Day with only the prospect of a blind date as comfort?

Dying that way would be *so* tacky. She spent several more minutes shivering in the cold, contemplating news stories until she felt so frozen, she decided to chance death anyway. People walked across wooden bridges all the time. Wood was a sturdy thing. She'd be fine.

She pushed the table up to the railing so she could step easily on the chair-bridge. Gingerly, she placed one foot onto it. Seemed fine. This was so stupid, so dangerous. If this thing slipped . . . She didn't let herself think about it, just put her other foot onto the chair as well.

Holding her breath, she hurried across. And then she was safe on the other balcony. She stood there for a moment, panting like she'd run a marathon. But she didn't linger outside. She darted through the door and shut it behind her with a sigh of relief. Finally, she could get her stuff and go home.

She was in a bedroom, a large one with flowered wallpaper and a matching bedspread on a queen-sized bed. A guest room? No, it was being used by someone. The clutter on an antique dresser attested to that. Well, it didn't matter whose room it was. She needed to find the master bedroom. She'd feel better once she had her jeans and shoes on and could look around for a coat closet. When she texted Mr. Dupont about the paint on the lawn, she'd tell him she'd borrowed a jacket and would return it Monday, once they were home.

Bethany stepped into the hallway and stopped short. This couldn't be right. The hallway should have led to the left in order to reach the master bedroom. Instead, it went straight ahead and to the right. Was there some other way to get to the Duponts' bedroom? Was she turned around? She'd never gone anywhere in the house except up the stairs and to the master bedroom. The rest of the house was unfamiliar.

She didn't let herself think about the other option—that she might not be in the right townhouse. She had to be. She just needed to find the stairs and reorient herself.

She went down the hallway until she saw the stairs. And then it became hard to breathe. Because instead of the black wrought iron staircase the Duponts had, this staircase was cherry wood.

She was in the wrong townhome.

Could this day possibly get worse?

An ominous clicking noise behind her announced that yes, things could most definitely get worse. She'd heard that sound before in movies—a gun safety being released.

"Don't move!" a wavering voice said behind her. An older man's gravelly voice.

Bethany slowly raised her hands to show she wasn't armed.

"This is a mistake," she said, her own voice wavering as well.

"I thought this was the Duponts' townhouse . . . your neighbors." She turned around, hands still raised. "I got locked out of their house while I was on the balcony—"

"Don't come any closer!" The man pointing the gun was probably in his seventies. What hair he had left was completely white. He was short and overweight with an overly large nose and glasses. His hand shook as he held the gun, which was not a good sign. Up until this moment, she'd thought that being found inexplicably sprawled dead on the lawn was the tackiest way to die. But no. Being shot dead in her underwear while breaking into a stranger's house was even worse.

"This is all a misunderstanding," she insisted. "Don't shoot."

"Stay where you are," the man barked, hands still trembling.

An elderly woman peeked out from one of the bedrooms and glared at Bethany. She held a phone in her hand. "The police are on their way. Don't get any ideas."

Ideas? What did these people think was going through her mind? Bethany kept her voice as calm as she could manage. "I'm not a burglar. I was painting your next-door neighbor's house, and I locked myself out—"

"Painting in your underwear?" The man scoffed. "I don't believe you. You're a burglar, and you dress that way so that if men catch you, they won't turn you in." He shook his head reprovingly. "Won't work on me, hussy."

"I've got paint splotches all over me." Bethany turned her hands, showing him the blue paint. "See?"

"That's your cover."

"My cover?" she repeated incredulously. "If I meant to break inside someone's home, I would have chosen an outfit that was less conspicuous than red underwear and a bit warmer than a coat of paint."

The woman scowled. "You thought you could get in here without us noticing, didn't you? Well, we heard you from the moment you laid that plank across our balcony."

Too bad they hadn't noticed a few minutes earlier, when she'd called for help.

Bethany slowly lowered her hands. "Look, I just finished a mural for Mr. Dupont. Really. You can call and ask him." She asked the next question with trepidation. "Do you know the Duponts?"

They wouldn't, of course. Because fate was determined to torture her.

"Oh, we know them." The woman said. "They're out of town right now, so you've no business at their home. Were you robbing them, too? Is that it?"

At least they knew the Duponts. That was a start. "Call Mr. Dupont and ask him."

The woman made tsking noises. "You're trying to get me to hang up with the police, aren't you?"

Bethany looked at the house phone the woman carried. "You don't have to hang up. Don't you have a cell phone?"

"Yes," the woman admitted. "But I don't use it much. It's just for emergencies." Then she didn't say anything else.

"Well," Bethany prompted, "this seems like an emergency. Why don't you use it now?"

The woman's eyes narrowed. "How do I know that you're not trying to get me to leave, so you can pull something?"

The woman was determined to believe that Bethany was enacting some devious plot. Clearly the result of watching too many TV cop shows. In reality, Bethany could hardly think at all—let alone come up with ninja moves that would allow her to escape Gun-wielding Grandpa.

She gestured to the man. "Your husband is pointing a gun at me. I'm not going anywhere."

The woman pressed her lips together in determination. "Fine. But I'll be right back." She disappeared into the room. A shuffling sound came from inside, the sound of drawers opening and closing. A minute passed. The woman reappeared. "Howard, what did we do with that phone?"

"Isn't it plugged in by the computer?"

"That's where I thought it was," the woman said. "But it's not there now."

"Are you sure?"

"Yes, I'm sure." The woman sounded offended. "Why don't you ever believe me when I tell you things?"

The situation just kept getting more surreal. Not only was she being held at gunpoint, she was being held at gunpoint by incompetent people.

"You must have taken it somewhere," the man said.

Bethany lifted her hand to get their attention. "The police officer you're talking to probably has another phone. You could ask them."

The woman didn't acknowledge that Bethany had spoken. "I put it in my purse when I went shopping." She shuffled out of the bedroom, passed her husband and Bethany, and went down the stairs.

Another minute went by. The up and down trill of a siren came from outside, growing louder. The police were almost to the house. It would have been nice if Mr. Dupont could have vouched for her before this moment, but at least with the police here, Bethany wouldn't have to worry about Howard getting too twitchy and accidentally shooting her.

She wrapped her arms around herself, cold again now that some of the adrenaline was wearing off. The siren grew louder, and then it turned off. Soon after, a knock sounded on the door. Without waiting to be let in, the officer opened the door and yelled, "Police!"

"Come in!" the woman called to him from downstairs. "We're holding the burglar on the third floor."

"Are you Mrs. Swanson?" the policeman asked.

They spoke to each other for a few moments in more subdued voices. Bethany couldn't make out what they said as they walked up the stairs.

Please let this be over soon, she thought. *And please let the officer be a reasonable person who has a sense of humor.*

When he came into view, she saw that her prayer had been answered—at least about the sense of humor part. She knew the man had one because it was the same cop who'd pulled her over for going through the light. Mr. October, himself. His must have been the closest squad car.

Bethany wasn't sure whether she should be glad he was the police officer on call or not. Was this good news because he seemed like a nice guy, or bad news because he knew she'd already committed another illegal offense today? She couldn't decide. Mostly, she had to fight the urge to laugh hysterically.

His eyes went wide when he saw her, although whether this was because of her state of undress, or because he recognized her, she couldn't tell. As he walked down the hallway, his head tilted in question. "Elisabeth Daniels, isn't it?"

"Yes," she said, and then because Mr. Swanson was looking impressed that the officer had ID'ed her right off, she added. "My old nemesis, we meet again."

The older man nodded smugly. "She's a wanted criminal, isn't she?"

Instead of answering, Mr. October said, "Please put away your gun, sir. And make sure the safety is on."

Mr. Swanson clicked the safety back on and lowered the gun. His wife finally reappeared from the stairs, holding her cell phone. "I found it," she announced.

As the policeman stepped closer to Bethany, she got a look at his nametag. *Hansen.*

He gave her an apologetic look. "Ms. Daniels, I need you to turn around and put your hands behind your back."

Bethany sighed and did as she was told. "Don't I get to explain before you cuff me?"

He came up behind her. "You can explain after." He took hold of one of her hands and she felt a cuff snapping around her wrist. "Sorry. It's procedure."

"Seriously? You can tell I'm not armed. I'm in my underwear."

He snapped the cuff on her other wrist. "I did notice that, yes." His voice went low. "Apparently, you have more interesting blind dates than the ones I go on."

"I'm not dressed this way for a date."

"These are your breaking-and-entering clothes?"

She turned to face him, ignoring how close he stood. "I didn't break anything. I only entered. And I only did that because I was lost."

He lifted an eyebrow. "You put a plank onto a stranger's balcony and entered that way because you were lost?" He obviously already knew the couple's side of the story.

"I was locked out on the balcony next door, and I thought this balcony was part of the same townhouse."

"I see." Officer Hansen took out a pen and a pad of paper to write notes. "Do you normally carry planks around with you?"

"It wasn't a plank. It was a wooden chair. You can go look at it."

Mrs. Swanson motioned to Officer Hansen to get his attention. "She always wants you to leave. I think she's going to run for it."

"I can't run anywhere," Bethany snapped. "My car keys are locked in the Duponts' house." As coherently as she could, she told the story of how she'd ended up locked out. "Look, all you have to do is call the Duponts. Or their housekeeper. They can verify my story."

"The Duponts are in France," Mr. Swanson said pointedly. "I know because we're watching their cat."

And that explained why the cat was on their balcony.

Mrs. Swanson shook her head in disbelief. "Lauren didn't say anything to me about someone coming in and painting while they were gone, and I'm sure she would have mentioned it."

"That's because it was a surprise," Bethany said. "A Valentine's Day present from her husband."

More head shaking from Mrs. Swanson. "Her husband took her to Paris for Valentine's Day."

"Right. He did two nice things for her. Some guys are awesome like that." Bethany swallowed. Even to her, the story sounded suspicious. Because really, how many men were that awesome? "Men can be nice," she insisted.

Officer Hansen wrote down something on his pad. "You don't have to convince me. I've already been nice today."

"Right," she said. "I'm hoping that streak continues."

Mr. Swanson nudged his wife. "See, she's trying to flirt her way out of this."

Bethany felt her cheeks flush. "The housekeeper knows all about this. She was the one who let me in each day. Her name is Marta something..." Bethany didn't remember her last name. It was hard enough to remember first names.

"Her accomplice," Mrs. Swanson said knowingly. "There's always an accomplice." She turned to Officer Hansen. "You're taking this woman to jail, right? I bet she's stolen something. If not from us, then from the Duponts."

Bethany let out a breath of frustration. "I obviously haven't stolen anything. Where would I put it? It's not like I have pockets."

Officer Hansen's gaze went over her, then snapped to her face as if he were embarrassed to be caught looking at her body. "Ms. Daniels, do you have Mr. Dupont's phone number?"

"Yes," Bethany said. "But it's on my phone that's locked in their house."

Officer Hansen's radio buzzed, and he answered it, listening for a couple of moments. Then he said into the mic, "I'm talking with Elisabeth Daniels. She claims she was working in the house next door, got locked out on the upper balcony, and so climbed onto the Swanson's balcony and came into their home."

The man on the other end of the connection said something that Bethany couldn't make out.

Officer Hansen's gaze cut to Bethany. "Yep, the same one." A pause. "Right. All she's got for a record is a traffic violation and a misdemeanor."

Mr. Swanson leaned toward his wife. "She's got a record. How much do you want to bet the misdemeanor is for burglary?"

"It was a college prank," Bethany said. "My sorority stole a football team's mascot costume."

Mr. Swanson nodded. "Theft. I told you so."

Officer Hansen spoke into his radio again. "Can you bring in a blanket for Ms. Daniels? She's in need of some clothing."

This time the response over the radio came in clear enough for Bethany to hear it. "You mean she's naked?"

Officer Hansen lowered his voice. "Mostly, yes."

The next response was also clear. Laughing, the man said, "How do you always end up with the interesting calls?"

Officer Hansen didn't answer. To the couple, he said. "My partner has checked the perimeter of the building and didn't see anything or anyone suspicious. The car parked in front of the Duponts' home is registered to Ms. Daniels. He noted a paint covered sweatshirt on the lawn, so that corroborates with her story. However, we really need to talk to Mr. Dupont, to be sure that he hired her. Do you have their cell phone numbers?"

Mrs. Swanson nodded and plodded toward the stairs. "Lauren wrote them down for me. I'll get them."

Bethany stood awkwardly in the hallway waiting. Officer Hansen's gaze kept sliding to her, and then turning quickly away as though he thought he should be watching her but didn't feel comfortable doing it.

Another police officer walked up the stairs carrying a thin yellow blanket. He was older than Officer Hansen, with dark hair and a stocky build. His name tag read *Martinez*. He draped the blanket over Bethany's shoulders without any of the amusement he'd displayed while talking on the radio. He probably hadn't thought she'd be able to hear those comments.

"I'll check the balcony," Hansen told Martinez, "and see how she actually got over here. Call the Duponts and get their story."

"Talk to *Mr.* Dupont," Bethany clarified. "He's the only one who knew I was coming."

While Officer Hansen went down the hallway to the flowered bedroom, Mrs. Swanson came back with a slip of paper. Officer Martinez called Mr. Dupont's number, and they all stood quietly, waiting to see if anyone picked up. Bethany tugged at her handcuffs. Time seemed to stretch out. Had the phone been ringing for one minute or two?

Finally the policeman said, "This is Officer Martinez calling from the Seattle Police Department. I need to speak with you about a possible break-in at your neighbor's home. Please return my call as soon as possible." Then he gave a phone number.

Just a message? Mr. Dupont hadn't picked up. Officer Martinez called Mrs. Dupont next. She didn't answer either. He left the same message then hung up the phone. "It's one in the morning in France. They may have turned off their phones and gone to sleep. Is there anyone else who could verify your story?"

"The housekeeper," Bethany said. "I don't know her number."

Officer Martinez turned to Mrs. Swanson. "Do you know which hotel the Duponts are staying at?"

The woman shrugged. "It had some French name with lots of syllables." She let out a little huff of indignation. "You're not going to let this woman go, are you? We want to press charges. She broke into our house. Probably would have robbed us blind if we hadn't caught her. A person can't even be safe in their own home anymore."

Officer Martinez's voice turned soothing. "We'll hold her at the station until we get to the bottom of this. In the meantime, you folks look around and let us know if anything is missing."

The police were going to take Bethany in? Did they mean take her to some waiting room, or were they going to put her in a jail cell? "I didn't touch anything except the door handle. You can dust the place for prints."

Officer Martinez turned his soothing voice on Bethany. "There's no need to raise your voice, ma'am. If this is all a misunderstanding, you'll be fine."

If? Honestly. "Come on, a real criminal would have brought a few accessories to a heist. Like a bag. And car keys. And the rest of her clothes."

"I agree," he said, still soothing.

She'd been speaking so loudly, she hadn't heard Officer Hansen come back into the hallway. He'd brought the chair with him and put it down in front of her. "This is what you used to get onto the balcony? A lounge chair?"

Officer Martinez let out a whistle and shook his head.

Officer Hansen stared at her, his blue eyes incredulous. "I was joking earlier about you having a death wish, but now I'm not so sure."

She shrugged. "It was cold and I didn't have a lot of choices."

"You had the choice to stay put, wait for help, and not plunge three stories to the ground. That seems like a viable option."

Shrugging had been a mistake. The blanket slipped from her shoulders, fell to the floor, and lay there like a yellow puddle.

Officer Hansen picked it up and began to drape it over her shoulders again.

"It won't stay put like that," she said. "You'll have to wrap it around me like a towel."

He hesitated, seemed reluctant to touch her.

"Trust me," she told him, "I feel more awkward about this than you do."

He nodded. "I'll take the cuffs off so you can handle the blanket. I don't think you're a flight risk."

While he did that, Officer Martinez spoke to the Swansons. "We're still going to take Ms. Daniels down to the station, but I don't think you folks need to worry that she's a criminal. They're usually much better prepared."

Chapter Three

When Bethany reached the police car, Officer Hansen opened the back door for her and waited while she slid onto the hard, plastic seat.

"Figures," she said. "I finally found a guy who'll open the door for me, and he's taking me to jail."

"We're only taking you to a holding cell. I'm sure Mr. Dupont will vouch for you." He didn't shut the door, just stood there eyeing her like he was mentally shaking his head.

"What?" she asked.

"I was waiting to see if you'd put on your seatbelt. I guess it shouldn't surprise me that you didn't."

"Oh." She let go of her blanket and buckled up. "I usually wear mine. Really."

"Glad to hear it." He shut the door and got into the front seat beside his partner.

Officer Martinez started the car and pulled away from the curb. Bethany watched out the window as they left her red Mazda behind. It seemed so forlorn, sitting there in front of the Duponts' townhouse.

The seatbelt made the blanket slide and she adjusted it back up, casting a glance at the camera that was perched on the car ceiling, pointing in her direction. Just what she needed—to know that footage was being taken of her. "You're not going to take a mugshot of me wearing this blanket, are you?"

"Not if you prefer the alternative," Officer Martinez replied.

Her bra? Not likely.

Officer Hansen shrugged apologetically. "Sorry, but trust me, it won't be the worst mugshot we've seen."

Yeah. It wouldn't even be *her* worst mugshot. Or maybe that's what Officer Hansen meant. Had he seen the picture of her in the mascot outfit? Did that show up with her record? "You don't have extra clothes down at the station for this sort of thing?" she asked.

"This sort of thing?" Officer Hansen repeated, amused. "You mean for all the other times we pick up women in lingerie?"

Which was really too much. "You know, I wouldn't have had to use my clothes as drop cloths in the first place, if you hadn't pulled me over and made me late getting back to the Duponts."

"And I wouldn't have had to pull you over, if you hadn't run a red light." He turned to Officer Martinez. "Is there a way to change my mind and retroactively issue her a citation? I don't think she learned anything from my generosity."

"Nah, bro," Officer Martinez said, suppressing a smile. "Best to let it go."

She tugged the blanket tighter around her. "What—you don't think I've paid enough for running that light? I'm being hauled to jail. This means I'm never going to be able to run for political office, for fear someone will dig up a mugshot of me wearing the yellow blanket of shame." She shook her head and leaned back against the seat. "Although, it turns out my mom's rule about always wearing clean underwear was right. I'll have to tell her. Oh wait, no I won't. Because I'm never going to tell anyone about this."

"See," Officer Martinez said to his partner. "She's learned something valuable. Mom is always right."

Officer Hansen seemed unconcerned about her mother, or Bethany's ruined political career. He turned in his seat, his gaze locking with hers. "The lesson I was talking about is that you only have one life, so you'd better start taking care of it. You used a lounge chair as a bridge—three stories off the ground."

"Okay, I admit that was impulsive, but I tend to be impulsive when I'm outside in my underwear." She cleared her throat. "That didn't come out right. But you know what I mean."

His eyes didn't leave hers. "Do you realize impulsiveness can kill you? You walked into a stranger's home without knocking or giving any warning. Some people would have shot you on sight. And let me tell you, the Swansons came pretty close to being those kinds of people." He didn't sound as though he approved of the Swansons, which made Bethany like him more.

"I thought their balcony was part of the Duponts' house." She had already explained this. "I was following the cat."

"Isn't that the sort of thing," he mumbled as he turned back around, "that got Alice in Wonderland into trouble?"

Bethany smiled despite herself. "She followed a white rabbit. I would have known better."

He looked over his shoulder, flashing his blue eyes at her again. "I'm not so sure. To be on the safe side for the rest of the night, you better not pick up anything that says 'Eat Me.'"

She laughed. Probably because their conversation had stopped feeling real. "Do you hear that a lot at the police station—'Eat Me'?"

"More than we should," he said.

"I can't imagine why."

His expression softened. "Just promise me you'll think twice before you do anything else that could lead to your untimely death."

She didn't answer. She'd thought about using the chair as a bridge more than twice, and she had still done it anyway.

The car left the residential area and headed toward downtown. Boxy brown buildings lined the street. The clouds above were blanketing the sky in its usual gray color, with only the slashes of black power lines to break up the monotony.

"What if you can't reach the Duponts tonight?" Bethany asked. "I mean, for all we know they don't have international phone coverage. I'm not going to have to stay at the police station until they fly home, am I?"

"I'm sure we'll be able to get a hold of them," Officer Hansen said.

That wasn't really a comforting answer. Granted, the Duponts probably had international coverage. They wouldn't have given their neighbors their phone number otherwise. But with the luck she'd been having lately, they wouldn't answer their phone at all. Would she be stuck in jail until next Monday? Could the police hold her that long for trespassing? How exactly did the whole bail thing work?

Bethany took several deep breaths to calm herself. No point in worrying about that. The police would get a hold of the Duponts. "After you release me, how am I going to get my phone, purse, and keys back?"

"You'll have to work that out with the Duponts," Officer Hansen said. "Maybe someone can let you into the house."

Maybe didn't sound reassuring enough, especially when she knew Marta was leaving for the weekend. "The housekeeper went out of town. Who else would be able to let me in?" She took more deep breaths. The extra oxygen did nothing to calm her. "I need my keys, or I can't drive to my next job. And my phone has all my contacts on it: my clients, my friends and—oh no." *James.* In all the commotion, she'd forgotten about their date tonight.

"What?" Officer Hansen said, finding her gaze in the mirror.

"My date tonight—I have no way to let him know I can't make it. He'll think I stood him up."

"Sorry," Officer Hansen said. "But look at it this way, if your date is a decent guy, he'll understand."

"He'll understand that I missed dinner because I was being incarcerated? If he's a decent guy, he'll stay as far away from me as possible."

"Nah," Officer Hansen said. "If he has a sense of humor, he'll think it's funny. This could be a good litmus test for you."

She sank into her seat. "I'm beginning to doubt how much you understand about relationships."

He shifted away from the mirror. "I think I understand enough."

She scoffed, refusing to relinquish her dark mood. "I bet you don't even have a girlfriend."

Officer Martinez laughed at that. "Ouch. She may have you pegged."

Officer Hansen tapped his fingers against the door handle. "I don't have a girlfriend because I'm busy." He said this as though it was something he'd discussed with his partner before. "And because the last girlfriend I had made me realize that there are some things worse than being single. Like being with her."

"But all that will change tonight," Officer Martinez said, "because you've got a hot date."

Officer Hansen made a grumbling noise in the back of his throat that indicated he was less than thrilled about his date.

Officer Martinez shot Bethany a quick glance over his shoulder and whispered. "It's a blind date. You know what those are like."

Apparently, she wouldn't tonight. But now she understood why he had let her go after she'd run the red light. He'd sympathized with her blind date plight.

"Hope that works out for you," she said.

Four

OVER THE NEXT hour, Bethany learned many things about the justice system. For example, despite the fact that Officer Hansen kept insisting she was going to a holding cell, not jail—yeah, she was pretty much in jail.

Any room with bars locking you in—that was jail. Four other women were there already. A sink and toilet sat in one corner of the room. No walls, no privacy around the toilet. And no way was Bethany going to use that in front of a bunch of other people.

The mugshot had been another scarring event. But Bethany had decided to make the best of it. She'd fluffed up her hair and pouted for the camera. If her mugshot ever showed up somewhere online, at least she could claim she'd been arrested with flair.

She also learned that despite what the movies claimed, the police let you make more than one phone call. They told her she could make as many calls as she wanted. Which would have been helpful if she could remember anyone's phone number. But she couldn't. She was so used to her phone storing her contacts that she only had Hannah's number memorized. And Hannah was off on a couples' cruise with all the rest of the fortunate people who had someone special in their lives.

Bethany could have called her parents collect but didn't. They were five hours away in Lewiston, Idaho, and it would only worry them to know she was at the police station. If she told her parents about this at all, it would be in the past tense. Such as, "Hey, did I ever tell you about that really horrible night ten years ago . . ."

She should have been able to call someone else, some friend who would be willing to help her. But her only friends were those handful of women on a cruise ship. So instead of making any phone calls at all, she waited numbly, sitting on the holding cell floor. There wasn't much to do except for contemplate where her life had gone wrong. As the minutes progressed, a few tears might have slid down her cheeks.

It wasn't the fact that she was here that made her cry. She knew she would get out. Eventually the police would get a hold of the Duponts, and her story would be verified. The thing that hurt was the realization that no one was worried about her right now. No one had even noticed she was gone. Truth be told, most of the people she knew were more of acquaintances than real friends. She hadn't put in the time to make them anything else. She was too busy with her career. Hannah was her only close friend, and now that Hannah was married, she was busy with Greg most of the time. So how long would it be until Bethany lost her, too?

This wasn't how her life was supposed to be.

She had planned on having a boyfriend and eventually settling down and raising kids in some charming cottage in a sleepy rural town. She'd already planned the murals she would paint in their bedrooms—forest landscapes with fairies, knights, and friendly dragons peeking between the trees. In that imagined life, she would chat with neighbors at the park, join a book club, and form playgroups for her children.

But none of those goals were getting any closer to being reality. She didn't meet many single, eligible guys while decorating other people's houses.

One of the other women in the cell noticed her crying and

came over to talk to her. She was a thirty-year-old bleached blonde in a tight miniskirt and fishnet stockings. She eyed Bethany, taking in her red bra straps that stuck out of the police blanket. "They got you for hooking, didn't they?"

Bethany nearly said, "No, for trespassing," but then she would have had to explain why she was trespassing in her underwear. And the story would only sound like a convoluted attempt to deny prostitution charges.

She shrugged miserably instead.

"Don't take it so hard," the other woman said and sat down next to her. "They'll only hassle you a little and let you go."

The woman then went on to give Bethany tips about avoiding the police in the future. She might have continued in this vein for quite some time, but a female officer came by holding a plastic bag. "Elisabeth Daniels?" she called, and then her gaze fell on Bethany. "I'm guessing that's you."

Bethany nodded. "How could you tell?"

"Your wardrobe gave you away." She held the sack through the bars. "Compliments of Officer Hansen."

Forms of some sort? Did those come in bags? Bethany took the offering. The woman didn't stick around for a response, just turned around and left.

Bethany opened the bag and found a note on top of some clothes.

I asked my sister to bring these to the station for you. I think you're about the same size. P.S. On the bright side, this experience will pretty much ensure that all your future Valentine's Days are better.

A nice gesture, especially since she hadn't given him many reasons to be kind to her. Now she regretted that comment she'd made about him not understanding women. And hopefully what he said about this experience was true. Because if there were any Valentine's Days in the future that were going to be worse than sitting in jail getting advice from a hooker, she didn't want to know about them.

Bethany pulled the clothes from the bag. Black yoga pants and a long-sleeved T-shirt. Putting on the clothes made her feel more respectable, although she wished she had shoes. Or even socks. The floor was cold cement. She folded up the blanket and sat on it.

About an hour after she'd arrived in the holding cell, the same female officer returned to release her.

As the woman walked her down the hall, she said, "Mr. Dupont corroborated your story, and the Swansons aren't pressing charges after all. So you're free to go. Mr. Dupont said to tell you their housekeeper will be available on Monday morning to let you in to retrieve your belongings."

Monday? Bethany tucked the blanket underneath her arm. "My keys, wallet, and phone are in their house. What am I supposed to do until then?"

The woman spoke with an, *It's your problem not mine,* tone. "You're free to call the homeowner and work out other arrangements. However, the call will be collect, and I'll tell you right now that Mr. Dupont wasn't all that happy the first time around, to be woken up in the middle of the night to talk to us."

Bethany was stuck then. Carless, moneyless, phoneless. It felt like the last straw. "I don't have a way to get to their house on Monday. I don't even have a way to get home tonight."

"Most people call a family member or a friend to come get them. But if you don't have any of those, you can always call a cab."

Bethany couldn't pay a cab because her wallet was locked up. She didn't point this out; she didn't want to let the woman know she had no friends who could help her. So she didn't even bother trying to call someone for a ride. She'd already mentally reviewed the list of people she knew. And even if she could look up their numbers, who could she ask to drop their Valentine's Day plans to pick her up at the police station? One of her artist friends, whom she saw occasionally at gallery openings? The neighbor she exchanged pleasantries with at the mailbox? A past client? An ex-boyfriend?

She didn't want any of those people to know she'd been to the police station, let alone beg them to come get her.

She strode outside, barefoot, and made her way down the sidewalk. She wanted to get away from this place. She'd walk home if she had to. Or at least she'd walk until her frustration died down, and she could think of a better plan. The street signs read Pine and 12th Avenue. She wasn't exactly sure where she was, but she knew her condo was miles away. Did cabs take PayPal? Was there a bus route around here? Maybe she could beg for some bus fare. That would be a fitting way to end this day—begging barefoot on some dark street corner.

The light changed and she made her way across the intersection, eyeing a liquor store on the other corner. She probably wasn't in the best part of town. Didn't matter. She kept marching along. The evening was cold, and she didn't have a jacket. Just this tacky yellow blanket. Well, she'd lost all her dignity already. She wrapped it snugger around her shoulders.

A couple of guys stood by some parked cars smoking. They gave her the once over as she went by. She picked up her pace.

When she came to another cross street, she stopped on the corner, wondering whether it was better to keep heading straight or to turn. Maybe she should go into a store somewhere and stay there until she figured out a solution. Asking someone to pick her up at a store wasn't quite as bad as asking someone to pick her up at the police station.

While she stood there debating which of her acquaintances was least likely to be busy on Valentine's Day, a white truck pulled up to her.

Her first thought was, *Please let this be someone I know, and not some stranger who thinks I'm standing on this corner because I'm a hooker.*

She looked at the driver and saw it was indeed someone she knew. Officer Hansen. He wore a jacket over his uniform so that only the dark blue collar of his shirt peeked through, but it was definitely him. Blue eyes, blond hair. Mr. October himself.

"What are you doing out here?" he asked. "Isn't someone picking you up?"

She shrugged, not wanting to explain. "I'm walking home. Oh, and thanks for the clothes. I really appreciate them. I'll drop them off at the station on Monday after I get my car."

"You can't walk home," he said. "You don't have any shoes on, and Pinehurst is nearly ten miles away."

She cocked her head at him. "How do you know where I live?"

"It was on your license."

Oh. Right. "You remember those details about the people you pull over?"

He fought a smile. "Well, you're more memorable than most of my cases." His gaze went to her feet. "Really, you can't walk that far. Don't you have someone who can come get you?"

"All of my friends' numbers are on my phone, which is locked up. I can't pay a cab, because my wallet is also locked up."

He kept staring at her, perplexed. "If you need help with phone numbers, the receptionist at the police station can look people up for you. Do you want a ride there?"

"No. I never want to go back there again." She held up her hands to stop further suggestions of that sort. "Do you know how I spent my time in the holding cell? A hooker gave me advice on how to evade police in the future."

"Hmm. It's not working so far."

He could afford to find this funny. He wasn't the one with

the yellow blanket of shame draped over his shoulders. She folded her arms. "Shouldn't you be working or something?"

"I'm done with my shift." He checked over his shoulder, then turned back to her. "Look, I'm not supposed to have contact with people I've brought in, but I can't let you walk home barefoot. You'll end up going through a rough part of town, and you have 'easy mark' written all over you." He unlocked his doors. "Get in and I'll drive you home."

She hesitated, then figured if she was going to accept a ride from a near stranger, a policeman was probably a safe bet. She opened the passenger side door and climbed inside. "Thanks." As she put on her seatbelt, she said, "So is it the paint splatters in my hair or the yoga pants that make me look like an easy mark?"

He pulled into traffic. "It's your bare feet. You can't outrun anyone."

"Oh. For a moment, I thought I was going to have to get rid of all my yoga pants."

He grinned. "Nope. You can keep them."

She stole a glance at his profile as he drove. He looked like a different guy without his uniform. Less imposing, but just as hot. His blond hair had a little bit of a wave to it. She hadn't noticed that before.

"Thanks again for the ride," she said.

"Just being a public servant."

She lifted an eyebrow at him. "That would seem more noble, if you weren't the one who'd dragged me off to the police station in the first place."

"I didn't have a choice," he said. "But if it's any consolation, I believed all along that you were innocent."

She made a tsking noise. "Actually, that makes it worse. I'd feel more forgiving if you'd thought I might be a criminal mastermind. As it is, you were only making things harder for someone who was already having a miserable day."

A smile tugged at his lips. "Well, the possibility of you being a criminal mastermind *did* cross my mind."

She fluttered her hand to erase his words. "Don't try to make things better now. You probably say that to all the women you meet."

He laughed, showing a set of perfectly white teeth. "Right. It's one of my best pickup lines."

Guys as good-looking as Officer Handsome didn't need pickup lines. They just walked into a room and let the women flock to them. "Yeah, go ahead and try that line on your blind date tonight."

He winced. "Crap, I forgot about that." He checked the time on the dashboard. Six ten. "I'm going to be late."

"You don't have to take me home." It was bad enough she was going to stand up her date tonight. She shouldn't ruin his evening, too. "Just drop me off someplace where the muggers look slow."

"I'm taking you home. I can't make things harder for someone who's already had a miserable day."

"Actually, I'm pretty sure we established that you can."

His chin dipped down. "I think what we established is that I got you away from angry homeowners who were waving around a gun and threatening to shoot you. Then I talked to them and convinced them to drop the trespassing charges."

When he put it like that, it was hard to hold a grudge. "Okay, fine. Thank you. Again. And trust me, I wouldn't usually say that to a guy who'd put me in handcuffs."

He glanced at her as though about to comment, then pressed his lips together and looked back at the road.

She realized how her words had sounded. "Not that I've ever . . . I mean . . ."

"Hey, I wasn't judging you. Or jumping to conclusions. Or trying not to form interesting visual images."

She ran her hand through her hair. "Every time I think this day can't get more embarrassing, it does anyway."

He sent her a sympathetic smile. "I'm just teasing. I know what you meant."

She put her hands back in her lap. "I suppose I shouldn't care what you think of me. After tonight, I'm never going to see you again."

"I don't know about that. With the way you drive, you might." His eyes slid to hers. "Still teasing. Well, mostly."

She didn't like the thought of never seeing him again, but wouldn't let herself dwell on that fact. Instead, she watched the buildings passing by outside. "Speaking of embarrassing moments, I'll probably run into the Swansons on Monday when I get my stuff from the Duponts. I bet they'll be watching for me."

"Shouldn't bother you. They know you're innocent now."

Maybe it shouldn't, but it would. How did you gracefully face people who'd seen you in your underwear? Although she was facing Officer Hansen now, and he'd gotten a good view of her in her unmentionables.

She let her gaze rest on him. Being with him wasn't so bad somehow. Her eyes stayed on him, and she couldn't help but admire his profile. From an artistic point of view, he had good lines, a square jaw, and perfectly symmetrical features. And from a woman's point of view, well, he was just nice to look at.

"If you want to wait while I change at my condo," she said, "I can give you your sister's clothes back."

He nodded. "Do you have someone at home?"

She didn't understand the question. Maybe because she'd gotten caught up in staring at him again. His broad shoulders were also artistically pleasing. "What?"

"A roommate. Someone who'll let you in. You don't have your keys."

"Oh, that. I'll be able to get in."

He shot her a questioning look. "Are you about to tell me that you don't lock your doors?"

"I lock my doors," she said. "But I have a spare key hidden under the welcome mat."

He let out a patient sigh. "Okay, that's only slightly better than leaving your doors unlocked. The welcome mat is the first place an intruder would look for a key."

"Well, I never claimed to be a criminal mastermind—no matter how many other people might have wondered."

He tapped a finger against his steering wheel. "Just promise me you won't put the key back there. Otherwise I'm going to worry that you won't make it through the night." He took his gaze from the road long enough to consider her. "How have you survived for twenty-five years?"

The question took her by surprise. "You know how old I am?"

"It's on your driver's license, too."

"You either have an amazing memory, or I should start worrying that you're a stalker."

"At least you'll worry about *something*. That's a start."

"I'm an artist," she said. "I worry so much about where my next job is coming from, I'm immune to all other worries."

He turned onto I-5, heading north toward Pinehurst, her neighborhood. "Have you always been an artist?"

"Except for that hour in the holding cell when I was a hooker, yes."

He raised an eyebrow. "Um, what exactly *were* you doing in the holding cell?"

She waved her hand in a careless motion. "It was easier to let my compadres think I was a lady of the night, than to explain why I was trespassing in my underwear."

"I see."

"Although, judging from what Cinnamon told me, hookers

get paid a better hourly wage than artists. So you know, a career change is always a possibility."

He laughed and his eyes flicked in her direction. "Do you ever give anyone a straight answer?"

"The truth isn't all that interesting. I'd rather appear enigmatic and shadowy. Is it working?"

"Nah, it's too late to be shadowy. I already ran your name through the records database."

Great. He probably knew more about her than her next-door neighbors did. She wondered what he thought of her. "Did you see the mugshot of me wearing the cougar mascot costume?"

"I wasn't going to bring that up, but as far as pictures go, it was, uh . . ."

"Choose your next words carefully."

"Cute."

She let out a sigh. "You probably didn't do anything stupid in college, did you?"

"Nothing I got caught for."

She turned to better see him. "What did you do that you didn't get caught for?"

He shifted in his seat. "We were talking about artists, weren't we? You were telling me how you became one."

"It can't be worse than what I did tonight," she pressed.

He chewed on his bottom lip, thinking.

"I won't tell anyone." She held up her hand in a pledge. "I give you my word as a criminal. We're a select and exclusive club."

"Okay. I may have set off some firecrackers with a friend."

She made a huffing noise. "Firecrackers hardly count as illegal."

"We set them off underneath his girlfriend's car while she was inside, making out with another guy."

"Oh. Well, in that case you can join the club."

He laughed and gave her another smile. It suddenly seemed ironic that the two of them were talking so easily together. Her date with Pre-law James probably wouldn't have been nearly as fun.

"You were telling me about how you became an artist," he said.

"I majored in art history in college and planned on teaching. But then I realized I didn't want to talk about art, I wanted to create it. So now I do oil paintings, watercolors, and sculptures, but it's the murals that pay the bills. Those and portraits."

"What's your favorite type of art?" he asked, and somehow they ended up talking about paintings for the rest of the drive. He knew the difference between romanticism and impressionism, which surprised her. She wouldn't have thought a cop would be up on his Monet.

At last they pulled up into the parking lot of her complex. The outside of the three-story building was a dreary brown, and the green awnings over the doors didn't do much to improve the general appearance. But the landscaping was nice. Pine trees towered everywhere.

He parked the truck and turned off the ignition. "I'll walk you to your door. Make sure you get inside."

She stepped out of his truck. "Are you being a gentleman, or are you afraid I'll get lost and go into the wrong condo?"

"Just being a policeman." He got out and locked his doors. "Actually, forget I said that. I stopped being a policeman when I gave you a ride home."

"Don't worry. I won't let your superiors know you were fraternizing with the—ouch!" In the darkened parking lot, she couldn't see well and had stepped on something sharp. It had embedded into the bottom of her foot. Grimacing, she leaned against the truck to pull it out.

Officer Hansen came around the front of the truck. "Piece of glass?"

"I think it was a sharp rock, but it's hard to tell."

"Is your foot bleeding? I've got a first aid kit in my truck."

Of course he did. He probably had supplies to see him through any emergency. All she had in her car were jumper cables and an empty Diet Dr. Pepper can. "I don't think it's bleeding. I can't really tell, though."

He stepped closer until he stood right next to her. "Sorry. I should have had my sister bring you some shoes, but I figured someone would pick you up at the station. Here . . ." He bent down, put a hand under her knees, and picked her up. "I'll carry you over the rough part."

She put her hands around his shoulders to keep from falling. "You don't have to do this." With his arms around her, and the feel of the muscles in his chest against her side, this suddenly felt intimate.

"It's okay. You don't weigh much—and yes, I know your weight from your driver's license, too."

She laughed and let herself relax against him. "You must have an amazing memory."

"At the traffic stop, Martinez saw your picture on your license and gave me a hard time about letting you off with a warning. Claimed I was showing favoritism toward beautiful women. He may have repeated your information to me a few times while I was running the paperwork."

"Well, just so long as you had a good reason for letting me go."

How long had it been since one of her boyfriends had carried her like this?

Justin, her ex from last year, had picked her up once, but then he'd thrown her into a swimming pool, so that hardly counted as a romantic gesture. Kyle, the guy before Justin, had never bothered to pick her up. And Patrick, the guy before him—well, he'd been so thin, he probably couldn't have lifted a suitcase, let alone her.

Figured. Bethany finally found a guy who was willing to sweep her off her feet, and after tonight she was never going to see him again.

His cologne had a warm, woodsy scent that brought forth images of fireplaces and hot chocolate. She breathed it in and sighed. Maybe she was going to have to start running through more red lights.

When they reached the walkway that led to her door, he set her back on her feet. "Does your foot still hurt?"

"A little." Hardly at all, but he kept his arm around her waist so she wouldn't have to put much weight on her foot. Who was she to reject such a sweet gesture?

Man, Hannah was right after all. Bethany needed a boyfriend. She was feeling ridiculously swoony.

She half-limped the last few steps to her door, glad she'd left on her porch light. She picked up the welcome mat. All that was underneath it was a layer of dirt.

Bethany blinked at the spot, and then searched the rest of her doorstep. "Where's my key?" She leaned closer to the area revealed beneath the mat, as though the key might suddenly appear.

"Are you sure you left it there?"

"Yes," she said, taking deep breaths. Hyperventilating really. Her key was gone. She had no other way inside. She was locked out.

"Would anyone else have taken it for some reason, a friend or neighbor?"

"No." She'd been able to handle everything else tonight, because she'd known that at the end of it all, she could come home, take a warm bath, and forget about the day. And now she couldn't even get inside. What was she going to do?

Officer Hansen placed his hands on his hips and scanned the area as though looking for burglars, or perhaps an escape route, because by now the guy had to be tired of helping her. And she couldn't blame him. She was equally tired of her non-stop stream of problems.

Undoubtedly, he was going to suggest that she go to a friend's house for the night. He'd probably even offer to drive her there. And then she would have to admit that she'd been too determined to stay self-sufficient to make room in her life for friends, that she'd been too wrapped up in her artwork to bother with relationships. She couldn't tell him that—couldn't admit the truth out loud. It was painful enough to admit it to herself.

While he used the flashlight function on his phone to look on either side of the doorstep, she plopped the mat back into place, sat down on it, and put her head in her hands.

She wasn't going to cry. She wasn't going to cry. Yes, she was, actually. Tears sprang to her eyes and flooded her lids before she could stop them. She wiped them away. *She wasn't going to sob hysterically. She wasn't going to sob hysterically.*

"When did you last see your key?" he asked, poking the light into a bush by the door.

"I don't know." The words wavered, sounding too close to hysteria, despite her best efforts.

He turned, his gaze zeroing in on her face. He sat down beside her and put his arm around her shoulder. "Hey, everything is going to be all right."

"My friends are out of town. I don't have anywhere to go tonight. And I'm locked out of my condo."

His voice turned reassuring. "We'll find a way to get you inside. If worse comes to worst, we'll break a window."

"Worst? Worst is already here." She rubbed her forehead and shut her eyes. "This has been the worst day of my life, and it's not even over yet."

His hand moved along her shoulder, a gesture of consolation. "If this is the worst day of your life, you're doing pretty well.

Believe me, I've seen a lot of people's worst days. I've seen addicts OD on just about every drug you can name. I've had to stop men from beating their wives, and I've arrested people for fraud and embezzlement. Your worst day consisted of some bad luck. But you handled the situation with humor and patience. That says something about you. You've got class."

"Class? I was taken into custody in my underwear."

"But you looked good in it. I mean, most women would love to look as great as you did in your . . . ." He broke off and started again. "Okay, that came out stalkerish. That's not what I meant."

He sounded flustered and sincere—as though he were attracted to her. She relaxed against his shoulder. "So you *didn't* mean that I looked good in my underwear?"

"No, I meant it. I just shouldn't have said it."

His arm around her was warm and strong. Nestling into his side felt so comfortable, like an embrace. It felt like the sort of thing couples did before they kissed. Perhaps the day had taken its toll on her in more than one way. Boundaries seemed like shaky things right now, things to be ignored. "What should you have said instead?" she murmured.

"Something that was more . . ." He was watching her and seemed to have lost his train of thought.

He looked adorable that way, searching for what to say. Adorable and attractive. If she kissed him now, would that go on her record? But then again, he'd said he stopped being a policeman when he'd picked her up to drive her home. She leaned over and pressed her lips to his.

He didn't move away, just sat in stunned shock. Not the best of reactions, not what she'd hoped for anyway. Maybe he hadn't been attracted to her. Maybe he'd only been comforting her to be kind, and now she'd made everything awkward.

She leaned away from him. "Sorry. You may have a point about me being too impulsive."

He let out a slow breath. "Impulsiveness isn't always a bad thing. I could change my mind about it."

She smiled and felt a warm glow inside. His lack of reaction hadn't been rejection, just surprise. She leaned over again and this time his lips met hers with more enthusiasm. He pulled her closer, gently holding her in his embrace. She wrapped her arms around his waist. The kiss was soft, gentle. His mouth tentatively moved against hers. She may have moaned.

He lifted his head, gauging her expression. "You aren't kissing me because this is an item on your bucket list, are you?"

"What?" she asked. She already missed his lips.

"This isn't part of some long-held policeman fantasy?"

"I didn't even realize women had policemen fantasies." She let out a sigh and shook her head. "I've *definitely* been working too hard. I'm missing out on all sorts of things."

"You'd be surprised how many women come on to me while I'm working."

She put her hand over his. "That's because you're hot, not because you're a policeman. They'd act the same way if you were a pizza delivery guy."

He lifted an eyebrow. "Would you have kissed me if I was a pizza delivery guy?"

"Bring me pizza sometime and find out."

He chuckled and pulled her close again. He dropped a kiss on her mouth, then his lips moved across her cheek, leaving a trail of kisses there. His voice took on a teasing tone. "So you've never had any policeman fantasies?"

"It's not too late to start."

That earned her another laugh. He had the most beautiful laugh, deep and resonating. She wished she could paint that laugh.

He wound his fingers through hers. "As much as I'd like to sit on your doorstep and enact your newly formed policeman fantasies, I have more important things to take care of."

Personally, she couldn't think of anything more important than her newly formed policeman fantasies, and then she remembered he had plans for the night. She tried not to let the sting of disappointment show. "Oh. That's right. You're meeting someone." She let go of his hand. "Now I feel bad about kissing another woman's date."

He shut his eyes and winced. "The blind date. I forgot about that." He pulled out his phone to check the time. "I'll call her and cancel."

Relief flooded through Bethany. He wasn't going to leave her. He wasn't just enacting some long-held artist fantasy.

While he flipped through his contacts, he said, "What I meant was that after we get you into your condo, I need to replace your locks."

"Replace my locks?" she repeated.

"You don't know what happened to your key. Anyone could have it. That means there might be somebody out there who could walk into your condo any time he wants. Maybe tonight, while you're sleeping." He found the contact he wanted and pushed call. "Do you see my point?"

"Yes." She took his hand in hers. "Thanks for offering to replace my locks. Your blind date is missing out on an awesome guy. I almost feel sorry for her, but not quite."

He put the phone to his ear. "I should tell her to connect with your blind date. Maybe they'll hit it off." He waited for a minute, and then ended the call. "She didn't answer. I'll text her and hope she reads it in time." He began typing in a message. "Otherwise Greg is going to be mad at me for standing up his friend."

Greg?

That was Hannah's husband's name.

Probably a coincidence. There were lots of Gregs in the world.

It occurred to Bethany that she didn't know Officer

Hansen's first name, and that she really should have learned that piece of information before she'd made out with him on her doorstep. Could he be . . . no. But then again, they both had blind dates tonight. "Your first name," she said slowly, "wouldn't be James, would it?"

He cocked his head in question. "Yeah, it is. Didn't I tell you that?"

She put her hand to her mouth, thinking. How should she break this news to him? "Your friend Greg—is his wife's name Hannah?"

James's eyes went wide. "Wait, you're not Bethany, are you? Your license said . . ."

"Elisabeth," she finished for him. "I was named after my grandmother, but I've always gone by Bethany."

"Hannah's friend," he said, as though he still couldn't believe it.

"I didn't call her to pick me up at the station—"

"Because she's on an anniversary cruise with Greg," James finished.

"Along with all my other happily married friends. Which is why Hannah felt the need to set me up." Bethany shifted uncomfortably, trying to judge his reaction. "I planned on looking better than this for our date."

He laughed and then rubbed his jawline. "And I planned on not hauling you down to the station beforehand. That sort of thing usually kills off a romance."

She smiled and felt relieved. "You said a decent guy would be understanding about my incarceration."

"Oh, I'm completely understanding. I understand one hundred percent, in fact."

She rested her chin in her hand, examining him. "Hannah said you were pre-law. I expected someone more . . . bookish."

"I'm going into criminal law. I guess I'm tired of putting the bad guys away, and then watching the courts let them out. I don't start courses until next fall, though."

"Hmm . . . Maybe then I'll be able to enact my lawyer fantasies. Every woman has those."

He grinned and shook his head. "I didn't believe Greg when he said you were my type. Usually the guy can't pick out pizza toppings for me, let alone women. I'm going to have to eat some crow about this."

Bethany put her hand over James's. "We don't have to tell Hannah and Greg how we met, do we?"

"We met at the Santorini Grill," James said. "You were a little late but you looked stunning."

"And I was completely dressed."

"Right," he said. "It was love at first sight."

"Was it?" she asked.

"Yeah," he said, and leaned over to kiss her again.

She slipped her arms around his neck and kissed him back. This Valentine's Day, it seemed, wasn't going to be so bad after all.

Janette Rallison (who is also sometimes C. J. Hill when the mood strikes her) writes books because writing is much more fun than cleaning bathrooms. Her avoidance of housework has led her to writing 21 novels which have sold over 1,000,000 copies and made her a *USA Today* bestseller. Her books have been on the IRA Young Adults' Choices lists, Popular Picks, and many state reading lists. Most of her books are romantic comedies or urban fantasies (with romance) because hey, there is enough angst in real life, but there's a drastic shortage of fantasy, humor and hot guys who want to kiss you. She lives in Arizona with her husband, kids, and enough cats to classify her as eccentric.

Visit Janette's website here: JanetteRallison.com

Follow her on Twitter: @JanetteRallison

Every Occasion

By Heather B. Moore

One

"THANK YOU, MR. FINCH." Maurie Ledbetter pressed END on her cell phone and collapsed onto the ratty floral couch. In two weeks, she'd be the new owner of the corner shop. Two weeks. Fourteen days. Three hundred and thirty-six hours, but who was counting? *I am.*

She dialed the number at the top of her contacts list, calling her best friend and one and only employee, Taffy.

"What's new?" Taffy answered, not one to stall with chit chat or other conversation conventions.

"We got it! We're about to open the bricks and mortar version of *Every Occasion*." Maurie squealed as the news finally started to sink in. She rose from the couch and walked around the boxes strewn about the living room, in a daze of excitement. "And the seller agreed to close in two weeks."

"Wow," Taffy said. "Not that I doubted it, but this is finally happening. Who would have thought the online hobby of selling gift baskets you started a couple of years ago would turn into this?"

"I know, right?" Maurie peered out of the newly scrubbed living room window, at the quiet neighborhood of her childhood. "When are you coming? We need to get the sign ordered and decide on a grand opening date and print off a million fliers—"

"Whoa," Taffy cut in with her bubbly laugh that seemed to complement her blonde, curly hair and energetic personality.

"Last I checked Google, Pine Valley only has 1200 residents. And even with the tourist ski crowd, our customer base wouldn't come close to a million."

Maurie released a breath. "You're right. I'm just up to my armpits in boxes, and I need to make a list of stuff to do now that the offer on the shop was accepted." Outside, two little girls rode along the cracked sidewalk, one on a red bike, the other on a blue one. They were laughing at something, and Maurie felt her stomach twist. She'd once been a carefree kid like those girls, but that was before . . . Well, the past was going to stay in the past, where it was meant to be. And the next step in Maurie's plan was renovating this dumpy house of her mother's, as soon as things at the shop were organized. She'd start with ripping out the carpets, then move on to burning all the furniture. Then—

"Hello? Are you still there?" Taffy asked.

"Oh, sorry. I'm already making more lists. You know me. When are you coming?"

"I just told you," Taffy said, indulgent laughter in her voice. "I'm packing tonight and leaving first thing in the morning. Should make Pine Valley by dinner time."

"Perfect. I'm already washing the new guest bedroom sheets I bought. And I might even venture to the grocery store before you get here."

"I can grab McDonald's," Taffy said.

"Don't you dare," Maurie said. "I'm trying a new chicken salad recipe I found on Pinterest."

"You're a nut. I mean, don't you have enough to do? Cooking should be at the bottom of the list."

"That's why you're coming to work for me," Maurie reminded her. "To keep my priorities straight." She turned away from the window, eyeing the boxes and a stack of wicker baskets.

"All right, boss. See you tomorrow."

Maurie was smiling when she hung up the phone. She

pressed the phone against her chest and turned back to the window. She'd done it. She'd returned to the hometown that she'd left ten years ago at the age of seventeen, moved into the house she'd inherited from the mother who'd disowned her, and now she would be an official shop owner here.

She crossed to the tiny kitchen area and fired up the laptop she'd left on the counter, to Google *handyman* in Pine Valley, a ski resort in Northern California. A couple of construction companies and their websites popped up. There were quite a few luxury cabins in the area, near the slopes, belonging to *who's who*. These construction companies certainly catered to the wealthy if their 10,000 square foot cabins were any indication.

She hovered over one link. "Briggs Brothers. Your hometown handymen. No job is too small."

She clicked and opened the simple website. In the top left corner was a picture of two men. Though with their ball caps on, shading their faces, Maurie couldn't see either of them clearly. Not that she knew a lot of people in Pine Valley anymore.

Her mom had home schooled her since middle school, insisting that the public system was failing her child. A notion to which for a long time Maurie had allowed herself to subscribe. It wasn't until she was removed from the home—after a raucous party her mother had thrown and was subsequently busted for—and placed in another city in foster care, that Maurie discovered she was academically nearly two years behind her peers. Her mother had gone to jail for six months for possession of illegal substances and endangering a minor. And when she was released, she'd written a letter to Maurie saying she was relinquishing parental rights to the state.

Ten years later, the memory of the letter still stung, although it had long ago been destroyed. Fortunately, Maurie had landed in a decent foster home and her foster mom, Gladys Ronning, had shown her what a real mother's love could be like.

Maurie wiped a tear off her cheek and took a deep breath as she stared unseeing at the Briggs Brothers website. Gladys had died when Maurie was in college. A year later, Maurie had been notified by the state that her mother had died as well. Causes unknown. It had been several more months before Maurie was contacted by a Pine Valley lawyer about her mother's estate. At first Maurie had laughed, and then she'd cried. Then, she'd called the lawyer back and told him to rent the house out. At the time she was still in college and hadn't been ready to change her life all over again and move back to her past.

That had all changed a couple of months ago, when Mr. Right had turned out to be Mr. Completely Wrong, and Maurie needed to start her life over . . . miles and miles away from Irvine, where she'd been living. Miles away from Brandon.

Pine Valley had suddenly seemed like a safe haven.

"Well, I'm here now," Maurie said aloud, knowing there was no turning back unless she wanted a lawsuit on her hands. She didn't think the seller of the corner shop on Main would be too happy if Maurie backed out of their deal. Since the house had been paid off long ago by Maurie's grandparents before her mother inherited it, years of rent, minus upkeep expenses, had been accumulating in an account. Eventually, it had added up to a sizable down payment for Maurie's new beginning.

She took a deep breath and dialed the number for Briggs Brothers. A woman answered, a secretary it seemed. She took down Maurie's address, then promised that someone would be out that afternoon to evaluate her needs and work up a bid.

"That's quick," Maurie said, surprised, not meaning to be rude.

"It *is* January, ma'am," the woman said. "Not much construction going on in Pine Valley this time of year."

"Oh, yeah, that makes sense." Maurie felt chagrined and annoyed at the same time, for being called *ma'am*. She was only twenty-seven. But the woman on the other end of the line had no way of knowing that. How old did Maurie sound? "Thank you so much."

When she hung up, she stood and stretched, then grabbed her notebook of lists and more lists. She turned to a fresh page and started planning for her site visit from Briggs Brothers.

Two

GRANT SHELTON STARED at his smart phone, at the address on his emailed work order. He looked back up at the dilapidated house and the street number stenciled on its mailbox. Yep. It was the right place. *Damn.*

He switched to his phone's contacts and called Julie. When his sister answered, he said, "Who called you from 462 Elmwood?"

"Uh," she said, and it sounded like she was typing something on her keyboard. "Maurie Ledbetter."

Grant's jaw clenched. "Okay. Hey, this might sound really weird, but do you think Dave could do this bid?"

Julie laughed. "Grant, you're funny. Yesterday over dinner you told my husband that you needed more hours. Ask and ye shall receive, hon."

"Yeah, you're right." Grant did need the extra income. His stupid legal battle with Joy was driving him crazy.

If ever a name was an oxymoron, it was his ex-wife's. And now Joy had revised their custody agreement so she could keep their five-year-old son, Trent, with her full time, limiting Grant's visits to little more than holidays and summers . . . because she'd moved a hundred miles south with her new boyfriend, Stone. Yep. That was his name. *Stone.*

"Sorry about that, Julie," Grant said. "I'm not thinking straight."

"You're going through a tough time." His sister's tone morphed from amusement to tenderness. "Keep your chin up and remember to enjoy the work."

"Thanks, I'm trying," he said.

His sister was right. After she'd married Dave Briggs, Grant had thought a partnership was the perfect solution to his problems. For years he'd been trying to make it solo as a carpenter, but he hadn't been able to hold his own for bigger contracts against the elite construction companies in the area. Together he and Dave had carved out their own niche, as hometown handymen, often cleaning up the bigger construction companies' mistakes. In between chasing her two kids around, Julie took care of their accounting and scheduling.

"Come over for dinner tonight," Julie continued. "You can't work a full day on a cup of coffee."

Grant hadn't even had coffee that morning, and at the mention of food he realized how hungry he was. Usually, he at least grabbed a sandwich from the local deli on his way through town, but there'd been no time today. Hanging up with Julie, he climbed out of his work truck and headed up the shaded drive. With each step, all kinds of thoughts and emotions churned within him. He didn't know if he had enough fortitude to face his past with Maurie Ledbetter.

There was no chance that she *wasn't* the Maurie he'd known when they were teenagers. It had been ten years, but Grant had never gotten over the guilt he'd felt after calling the police that night—which had turned out to be Maurie's last night in Pine Valley with her mom.

When Grant had found out that Maurie had been taken into protective custody and put into foster care, he'd been gutted. He had only wanted to protect her from her mother's deadbeat boyfriend. Everyone had known that Joe was bad news—Joe being Grant's mom's cousin, so Grant had known more about him than most in town. And when Grant had seen Joe coming out of Maurie's home one afternoon, Grant's blood had frozen in his veins.

At the time, he'd assessed what he knew about Maurie—she'd been a couple of years younger than him, was being homeschooled, sat on her porch to watch the kids walk home after school, and had been friendly with the other neighbor girls for the most part. He'd lived down the street from her and had passed by her house often. Mrs. Ledbetter had been a single mom who lived in her deceased parents' home. Grant had heard the talk around town about Mrs. Ledbetter's string of boyfriends, but Joe had been the baddest yet of those bad news guys.

Grant shook the memories from his mind as he climbed the front steps to the Ledbetter house. Once he rang that doorbell, there'd be no going back. He'd have to face the woman whose life he'd changed forever.

The door swung open while Grant was still gathering his courage.

"Oh, sorry," a female voice said, opening the screen door as well. "I thought I saw the truck out front and wondered . . ." Her voice trailed off as she stared at him.

Grant couldn't stop staring back. The Maurie he remembered had been a thin, pale girl with a mop of black curls and round glasses hiding bright green eyes.

This Maurie was the same person . . . but grown up and transformed. It was the only way to describe her. Her dark hair was still curly, but now it lay in soft waves, skimming her shoulders. Her glasses were gone, and her eyes were just as green as ever. She was fair, yes; but not pale. In fact, her skin was more of a honey tone, as if she spent time outside. And she had a smattering of light freckles across her nose.

"Grant Shelton?" she said in a disbelieving half-whisper.

"And you're Maurie, right?" He held out his hand to dispel

the awkwardness. How much did she remember of that night? Did she hate him for it?

She took his hand, surprising him with a firm grip.

"It's been a long time," she continued, releasing his hand.

It was all that Grant could do to nod as he swallowed against his dry throat.

"Come in," she said. "I didn't mean to leave you standing on the porch."

She was normal. Totally normal. Friendly and . . . beautiful, if Grant was to be honest with himself. She was taller than he remembered, only about six inches shorter than him, and as he followed her inside, he had to drag his gaze away from her curves. She'd definitely grown up from that skinny girl he remembered.

They walked into the kitchen and Grant had to force himself not to gawk. The place was a disaster. Nothing had been updated in decades, and it looked as if Maurie had moved from one of those luxury resort cabins and crammed everything into this small house.

"Here." Maurie handed over a piece of paper. "My list of to-do's. Just so we're on the same page, and I don't repeat myself."

He looked away from the intensity of her green eyes—instead of all green, there was a fair amount of brown. So, hazel. He tried to read the list, but his thoughts wouldn't compute. Were the two of them not going to talk about the last time she'd lived in Pine Valley? How her mother's boyfriend had driven his car into the elm tree across the street, and how her mother had thrown beer bottles at Joe from the front porch?

"I know there's a lot of little things on the list," Maurie continued, pulling Grant from his revelry. "But I'm opening a shop in town, so anything you can do here will free me up to focus more on my shop."

Grant's mind caught up with what she was saying. "What kind of shop?"

When she smiled, Grant tightened his grip on the paper he held. He felt that smile all the way to his feet.

"It's a gift shop called *Every Occasion*. We specialize in gift baskets. I've been running it online for a couple of years now." She waved a hand at all the boxes and clutter. "Orders arrive daily, and I can't wait to move all of this to the shop. I close in thirteen and a half days."

Grant lifted his brows. "Thirteen and a half, huh?"

Her cheeks pinked, and Grant couldn't decide what he liked more: her smile, or her blush. Then he chastised himself for letting his mind wander to places it shouldn't. His life already had plenty of relationship baggage. And if Maurie thought Grant was attracted to her, after everything that had happened between them, she'd probably give him a well-deserved punch.

But here he was. Grant was trying not to ogle Maurie as she led him through the house and pointed out the repairs.

"Mind if I add a few things?" Grant said, taking a pen from his pocket and writing on the note paper that Maurie had given him. "For instance, this door frame is rotting and growing mold. And instead of replacing the door, the entire frame should be changed."

Maurie frowned.

Grant rushed to say, "If it's a matter of cost, I could start with the repairs that are most dire, and then once you're ready, move on to the others."

"That's not it," Maurie said. "I just remembered something, that's all." She flashed him a smile, but it wasn't like the genuine one earlier. "Yes, write down any additional repairs that you think are necessary. I want this place livable again."

Her life in this house must not have been too horrible, Grant decided, if she was willing to live here. A thought that made him feel even more guilty about his role in her becoming a foster kid.

"Do you want a total bid for everything on the list?" he asked as they moved into one of the bedrooms. He assumed it was where she was sleeping. It contained fewer boxes, and the bedding was rumpled but new. "Or do you prefer it itemized?"

"A total cost will be fine," Maurie said. "It all needs to be done, and I'd rather have it finished sooner than later." She pointed at the yellowed plastic blinds on the window. "Do you replace blinds, too?"

"Sure," Grant said. "What about the carpets? It's not on your list, but it's pretty threadbare."

"You noticed that, did you?" Maurie's mouth turned up with amusement.

Grant felt his face warm for some reason. Perhaps it was because he was standing in this beautiful woman's bedroom, or because he didn't want her to think he was trying to get more money out of her. "One of my friends is a carpet layer."

"Who?" she asked.

"Shawn Anders. He was a couple of years older than me in school. Not sure if you knew him."

"Doesn't sound familiar."

They inspected the second bedroom—where, Maurie informed him, her friend Taffy, also Maurie's employee, would soon be moving in.

For some reason, Grant was happy that Maurie seemed to have a close friend.

"Would you like a drink while you run the numbers?" she asked as they moved back toward the front of the house.

Everything about Maurie was unaffected. She was kind, generous, smart, and obviously talented. Not to mention gorgeous. Curiosity burned through him, and he wanted to know more about her. He wanted to know what she'd been doing for the past ten years. His answer to her question was simple, "Sure."

Three

Maurie opened the refrigerator, trying to figure out why she'd offered Grant a drink. It would mean he'd stay longer and put his bid together right in her kitchen, instead of calling back tomorrow or the next day with the numbers. Maurie already felt like a nervous mess around him. She'd had a major teenage crush on Grant Shelton.

She'd wondered if she was dreaming when she'd first opened the door to see him standing there. How many times had she thought of him after she left Pine Valley? How many men had she compared to him? More times than she wanted to admit.

She'd only shared a handful of words with Grant before her mom had been arrested. But he'd done things around their yard when he'd thought no one was home. Of course, Maurie had always been home. She'd been a homeschooling recluse, and when her mom was gone Maurie had stayed inside. Only in the afternoons when her mom had been sleeping had Maurie dared to sit on the porch and watch the other kids walk home from school.

She'd often imagined she was one of them. She had been until she was about eleven. But then her father had left, and everything had changed. Her mother had started drinking and inviting other men over. She'd slept most of the day and watched television all night. Then after an argument with the principal, she'd pulled Maurie out of school when Maurie was too young to fully understand what was going on.

She remembered early mornings during the winter when Grant had shoveled snow from their walkway. He'd even mowed their lawn when her mother had been gone and there'd been no car in the driveway. He'd probably thought Maurie had been gone, too. But once her mother began shoplifting and hanging out in the next town's bar, Maurie stopped going anywhere with her.

Grant had come around the corner from his own neighborhood once, when Maurie had gone out to the mail box. He slowed down and asked her how she was doing.

She'd told him, "Thank you for helping with our yard."

He'd turned bright red, and she'd fled, running up the driveway and into the house.

But now she was a college graduate, ran a successful business, and had had her share of boyfriends. Of course, she could credit her foster mom and dad for showing her what normal was. Oh, and a few dozen therapy sessions in high school.

"What made you decide to return to Pine Valley?" Grant asked in the here and now.

His deep tone sent a wave of warmth through her. She'd always loved his voice, the few times she'd heard it. Voices seemed to have more power over her than a man's looks. But Grant had plenty of looks as well. He was taller than she remembered, and his muscular frame was a testament to his construction-type profession.

She turned to him, holding a carton of cream and a pint of milk from the refrigerator.

"My mom left me the house, apparently, and well . . ." She shrugged. "I really needed a change of scenery."

He was watching her closely. Quite intensely, in fact. It felt as if he were trying to read her thoughts.

She set the things on the counter and tucked a curl behind her ear. "Have you ever needed a do-over?"

He nodded. "Several times."

When he didn't offer more, she folded her arms and tilted her head and said, "What about you, Grant Shelton? What have you been up to in Pine Valley all these years?" She tried to sound lighthearted, but in truth, her heart was pounding. Here it came . . . the story about his beautiful wife and two kids. Or his live-in girlfriend who was a supermodel.

"Uh, that's a depressing tale," he said, leaning back in his chair and scrubbing a hand through his hair.

Depressing? Not what she expected at all. Grant Shelton didn't seem like he had a depressing life. His light brown hair was trimmed, his face shaved, although a five o'clock shadow was making an appearance. And his nails were clean, even though he worked construction. Not to mention, she'd caught his clean and spicy scent more than once as they explored the house.

No, Grant Shelton was no deadbeat.

She took the dark chocolate mix out of the cupboard and poured milk into a pan.

"You're making me hot chocolate?" he asked.

She laughed. "Cocoa," she clarified. "And you've never tasted anything like it, believe me. Besides, I want to hear your depressing tale."

He visibly swallowed, and a thought hit her. Maybe he was as nervous as she felt.

"All right," he said, writing down some numbers on the note paper. "If you're sure you want to hear it."

She turned on the burner and watched the gas flame leap to life. "I'd love to." After mixing in the cream and several scoops of dark chocolate powder, she lowered the temperature to a simmer and said, "I'm listening."

Grant pushed the note paper to the side with a grimace.

Then he met her gaze. "So, right now I'm in a custody battle for my five-year-old son. His mother wants to keep him in another city and raise him with another man."

"Oh," Maurie said, moving to the table and sitting across from Grant. He was divorced, and he was a father. Wow. "What's your son's name?"

He looked surprised at her question. "Trent."

Maurie nodded. "Trent Shelton. I like it. He'll be a strong and good man, like his father."

"How would you know?" Grant asked, although he sounded more curious than bothered by her pronouncement.

"A kid takes after the good parent," she said in a quiet voice. "Believe me, I know. My father might have left us, but I think I must be like him. I am nothing like my mother."

"That's pretty clear," Grant said, his tone also subdued. "I appreciate your compliment, but I just can't see through much more than the court battles right now. I had him for three days over Christmas, and now I won't see him until Spring Break."

Maurie stood and stirred the hot cocoa. "When's that?"

"Middle of March."

She shook her head. "That's a long time for a little kid. Can you call him at night?"

"Joy usually tells me he's asleep."

"Does he have an iPad or a phone?"

"He has an iPad."

"Perfect," Maurie said. "Then you can Facetime."

"Is that like Facebook?" he asked. "I hate social media."

Maurie scoffed. "Me, too. But it's a great way to reach my customers. Here, let me see your phone." He handed it over, and she turned on Facetime in his settings, then handed it back.

"What's your number?" she asked. Typing the numbers he recited into her phone, she then Facetimed him.

"What do I do?" Grant said.

She leaned over his shoulder and pointed at the answer button. "Answer it and keep it in front of your face."

He did, and his eyes widened.

"Hi Grant," she said into her phone, smiling at his image on the screen.

"Hi," he replied as he stood. He walked about the small kitchen, angling his phone this way and that, experimenting with her image.

"Is the bid ready yet?' Maurie asked as Grant brought his phone really close to his face until only one blue eye filled her screen.

He laughed at his copied image in the corner of his phone, the sound sending warm prickles along her skin. "I'm nearly finished."

"Great. What's the estimated completion date?"

He paused by the table and looked down at the note paper. "At least two weeks." Then his blue gaze was back to staring at her through the screen, even though they were standing only a couple of feet apart.

She ignored his closeness and his spicy clean scent. "Sounds good. When can you get started?"

"Does tomorrow work?" He slid a sideways glance at her, smiling.

"Perfect." Maurie ended the call. She looked at the Grant in the flesh. "What do you think? Will Trent like it?"

"He'll love it," Grant's smile turned into a grin.

And then he pulled her into a hug. It was brief, enthusiastic, and over way too soon.

"Oh, uh." Grant took a step back and scrubbed a hand through his hair. A nervous habit of his, apparently. "Sorry. I'm just really grateful."

She wanted to laugh, but it would be a nervous laugh. Instead, she turned calmly back to the hot chocolate. "I can't wait to hear what Trent thinks of Facetime."

"Yeah," Grant said. "I'll let you know. I'm going to talk to him tonight about using it on his iPad—if Joy lets me get through to him."

Maurie touched Grant's arm. "Good luck." She decided that the stove was making the kitchen warmer than usual. She released him and said, "The hot cocoa smells ready."

"Smells?" he said.

"Yeah," Maurie said with a shrug. "Can't you smell the richness of it?"

He inhaled. "It smells good, that's all I know."

Their eyes connected again, and before Maurie allowed herself to blush, she turned toward the cupboards and took out two mugs, each of them different. She never bought two exactly alike. She poured in the steaming cocoa, and then used a peppermint stick in each to stir. Leaving the peppermint sticks in the mugs, she topped each with a dollop of whipped cream and a sprinkle of cinnamon.

"Wow," he said as he sat and she placed his mug on the table in front of him. "This is too fancy to drink."

"I can make you another if you'd just like to look at that one," she teased.

"No," he said with a grin. "I'm drinking this." He took a sip and swallowed. He closed his eyes. Then he reopened them. "It's like perfection. How did you do this?"

"Years of practice. My foster mother was a gourmet cook. You should have seen her meals—even the simple ones. I was pretty desperate for a normal mom, so I stayed with her in the kitchen after school and on the weekends, instead of being social."

When Maurie looked over at Grant, his face had paled. Had she said something to upset him? She didn't remember much about his parents, but his family had seemed a decent lot. Maybe his ex-wife cooked?

"Well, this is delicious," he said after a moment, finishing his drink, surely scalding his throat. "I'd better get going." He stood and picked up the mug and rinsed it in the sink.

"You don't have to . . ." she started, but he was finished before she could protest.

"Tomorrow?" Grant asked.

Maurie nodded, stunned out of a reply.

"I'll be here around 8:00 am."

Then he was gone.

Four

As Grant strode to his truck, it sank in that Maurie didn't know he was the one who'd changed her life. The wintry air had turned sharp, and he cranked on the heater. Had he done the right thing ten years ago? Looking at how successful and seemingly content Maurie was now, he could probably talk himself into believing it had all been for the best. But a thirty-minute visit with her couldn't erase ten years of questions and guilt. There had to be much more that she wasn't telling him, and probably not telling anyone. If the roles had been reversed, he couldn't imagine what he might be feeling.

What if it had been him taken from his family and placed in foster care?

He pulled away from the curb and started driving to his last appointment of the day. He'd spent the last two weeks building and painting cupboards for Mrs. Jones, two blocks over. Today he'd mount all of the cupboards and install the hardware. He couldn't wait to see the finished product, and it would be a welcome distraction to take his thoughts away from the beautiful woman he'd just spent time with.

Mrs. Jones turned out to be little distraction. The install went quickly, and soon Grant was home from work. He texted Julie that he wouldn't make dinner that night, and instead he turned on his too-slow laptop and Googled Maurie Ledbetter.

Before he knew it, he'd spent two hours reading links

associated with her name. She'd graduated high school with honors and earned a Bachelor of Arts degree in college. When he poked around on her Facebook page, he unearthed only a few pictures. To see more he'd need to friend her. But she looked happy and healthy and successful from what he saw.

Grant shut off the laptop and leaned back in his chair. Night had fallen around him, and there were no lights on in his apartment, so he sat in the dark, thinking. Why rock the boat now? Maurie had turned out fine, better than fine.

The guilt that churned in his stomach would fade with time. He'd spend the next couple of weeks fixing up her house, while she'd probably be putting together her shop. How much would he really see her anyway? Then after his job was completed he might see her once in a while about the town, but to have a congenial relationship with her, it wasn't as if he'd need to bare his soul.

He flipped on a couple of lights and called Joy. Not his favorite thing to do, but for now it was the only way to get through to Trent. He hoped that Facetime would change all of that. Tonight must be his lucky night because five minutes later, Trent's small face popped up on Grant's phone screen. They spent the next twenty minutes talking and laughing as Trent told Grant every joke he'd heard at school. Most of them were told wrong, but Grant didn't mind one bit.

The following morning, he knocked on Maurie's door, confident with his decision to not tell her about that night he'd called the cops on her mother. When no one answered, he knocked again, then looked for a note she might have left. Maybe she had already gone to her shop. But there was no note, and with still no answer to his knocking, he tried the door knob and found it unlocked.

"Maurie?" he called as he pushed open the door and stepped inside.

The house was quiet, but for some reason it didn't feel empty.

"It's Grant. I'm here to start working." Still nothing.

He peeked into the kitchen, surprised to see the mug of hot chocolate that she'd drank from still on the table. His bid was where he'd left it on the table, seemingly untouched.

"Maurie?" He moved into the hallway and started peaking around doorways. The bathroom was empty, so were the bedrooms. And then he heard her voice.

"Grant?"

The sound came from above . . . the attic. He hurried toward the sound and saw the open hatch in the corner of the second bedroom.

Two feet dangled from the opening.

As he strode toward the hatch, Maurie's legs appeared as she lowered herself to the chair beneath the hatch. He grasped her arm to steady her as her feet touched the chair.

"Thanks," she said, smiling as she started to brush off her clothes. Then she sneezed.

"Bless you," he said, smiling back. Her hair was pulled up into a knot, and her black leggings and oversized shirt were covered in dust and lint. "Are you all right?"

"Yeah," she said. "It's really dusty, but I was checking to see if my mom had put anything up there."

He held out his hand again and she took it, using his support to step down from the chair. She brushed against him as she reached the carpet, and he exhaled as heat swept through him at her nearness. Even though she was grimy from the attic, she was even more beautiful than yesterday.

He released her hand and stepped back, giving her space to pass him.

"Find anything?"

She halted and looked up at him. They were standing about

three feet apart, but it felt as if the room had shrunk and they were mere inches away from each other. "I did. I've been up there for over an hour looking through old albums that my grandmother probably put together. Pictures I've never seen."

"Do you want me to bring them down?" He asked, noticing a piece of lint in her hair. He said, "Hold still," and stepped closer to pluck it out.

"Thanks. But you don't have to go up there."

He lifted his hands. "Free of charge."

"All right, I'd appreciate that."

"No problem." He stepped onto the chair and poked his head through the hatch opening. The attic's mustiness attacked, and he sneezed.

"It's really dirty."

"I got it," he said, bracing his elbows on the edges and pulling himself up. "I'll hand down the boxes to you."

"Okay," came her muffled reply.

He scanned the small area. There were about a dozen boxes—handmade boxes, with their taped edges and corners. A small crib that was more of a bassinet stood in one corner. And a huge stack of *National Geographic* magazines teetered in another corner. Grant picked up the top magazine. 1968. He put it into one of the boxes, then handed it down to Maurie.

He looked down through the hatch. "Did you see all of these *National Geographic*'s up here?"

"Yeah, I think they were my grandpa's," she said peering up at him. "He died when I was pretty young, so I don't remember much."

"Well, if you want someone to take them off your hands, let me know," he said.

"Really? You want them?"

He shrugged. "Only if you don't."

Her smile was soft, and it traveled all the way to his heart. "They're all yours, Grant Shelton. Hand them down."

So he did, right after they finished with the other boxes. By the time the attic was mostly cleared out and Grant had lowered himself down through the hatch, he was even dirtier than Maurie had been.

"Look at us," she said. "Do you need to go home and get cleaned up?"

"I'm used to these working conditions," he said, winking at her. This gave him pause. It had been a really long time since he'd winked at a woman.

"Well, I need a shower," she said. "Help yourself to whatever you need."

He nodded. "Thanks, I plan to start in the kitchen so you'll have it functional first."

They parted ways, leaving the boxes from the attic in the second bedroom for now, and he set to work repairing the two broken cupboards and adding two shelves to the pantry. As he moved back and forth between the kitchen and the saw table he'd set up on the porch, he tried not to think of Maurie in the shower only a couple of walls away. She definitely trusted him. And it wasn't that he *wasn't* trustworthy, but he was definitely attracted to her and his imagination wasn't exactly behaving.

He chalked it up to the fact that he hadn't allowed himself to relax around a woman in a long time. He'd gone on exactly two dates since his divorce—one was set up, and the other a spur of the moment connection. Neither had led to second dates. But now it was all that he could do to not let his imagination get away from him as he thought about what it would be like to take Maurie out for dinner, or maybe on a long walk near the ski resort, or even just grabbing a coffee at the Main Street Café.

"Snap out of it," he mumbled as he hammered the support two-by-four that would hold the new pantry shelf.

"Did you say something?" Maurie asked.

He turned to see her standing in the kitchen doorway. Her

skin gleamed pink from her shower, making her eyes more green than brown. Her hair was still wet with small water droplets marking the shoulders of her long sleeved shirt. She wore ratty jeans with holes at the knees, the jeans fitting her curves as if they'd been painted on.

Oh boy. "Uh, I should have warned you," he said, swallowing hard. "I talk to myself when I work."

"Hmm," Maurie said. "I'll be sure to stay close by then." She crossed to where he was working and placed a hand on his shoulder. Her touch was like a mini-heater on his skin. "Did you and your son hook up Facetime?"

"Yes. He loved it, and I loved seeing his face while we talked. Well, I sort of hated it, too, because it made me miss him more. But now I don't have to go through Joy every time I want to get in touch with my kid."

"Good," Maurie said, squeezing his shoulder slightly, then moving away. "I'm glad it worked out."

"Me, too," Grant said and watched her walk out of the kitchen, the feel of her hand on his shoulder still lingering. Then he went back to work before he allowed himself to get even more distracted.

Five

WHILE GRANT WAS working in the kitchen, Maurie texted Taffy. *Just a warning. An old friend of mine is doing repair work on the house. Grant Shelton. And I'm only going to tell you once. I'm not interested in him.*

Her phone rang thirty seconds later.

"*Grant Shelton?*" Taffy practically shouted. "The neighbor guy who used to mow your lawn when your mom was gone?"

Maurie groaned. She'd told Taffy about everything in her past, and apparently that had included everything about Grant, too.

"Is he still drop-dead gorgeous?" Taffy pressed.

"Is that how I described him?" Maurie asked.

"Pretty much." Taffy laughed. "So what's his story? Is he married?"

"Divorced, with a kid. Custody battle. And he's still gorgeous, but before you say anything, he's like a million miles away emotionally, and no . . . I'm not interested. When I start dating again, it's going to be someone with no baggage. I have enough on my own for two."

Taffy scoffed. "Yeah, good luck with that, Maurie. I mean, I love you, but you're twenty-seven. What are you going to do, marry a twenty-year-old? Every man your age will have baggage. And if they haven't been married or in a serious relationship, then you probably don't want anything to do with them."

This was not the first lecture Maurie had received from Taffy. "Okay, okay, when you put it like that . . ." her voice trailed off.

"When I put it like what? Are you admitting that you're still attracted to Mr. Hot Guy?"

"Don't call him that. I mean, he's a *dad*."

"Oh my heck, girl, you've still got it for him," Taffy said, delight in her voice. "I can't *wait* to meet him. Which will be, incidentally, in about seven hours."

Maurie leaned back against the pillows in her bed, where she'd sequestered herself with her laptop to input her recent orders. Grant was still working in the kitchen, replacing a couple of broken tiles on the floor. He was like a renaissance man, but she didn't need to tell Taffy that.

"I can't wait to see you," Maurie said. "I think this will feel *real* once you're here, and we can start moving everything into the shop."

Once she hung up with Taffy, Maurie listened for a few minutes to the sound of whatever high pitched drill Grant was using. Curiosity got the better of her. Climbing off her bed, she checked her reflection in the mirror above the dresser. Her hair had dried in a riot of curls, so she smoothed it back and knotted it into a ponytail.

She found Grant in the living room, removing screws from the dark wood paneling that lined the walls. He'd taken off the flannel shirt he'd worn over a navy t-shirt. His forearms were strangely tanned for the middle of winter, and not so strangely muscled. She blinked to clear her mind of the memory of his hug yesterday.

"You're taking the paneling off?" she asked, when there was a short break in the noise. "I thought you were going to paint over it."

He bent to the floor and picked up one of the panel pieces. When he turned it over, she saw the black on the other side.

"I think it's mold," he said. "But it looks like it's only embedded on the paneling and not the walls."

"Oh, wow," she said. "I'm glad you caught that."

"With material this old, I have to check," Grant said. He scanned the rest of the room, and then his gaze settled on hers. "If you need help taking all your boxes to the shop, I've got a truck."

"Well, that would be nice, but my friend Taffy is arriving tonight. We'll probably rent a trailer."

Grant lifted a single brow. "Since I have to remove the paneling, I was thinking you and I could take a truck load over today. I mean, it's a bit crowded in here."

"Yeah." Boxes were everywhere, and she couldn't really expect him to work when there was hardly room to walk. "But I don't want to put you out. And I'm not sure if I can really move stuff into the shop until I officially close."

"Why don't you call the realtor? Is it Jeff Finch?"

"Yeah, do you know him?"

Grant smiled. "It's Pine Valley. We go back a ways. Let me know what he says." He turned back to the next part of the panel and started up his drill again.

Well, then. Grant was a bit bossy, it seemed, she decided. But she'd hired him to do the renovations, so she returned to her bedroom, shut the door and called the realtor. Mr. Finch told her to stop by his office for the key on her way over there.

"I just won't be able to let you keep the key," he added. "You'll have to bring it back after you're finished."

"No problem," she told the realtor. "Thanks for this. Grant needs the room to work on the house."

"I get it. How's he doing, by the way?"

"Fine, I think." The turn in the conversation surprised her. Things with Mr. Finch had never veered toward personal before. "Should I be worried about him?"

"Oh, it's nothing, I'm sure. He's cancelled on everything that we've tried to set up with the guys. We go way back to high school, and since his divorce, we've tried to reach out to him, but no dice."

"He mentioned some frustrations with the custody issues over his son. But I don't know him that well."

"Yeah, sorry," Mr. Finch said. "Don't mean to get you involved."

After she hung up, she stood and paused in the middle of her bedroom. If Grant had isolated himself from pretty much everyone, he probably wasn't dating. The thought made her feel fluttery and guilty at the same time. Fluttery that he was available, guilty because he seemed to be under a lot of stress.

She walked into the living room, and when he saw her, he turned off the drill.

"The realtor gave us the green light," she said. "We just need to pick up the key from his office."

"Great," Grant said, setting down the drill. "Which boxes do you want to go first?"

"Now?"

He nodded. "Yep."

"All right, then." She looked around the room. "Everything in this room goes, except for the baskets. I'll be doing some orders over the weekend."

"Great," he said, then picked up a double set of boxes.

Maurie opened the door for him and then went to grab her jacket. He might be able to stand the cold, but it seemed to go straight through her.

Twenty minutes later, the bed of his truck was loaded with boxes, and while she was trying to catch her breath, he closed the tailgate, and then jumped into the truck.

She climbed in, noticing that he didn't look the least bit winded. He wasn't even perspiring, and he was still in his t-shirt.

Which meant Maurie couldn't let herself stare at him too long. Apparently her teen crush hadn't completely died. She was just glad he wasn't married anymore; it would have been even more awkward crushing on him.

"How did you get into gift basket sales?" he asked.

Maurie leaned back on the seat and said, "Probably something to do with my foster mom. Not only was she a fabulous chef, she always put together the most amazing presentations for neighbor gifts and fundraisers."

"So you're a dot.com, too?"

"Yeah, but Taffy will do most of the online stuff now, and I'll focus on the retail location. Taffy isn't a hundred percent sure she wants to live in Pine Valley forever. I'm hoping to convert her, but she's the type who wants to get married and have a bunch of kids."

"And you aren't?" Grant treated Maurie to an endearing blush. "I mean," he backtracked, "that didn't quite turn out right."

"It's okay." Maurie was certain she was starting to blush as well. "I suppose if it happens, it happens. But if there's one thing I learned in my months of therapy, it's to be happy wherever I am. Happiness comes from my choices in life, and not worrying about what is beyond my control."

He looked over at her. "You're pretty amazing, you know that?"

She was definitely blushing now. "And you have way more energy than I'll ever have."

"Working hard keeps my mind off the other stuff."

"I completely get that," she said, and it was true.

He slowed the truck in front of the realtor's office, and she said, "I'll grab the key." She jumped out of the truck as Mr. Finch came out of the front door of the office.

He held up the key as he walked toward the truck. "Hello,

Maurie," he said, then peered around her. "Grant. How's it going?"

"Keeping busy, Jeff. How about you?"

"Work. The usual. Are you up for the ski trip next weekend?"

"About that . . ." Grant said in a hesitant voice. "I might be seeing Trent, so I'd better not commit to anything."

"No problem. If you change your mind, even at the last minute, we'll have room for you."

The two men said goodbye, and soon Grant and Maurie were on their way again.

"So you ski?" she asked.

"Yeah," he said, and then grew quiet.

"You didn't seem too excited about making plans with Mr. Finch," she asked after a few moments.

"Call him Jeff," Grant said, sounding exasperated. "He's hardly Mr. Finch." He paused. "Sorry, I'm just not . . . Well, I was married, and I really don't feel like I fit into the single life anymore. I mean, skiing all day, then going to the bar and picking up women isn't really on my priority list."

Jeff Finch was a good-looking man, though not someone she was really attracted to, and she hadn't considered what his personal life might be like. But what else did handsome, single men do on the weekends?

"I'm way past high school, if you know what I mean," Grant added.

"I never really got the regular high school experience," she said, her face heating for some unknown reason.

"Yeah, and I'm sorry for that," he said. "I wish things could have been different for you."

She looked at him with surprise as he slowed the truck once more, this time stopping at the corner shop that was soon to be hers.

"We can't all get what we wish for," she said in an overly bright voice.

He didn't make a move to open his door. Instead he said, "What did you wish for, Maurie?"

She looked away from his blue gaze, down at her clasped hands. "A mom who'd cared about me." Blinking against the building tears, she said, "In the end, I did get that. Even if for only a couple of years, and even if she wasn't my biological mom. I was lucky for the time I had with her." She brushed at her cheeks. "Sorry, this moving stuff has made me unusually emotional."

"It's okay," Grant said. "I get it. Changes can be really hard."

"Come on," she said, and this time Grant turned off the engine and popped open the door.

They climbed out, and she unlocked the door to the shop, then propped the door open with one of the boxes. Grant carried boxes two at a time, while she only managed one. The work went fast, and when they finished Grant stood, his hands on his hips. "This is the place, huh?"

The shop had been cleaned out by the previous owners. But there was some trash on the ground, and the main counter was in a sorry state. It had been a clothing boutique. Framed posters of models had been taken down, leaving a dingy outline on the taupe walls. Maurie had already decided to paint the walls a soft yellow to give a warm and friendly ambience.

"What are your plans?" Grant asked, coming to stand beside her.

And she knew he wasn't asking out of politeness. As she told him of her design ideas, he nodded along the way, asking a few questions and even throwing in some feedback. The more she talked, the more she realized how easy he was to talk to. He really listened, he didn't act as if he was in a hurry, and he didn't take over the conversation. In other words, he was the complete opposite of her last boyfriend, Brandon. At first she'd chalked it up to Brandon's busy schedule with his software start-up. But even when they spent a weekend on vacation together, he'd still been so self-involved, she had felt like a decoration at his side.

When she and Grant left the shop, the excitement of finally having her own shop buzzed through her. The guests at the Pine Valley ski lodges would find a great variety of gifts in her shop and wouldn't have to rely on packing what they needed for special celebrations. And the items she offered would be more unique and desirable than the touristy items offered in gimmicky lodge stores.

They walked outside, and Maurie locked the shop door. Mr. Finch had told her to bring the key back in a couple of days, so for now she'd keep it. Grant opened the truck passenger door for her, and she said, "Thanks," before climbing in. Then she said, "How are you not cold?"

He shrugged those muscled shoulders. "I run hot, I guess."

Yes. Maurie watched him walk around the front of the truck, silently agreeing with him one-hundred percent.

Six

WHEN GRANT ARRIVED at Maurie's house the next morning, another car was parked in her driveway. He assumed it was her friend Taffy's car, and when he knocked on the door a minute later, it opened to a blonde woman.

She was a petite woman with a huge smile. "You must be Grant."

"Yep, and you must be Taffy."

She laughed. This woman seemed pretty peppy, if he were to go on first impression.

"Come on in," she said. "I've got the coffee on." Then she gave him a wink.

Grant wasn't sure exactly how to take that. He'd met this woman all of ten seconds ago.

"Maurie slept in," Taffy continued their one-sided conversation. "She'll be out in a minute. She was up half the night looking at those blasted photo albums of her grandparents. I told her not to, but would she listen to me? No. Now she'll be all weepy today."

"Weepy?" Grant asked, a knot forming in his stomach. Should he not have brought the albums down from the attic?

"Well, don't tell her I told you anything. But she's worked really hard to get over her crappy childhood. And I don't want those albums to send her back to that dark place, if you know what I mean?"

She didn't give Grant time to respond, not that he knew what to say. His mind was trying to compute all that Taffy was saying.

"I'm so glad you're renovating this place," Taffy continued. "It looks like a dump, and that can't be good for Maurie's morale either."

Grant opened his mouth to speak, but then the coffee timer went off.

"Perfect," Taffy said, flashing him a stunning smile.

If Grant were into talkative blondes, he might find her fairly attractive. But as it was, he already knew his thoughts were otherwise occupied with a dark-haired lady, if his restless sleep last night was any indication.

Taffy took out two mugs and poured the fragrant coffee. "Don't tell Maurie, but I made this straight-up black. You can add some sugar or cream if you'd like. Maurie likes to add flavors and other fancy stuff." Taffy waved to a row of bottles lined up on the counter that Grant hadn't seen the day before.

"Black is fine," he said, taking the steaming mug.

She grinned at him in a familiar way that left him wondering if there was some inside joke he was missing.

He took a careful sip of the hot liquid, and Taffy said, "Well, look at you. All handsome and rugged."

He nearly spat out the sip he'd taken.

"What?" Irritated, he couldn't tell if she was flirting, or if she just thought he was her instant best friend. He could imagine her working at a trucker's diner, calling everyone "hon" or "sweetheart."

She took a slow sip of her coffee, her gaze locked on him. "I'm sure you know what you look like, and I'm sure you've got a lot of ladies in your back pocket."

"Uh," Grant started, utterly dumbfounded. The coffee was suddenly way too bitter. And he was not in the least prepared for this onslaught this morning. But he had lived long enough to know that it needed to stop, now. "I'm not sure what you're talking about, but I'm not a player, if that's what you're asking. And we're *not* hooking up."

Taffy's eyes practically bugged out as she raised her brows. And then she burst out laughing.

Grant couldn't move. This was perhaps the strangest and nuttiest woman he'd ever met.

She lifted a finger to point at him, still laughing so hard she could barely speak. Then she finally burst out, "You're a gem, Grant Shelton. You have my 110% approval."

"Taffy!" a voice came from the hallway. Seconds later Maurie joined them in the kitchen looking as if she'd just tumbled out of bed. Not that Grant was complaining. Her fitted t-shirt had a row of Z's on it, and her PJ bottoms hung low on her hips.

"What are you feeding him?" Maurie strode up to Grant, took the mug from him and sniffed. "Not in my kitchen," she said, and then poured out the whole thing into the sink.

"Hey!" Grant said "I was drinking that." What was up with these two women?

"You're on your own, sugar," Taffy said, then sashayed out of the kitchen with her mug. "I'll be in my room processing orders. Let me know when lunch is ready." She stopped at the edge of the hallway. "Oh, and Maurie, he's all yours." She winked, and then she was gone. Her bedroom door clicked and seconds later, music began playing.

Grant looked over at Maurie who was staring at him.

"What did she say to you?" she asked, picking up the can of instant coffee and dumping it into the trash. Then she pulled out a bag of roasted coffee beans from the cupboard.

"What *didn't* she say to me?"

Maurie's eyes widened.

"Hey, are you all right?" he asked, stepping toward her. "Taffy said you had a rough night."

"She did?" Maurie's face paled. "I'm really sorry, she can be a bit . . . transparent."

"That's one way to look at it," he said. "But what about you? I mean—"

"She told you about the albums, didn't she?"

He nodded. He wished he had his coffee mug back for some sort of distraction. The knot in his stomach was tightening.

"I had a pretty bad childhood," Maurie said, "which you know. But there were good times, too . . . when I was a little kid—too young, mostly, to remember. Those albums showed me what might have been, I suppose. If my grandparents had lived longer, and my mom hadn't gone off the deep end."

"I'm really sorry," he started. "I—"

She held up a hand. "It's all in the past, and"—her voice cut off. And when she spoke again, it was trembling—"I've been lucky in many ways, but I wish that my dad hadn't left, and that my mom could have been stronger." Tears rolled down her cheeks. She closed her eyes.

"Hey," he said in a soft voice.

He closed the distance between them and pulled her into his arms. She came easily and rested her head against his chest as if it were the most natural thing in the world. And Grant had to admit that she fit there perfectly. He was just being kind, right? He rubbed her back for a few moments as she sniffled and her body trembled. Even though she'd just woken up, she smelled sweet, like chocolate and mint . . . Perhaps she'd had her gourmet hot chocolate the night before.

The thought made him smile. Then she took a few deep, calming breaths. Grant's skin had warmed up considerably where they'd touched, and his heart was thudding by the time she pulled away. He told himself space was good between them. Her smell and her touch were intoxicating.

"Thanks," she whispered, looking up at him, her smile tremulous.

They were only inches apart, yet Grant craved to be closer. He hadn't wanted the embrace to end yet, which was ridiculous. He hardly knew Maurie, and she was in distress. Even as he talked himself out of pulling her into his arms again, he knew that he *did* know Maurie. More than he should admit. And that his comforting of her wasn't exactly platonic.

"You're a good man," she said, touching his arm and raising up on her toes to kiss him on the cheek.

Her scent swept over him again, and his skin tingled where she'd pressed her warm mouth.

"Maurie," he said, grasping her hand to stop her from pulling away too soon.

She stilled, her gaze meeting his. Her breathing seemed rapid, and he couldn't help but look at her parted lips.

"I've been wondering what happened to you over the years," he said.

She seemed to move a fraction closer, or was that his imagination? Her fingers threaded through his, and a warm shiver ran up his arm.

"I've been wondering about you, too," she said softly, almost a whisper. She'd stopped crying, but her eyes were luminescent with her tears. "I had a huge crush on you."

When she smiled, Grant smiled back. His heart sounded like a freight train in his ears. He had to tell her. He couldn't stand her gazing at him as if he were some sort of nice guy. She had to know the truth about her last night in Pine Valley.

"Maurie, I always wanted to get to know you better," he started. "Being a teenager was complicated, and you were like a shadow that came and went. Sometimes, I hoped that when I did yard work at your house that you'd come out and talk to me."

"You knew I was home during those times?"

He chuckled. "Of course. I'd wait for your mom to leave, and then I'd come over. For some reason I couldn't bring myself to knock on your door and talk to you." This was it; the time was now. "Maurie, I need to—"

And then it happened.

She moved forward and wrapped her arms around his neck, pulling him toward her. She pressed her mouth against his, and he forgot all reservations and drew her closer to taste those inviting lips. She kissed him with unexpected depth and passion, yet it was gentle and exploring, too. His heart seemed to hammer in time with the music thumping from the back bedroom. He didn't want to scare her off, but he also couldn't get enough of her. He backed her up against the counter and continued to kiss her, taking the lead.

She practically melted into him. When he finally needed air, she was equally breathless.

"Wow," he said, leaning his forehead against hers, trying to calm his breathing.

"Yeah, wow," she answered.

"I think I need to get to work," he said.

"Too hot in the kitchen?" she asked with a laugh.

"Yeah," he said, grinning. "Mind if I open a couple of windows?" He pulled her close again and kissed her lightly on the mouth. "Dinner tonight? Without Taffy?"

"Hey, she's my friend," she said, playfully pushing against his chest. Then she raised a brow, looking up at him. "I'd love that."

Seven

WHAT HAD HAPPENED today?

Maurie still couldn't get over it, as she got ready for her dinner date with Grant. He'd gone home to shower and change, and she felt as if she'd been floating all day. She still couldn't believe that she'd kissed him, and then of course he'd kissed her back. Just remembering their adventure in the kitchen made her blush again. There was no way she was telling Taffy about the kiss, or kisses, at least not yet.

Maurie didn't need to hear Taffy's lecturing about how it was too soon to fall for a guy. It had only been a couple of months since Maurie's breakup with Brandon. Her friend would say that Maurie was on the rebound. But Taffy had also said she was giving Grant her 110% approval. But when Maurie told her she and Grant made dinner plans, her friend had put her hands on her hips and said, "You be careful, girl, with that heart of yours."

A knock sounded at the front door as Maurie examined her collection of lipsticks.

Taffy passed the bathroom. "I'll get the door."

Maurie stepped back from the mirror and surveyed her appearance. She wanted to look nice, but not as if she was trying too hard. She wore a long black sweater over dark gray leggings, ending in black ankle boots. She'd chosen her pearl earrings and pearl drop necklace, inherited from her foster mom.

Taffy's laughter streamed from the front room, and Maurie

decided on a simple lip gloss. She didn't want to have to maintain the lipstick look, especially if Grant decided to kiss her, or . . . the other way around.

When she exited the bathroom and turned the corner to the living room, she slowed her step, stunned.

She'd seen Grant only in work clothing so far, which had been pleasing enough. But now that he was dressed up, Maurie wondered how this guy had stayed single for so long after his divorce. He'd shaved, and he wore dark slacks with a black leather jacket over a pale blue button down shirt that was open at the collar. His brown hair looked slightly damp, and as she neared him, his cologne became distinct. His blue eyes seemed to glitter.

"Hi," he said, his gaze soaking her in, from her hair waving about her shoulders, down the length of her body.

She was glad he was checking her out because when their gazes met again, she only saw appreciation in his, and her pulse thrummed to life. "Hi," she said back.

"All righty, then," Taffy said. "It looks like you two are ready to go. Have a great time. And don't worry about me here alone. There's a new series I want to binge watch on Netflix."

Maurie turned to Taffy. "Do you want me to bring you something back?"

"Ah, no," Taffy said with a wink. "I'm not so fond of leftovers. This will give me a chance to eat some of the contraband food I snuck into your house."

"Funny," Maurie said and hugged her friend. "We won't be too late."

"I'm not planning on staying up," Taffy said.

Maurie was really glad she hadn't told Taffy about the kiss. Otherwise, her friend would probably be giving her a much harder time. Taffy would have reminded Maurie about her recent breakup and about Grant's newly divorced status, combined with all that went into opening a new shop. As it was, Taffy practically pushed Maurie and Grant out the door. Maurie stopped on the porch, taking in the SUV parked in the driveway.

"No truck?" she asked.

"I wasn't going to bring my work truck on a date," Grant said, slipping his hand into hers and guiding her down the steps and along the icy walkway to the driveway.

"I'm not complaining," she said as a thrill ran through her at his touch. The affectionate gesture told her so much: that he remembered their kiss as well, and that he was definitely interested in her.

He chuckled and opened the passenger door. She climbed in, finding the interior warm. She leaned back against the seat and released a sigh as he walked around the front.

When he climbed in, she said, "Any Facetiming with Trent tonight?"

"Yeah, actually. A couple of times," Grant said as he started the engine. He backed out of the driveway. "He's been sending me selfies like crazy, too. I might have created a monster."

After he straightened out the wheel of the car, he handed her his phone. "Here, look at the texts he sent."

She took the phone and opened up the discussion labeled "Trent" and laughed when she saw the pictures of the different expressions of a little boy that looked like a mini-me of Grant. "Wow, he looks so much like you."

"That's what everyone says. The good news is that it means I'm his real father."

"What do you mean?" she asked with a sinking heart.

He turned the wheel, steering around the corner and onto Main Street. "Joy believed in sharing her love with more than just her husband."

Maurie nodded, not sure what to say. She felt awful for him, and she was having a hard time imagining a woman who wouldn't find satisfaction with one man, especially a man like Grant. "How long were you married?"

"About a year. Most of it was pretty miserable. But she was pregnant, and I tried to stick it out for the kid." Grant blew out a breath. "I had a hard time believing the child was mine, until he was born, that is."

"Well, he's adorable," she said, scrolling through the last of the pictures. When she finished, she set the phone in the middle console. "What does he like to do?"

"He's pretty much obsessed with all reptiles and dinosaurs," Grant said, his tone softening. "Despite all the crap that's gone on with Joy, I wouldn't trade my son for anything."

She admired his profile. In it, she saw pain and determination and resilience. And, most of all, loyalty. "I'd love to meet Trent sometime."

Grant flashed her a smile. "I think that can be arranged."

His answer made her heart flutter. She wasn't sure when Spring Break was, when he said he'd have his son for a visit. But if Grant and she were still friends—still dating—that sounded perfectly fine with her.

"Where are we going?" she asked as he turned onto the canyon road that led to the ski resorts and mountain slopes.

"The Grille has a great menu. Have you been there before?"

She laughed. "Hardly. I pretty much ate out of cans and boxes growing up. My mom wasn't much of a cook. It wasn't until I moved into foster care that my eyes were opened to the heaven that good food can bring."

He smiled as he pulled off the turn in the road, and drove up to a large lodge blazing with lights. He slowed as he drove through the parking lot. "Was it hard? Leaving Pine Valley and everything you knew?"

"It wasn't like I could be more miserable than I already was," she said in a quiet voice. She took a deep breath. "Honestly, the only thing I missed was you."

He snapped his head to look at her with surprise.

"Don't get creeped out, okay?" she clarified. "I mean, yeah, I did have a crush on you, but it was that the things you did around our yard gave me a sense of comfort. Like someone was watching out for me. I missed that once I left." She shrugged. "After a few weeks in foster care, I realized how messed up my life had been, and I felt lucky to have escaped when I did."

"Truly?" he asked, as he pulled into a parking place. He turned to look at her, his gaze intense.

"Yes, truly." She was surprised at his intensity, as if he somehow he felt responsible for her happiness.

"So . . ." he said, amusement replacing the intensity. "You had a pretty big crush on me, huh?"

"I think I already made that clear. Maybe more than once."

"Hmm." He leaned toward her, capturing her hand in his and pulling her close. Then he kissed her, slowly, as if he were savoring the feel of her. When he drew away, she had to catch her breath.

"I'm glad you came home." One side of his mouth lifted into a smile. Then he popped open his door, climbed out, and hurried around the SUV to open her door.

The best part of the night had already happened, she decided as he took her hand again. She could get used to this really fast.

Inside the lodge, they walked to the hostess stand.

"Grant?" the petite, dark haired woman said. She wore a nametag proclaiming her name as *Alicia*.

"Oh, hi," Grant said. "You work here now?"

"The Aspen Lodge had too many politics, if you know what I mean." She gave him a long glance.

Heat burned through Maurie, all the way to her toes. The other woman hadn't even acknowledged her . . . even though Grant was holding her hand.

Alicia leaned forward on the podium, giving anyone who cared to see an eyeful of the cleavage spilling from the low-cut neckline of her navy dress. "I haven't seen you around for a while," she said in a sultry voice. "What have you been up to?"

"Working," Grant said," and trying to fit in time with Trent."

Maurie's stomach churned. This beautiful, sophisticated woman knew Grant well enough for him to discuss his son with her.

"You poor thing," Alicia practically cooed. She started to say something else, but Grant cut her off.

"We're here for dinner," he said. "I made reservations."

Alicia's eyes cut to Maurie, giving her a passing glance. Maurie had the feeling that Alicia had already checked her out, long before they arrived at the hostess stand.

The woman looked back at Grant without greeting Maurie. "Follow me," she said, turning with a smug smile and walking through the restaurant until they reached a round booth. "This will keep you cozy." Her smile was for Grant alone.

He and Maurie sat and made themselves comfortable, and soon a waitress appeared with more smiles. When she looked at Grant, her smile became even wider. "Hi, Grant, it's been a while."

Oh great. Maurie studied the waitress. Long blonde hair. Flawless makeup.

"Hi, Gwen," Grant said smoothly as if the woman's mega-watt smile had no effect on him. "Looks like it's busy tonight."

"Yeah, Fridays are usually like that," Gwen winked. She glanced over at Maurie, and then said, "What drinks can I start you with?"

After they ordered and Gwen left their table with her smile still in place, Maurie leaned forward. "You've got a lot of lady friends here."

His blue eyes met hers. "None of them are as interesting to me as you."

She looked down at her hands. "I'm not fishing for a compliment, Grant."

"I know you're not," he said, lowering his voice. "I'm letting you know that I'm on a date with *you*, not any other women."

She looked back up. It was silly to be jealous. They'd shared a couple of kisses, and this was their first date. She had no claim on him. But she had to know. "Did you date either of them?"

He leaned back and glanced over at the other tables in the restaurant. "Alicia and I went out with a group of friends. We texted off and on, but our schedules never lined up. And to be honest, I wasn't all that interested in her. Joy was so high maintenance, and Alicia seemed more of the same."

"What about Gwen?"

"Nothing with Gwen. She's just flirty."

Maurie lifted a brow. "I'll bet you get that a lot."

With a shrug, he said, "One of the cruxes of being single and in a small town—everyone knows you're available." He paused. "I got tired of the pickup scene pretty quickly. It's why I don't go out much with the guys."

"Yeah," Maurie said. "I get it."

Gwen came back, pen and notepad poised to take their orders. Maurie hadn't even looked at the menu. After Grant ordered top sirloin, she selected the grilled salmon salad.

Gwen was still friendly and flirty with Grant, but it didn't bother Maurie anymore. When the waitress left to put in their order, he asked Maurie questions about college and why she'd decided to start up an online retailer outfit.

Their food arrived, and by looking at her salad, Maurie knew she'd enjoy every bite. As they ate and talked, Grant told her about his two years at a community college—where he'd met Joy—a little about their marriage, and then their move back to Pine Valley, where Grant had worked as a handyman at the lodge, and then joined up with one of the larger construction companies in the area.

Every Occasion

"Did you always want to strike out on your own?" she asked.

"I was much happier doing certain jobs than others," he said. "I learned that working with a large construction company meant I always had to listen to the boss before I could make decisions and dive into a job."

"And now?"

"Now I have to listen to my sister Julie who does the scheduling."

Maurie laughed.

"But really," he continued. "I can't complain. I make more money now, and I have more time to myself. I can set my own schedule and take off holidays if I want to. That's especially important when Trent's with me."

Gwen returned, asking if they wanted dessert. Maurie declined, and Grant asked for the bill.

"Being with you is different," he said when they were waiting for the check.

Maurie stared at him. "How?"

"You're . . ." Grant held her gaze. "I don't know how to explain it."

Her face heated. "Is 'different' good, or bad?"

"Oh, definitely good," he said with a smile.

Now she blushed.

"Maybe it's because I knew you as a kid," he said. "And all these years, I've wondered about you."

She found herself smiling. "It's hard to believe you still remembered me."

"Here's the thing," Grant started. "I need to make a confession. And I don't know if you'll even want to see me after. I was going to wait until I finished with your house."

"What is it?" Maurie asked, a hard knot forming in her stomach.

Gwen appeared with the bill and thanked them for coming.

Grant added a tip to the receipt and signed it, and then he stood and held out his hand toward Maurie.

She wasn't sure if her heart was pounding because Grant had taken her by the hand again and was leading her through the restaurant, or if she was nervous about his "confession."

Once outside, he steered her toward the outside gardens that were strewn with lights. They walked along the frozen paths, and finally Grant said, "All right, here it goes . . ."

Eight

GRANT SLOWED HIS step, glad the night wasn't as cold as it had been lately. Maurie looked beautiful in any setting, but outside with the lights twinkling around them she seemed ethereal. It was all he could do not to stop and pull her into his arms and kiss her. The memory of their earlier kissing was still fresh in his mind. And he'd actually liked that she seemed a bit jealous of the attention other women had given him. Not that either of them meant anything to him.

But he couldn't hold to his decision not to tell her about his role so long ago. He now knew that he had to tell her before anything more happened to progress their relationship.

"What's going on, Grant?" She tugged him to a stop and looked up at him.

Why did her eyes have to be so beautiful, and her lips so inviting? His heart hammered with a combination of anticipation and fear. He exhaled. "First, I need you to know that when I said that I've been wondering how your life turned out, it wasn't just because I was curious."

A slight smile touched her face.

"I was worried, actually," he said, looking away for a moment.

"You're a sweet man, Grant Shelton," she said, moving closer.

He didn't move away. In fact, he grasped her other hand.

"Don't say that," he insisted in a quiet voice. "I . . . your last night in Pine Valley, I was on my way to your house. I was going to invite you to the high school dance."

Her lips parted with surprise.

"I wasn't going to do anything fancy. Just knock on your door and actually talk to you."

She laughed, but Grant couldn't make himself join her.

"It was probably about 9:30 at night, and I knew it was late for a school night, but the lights were on at your house."

Her face sobered, and Grant's heart rate sped up.

"My mom's party . . ."

"Yeah," Grant said. "The music was loud, and there were a few cars in front of your house. I figured they were your mom's friends. So I waited a while, trying to build up my courage. I didn't really want to face a bunch of people when I tried to talk to you."

Maurie nodded her head slowly.

"But then . . ." Grant looked down at their clasped hands. Surprisingly, he was no longer cold. He felt too warm. "As I started up the walk, the front door burst open, and a man came stumbling out. Your mom was right behind him. Yelling at him for cheating on her. She threw a beer bottle at him."

Maurie's face had gone still.

Grant had to continue, get it all out. "The man ducked, but then he turned back around and charged after her, cursing. I think I was in shock, and I didn't really know what to do. I could only think of you inside that house and being hurt by that man, or even your mom." He paused. Maurie was looking down. Tears had dripped onto her cheeks. "So, I called the cops. By the time they came, everyone else had gone home. I was watching from the other side of the street. Things were calm again, so maybe I'd jumped the gun too fast."

Maurie released his hands and wiped at her cheeks.

His eyes burned with his own tears, and he looked away. "I

had no idea that you'd be taken from your home and put in foster care. And I didn't intend for your mom to get arrested." He blew out a breath and rubbed his face. "If I could go back, I wouldn't have called. I feel like because of me, your whole life was turned upside down."

Maurie was quiet for a moment, and then she said, "My life was already upside down." She was looking at her twisting hands, and Grant wished he knew what she was thinking.

"Sorry." She wiped at her cheeks again. "I just need some time to digest this all." She seemed to be thinking about what he'd said, but she'd also stepped away and wasn't looking at him. She started walking through the frozen garden, Grant following, and after a few minutes, he said, "We can get in the car, it's getting pretty cold."

Maurie didn't say anything more, and the drive home was very quiet. It wasn't until they reached her neighborhood street that she said, "Thanks for dinner. The food was great."

He felt relieved that she was at least speaking to him again. He pulled into her driveway. "You're welcome," he said, glancing at her to gauge her expression. He couldn't read her eyes. "And I'm sorry I didn't tell you earlier about what happened that night."

She reached over and placed a hand on his arm for a brief moment. "You did what you thought was best. And I've learned more than anyone that we can't change the past. We can only go forward." The last few words came out shaky, and she opened the door before he could say anything more.

He opened his door to walk her to the porch, but she hurried up the walk and slipped inside before he could get his feet on the ground.

For a long moment, he stared at the house, his heart heavy and his throat thick. He knew he'd done the right thing by telling her. He wished things between them hadn't been so fragile. He drove home, feeling like he'd just shed a warm coat and was standing in the middle of an icy blizzard.

Over the next two weeks, he saw very little of her. Truthfully, they crossed paths only a handful of times when he arrived at her house to work and she was on her way out the door to work at her shop. Their conversations were short and never referred to their last date. As far as he knew, and overheard between Maurie and Taffy when he heard them talking in the house, the closing paperwork for the shop had gone well. And Maurie and her friend were busy setting things up. The shop's grand opening was scheduled for the Friday before Valentine's, and he'd offered to help them move things in. But they'd arranged to pay a couple of neighbor kids who were looking for some extra cash.

So, Grant had kept his head down and worked, hoping that it wouldn't be too much longer before he and Maurie could at least clear the air between them. But on his final day working on her house, they hadn't spoken privately. Everything said between him and Maurie had happened with Taffy near enough to overhear.

At least Taffy had stopped her teasing and was behaving normally toward him now.

Grant checked the time. It was well after 7:00 pm, and he'd been finished for almost an hour. He'd checked and rechecked all of his work. He'd cleaned up everything and loaded his tools in his truck. But there'd still been no sign of Maurie or Taffy since they'd left earlier in the day.

Maybe he could run by the store, see if they needed help, and let Maurie know he was completely finished with her house.

Outside, he was slipping off his tool belt and setting it on the passenger seat of his truck when his phone rang. Joy. Surprise shot through him.

"Hello?" he answered.

Joy's breathless voice cut in. "Stone's taking me on a surprise

Valentine's getaway," she said. "Can you pick up Trent for the weekend?"

Grant wasn't sure if he heard right. He'd been counting down the days until the first week of March and Trent's Spring Break. "This weekend?" It was Thursday night.

"Yes," she said. "We're leaving first thing in the morning, so tonight would be best. I don't want to have to deal with him in the morning."

Grant's mind spun. "Uh, I need to switch to the SUV, and then I can head over."

"Great," Joy said. "He needs to be home by Sunday night, 6:00 sharp. I want to make sure he gets a good dinner in him and full night's sleep for school the next day."

"All right," Grant said. It was completely last minute, but he wasn't going to complain. He could bring Trent along to his job that started tomorrow.

"Oh, I hope you didn't have Valentine's plans," Joy said. "Well, if you do, I guess Trent will be a third wheel."

"I . . ." He hadn't even thought of making plans. Valentine's Day was Saturday, but it wasn't like he was dating anyone. At all. It would just be him and Trent.

By the time Grant arrived at Joy's condo, he was met with a very sleepy Trent. Grant pulled the little guy into a tight hug. Trent started to squirm and make fake choking sounds. "Lemme go, Dad."

Dad.

It felt good to hear it again in person, and Grant realized how much he missed it. With hardly a glance at Joy and Stone, who looked as if they'd just returned from a high dollar fundraiser, which they probably had, Grant lead Trent to the SUV and buckled him in.

The kid fell asleep about ten minutes into the drive. Grant couldn't be more grateful for this stolen weekend with his son, and it almost made up for the disaster with Maurie. Almost.

Nine

MAURIE COULDN'T SLEEP. The grand opening for *Every Occasion*'s storefront was in a few hours, and although she and Taffy had finished the final touches on the shop the night before, Maurie's thoughts were like a merry-go-round.

And it hadn't helped when she'd arrived home at 10:00 pm to find her house completely finished and cleaned up. Grant had left a handwritten note.

Maurie,
Sorry I missed you tonight. I hope everything meets to your satisfaction. If not, please let me know. Best of luck with the grand opening. Julie will be getting the invoice to you in the next couple of weeks. No rush on payment.
Grant

Maurie had sunk into the kitchen chair after reading it the first time. Then she read it through again, this time paying attention to the strong, masculine handwriting that reminded her of the man behind the pen. She'd spent the last two weeks working through what he'd told her after their dinner. And she really didn't blame him for calling the police that night . . . and it was all in the past, anyway.

But she'd struggled with how to reconcile herself to the fact that Grant had seen how desperate her situation had been.

Strangely, she was embarrassed. Although the therapy she'd received had taught her to be open about her challenges, and to face them head-on, Grant's confession had made her feel vulnerable. She'd found it easier to avoid him for a couple of days, rather than admit to her thoughts. And then the days had turned into another week, then two weeks. She'd kept busy, but her heart grew heavier by the day. She missed Grant and what had been budding between them. Plus, Grant deserved an explanation and not the cold shoulder she'd been giving him.

So, with the digital clock in her bedroom glowing 4:05 am, she got out of bed, drew on her robe, and went into the kitchen. She made herself a steaming mug of hot cocoa, and then sat down to write to Grant. This way she couldn't put it off any longer, and she couldn't keep chickening out.

Once her letter was written, she bundled into her car, let it warm up for a few minutes, and then drove to his place. It wasn't hard to find his work truck in the parking lot, and she hoped no one would take the letter. She placed the envelope beneath the driver's side windshield wiper. Thankfully, the sky was clear and the wind was nonexistent. Barring a sudden storm or a curious passerby, the letter should stay safe until Grant saw it.

Her heart pounded at the thought of him reading her words, reading her own confession, but she forced herself to walk away and drive back home.

Hours later, when she and Taffy drove to their corner store, the rear seat of Maurie's car stacked with ten dozen donuts to give away to grand opening customers, they were shocked to find no less than fifteen people lined up outside the shop's door.

"Are they here for us?" Taffy squealed.

Maurie gave a numb nod.

"Oh. My. Heck!" Taffy continued. "My fliers worked!"

Maurie laughed at that, as a thrill buzzed through her. The small crowd looked to be a mixture of locals as well as the touristy ski bunnies.

They drove to the rear parking lot and parked in the last available slot, then entered the rear door. It was still thirty minutes before opening, but Maurie told Taffy, "We're opening early. I'll get the hot cocoa machine heating up."

Taffy flipped on all the lights, then sauntered to the front door and unlocked it. "Come in, come in! Free hot chocolate and donuts. And don't miss out on the 50% off coupon we're offering today. Valentine's Day is tomorrow, folks!"

Maurie could only grin at Taffy's enthusiasm, as Maurie set out the donuts on a side table she'd decorated the night before with all things Valentine's. Then Maurie greeted the customers, too, one by one, introducing herself and what her store was all about.

The morning sped by, and soon it was nearly 2:00 pm Several customers were browsing when Maurie told Taffy, "You can take a break if you want. Why don't you grab us a couple of sandwiches from the café down the street? Ham and Swiss on country sourdough sounds good."

Taffy looked around at the milling customers. "Are you sure?"

"Yeah." Maurie flashed her a smile. She was more than exhausted, but she also needed to eat. So did her friend. "And maybe a Diet Coke."

"Got it," Taffy said. "I think I have a sugar headache from too many donuts."

Speaking of donuts, there was only one box left, a testament to the number of visitors they'd had. It was amazing, really. Maurie folded the two empty boxes on the table. She checked the contents of the hot cocoa machine.

"Uh, Maurie," Taffy said, "you might want to change your lunch order."

Maurie looked over to see a man entering the store. He was tall, broad, with familiar brown hair. He was holding the hand of a little boy who was carrying a large sack with "Main Street Café" printed on the side. In the man's other hand was a bouquet of red roses.

"Grant," Maurie said, not realizing she'd spoken out loud until the little boy spoke.

"Is that her, Daddy?"

"Yeah," Grant said, his eyes locking onto Maurie's. His expression was wary, perhaps even vulnerable.

One of the customers approached Maurie, but Taffy intervened, and soon it was just Grant and the kid who had to be his son and Maurie standing at the refreshment table.

"Can I have a donut?" Trent asked, tugging on Grant's hand.

"Sure," Grant said, not taking his gaze from Maurie's.

"Did you get my letter?" she asked, her voice a whisper.

"I did."

"Daddy, can I have hot chocolate, too?"

Grant smiled at his son. "Sure. And I can promise, it's really good."

"Are you Trent?" Maurie crouched down and held out her hand.

"Yep!" Trent said, shaking her hand as if he considered the exchange very formal. "We brought you lunch, and my daddy got you flowers for Valentine's."

Maurie's heart hitched. Goodness. "The flowers are beautiful, and thanks for bringing lunch, too. You can have as much hot chocolate as you want, although I like to call it cocoa."

"Cocoa?" Trent said with a shrug. "It's the same thing, though, right?"

"Yes." Maurie straightened.

"Aren't you going to give her the flowers, Daddy?"

Grant's face flushed, and Maurie smiled.

He cleared his throat, and said, "So, I was wondering if you had plans tomorrow—for Valentine's Day. I mean, I'd love to take you out after the shop closes, but it would be the three of us."

He looked toward the front of the store. "Except if Taffy wants to come, too. Then it would be four of us."

"Unless you're too tired," Trent piped up. "My dad said you've been working a lot, and that opening a store is a super big job."

"Well," Maurie said, looking down at Trent. "I have been working really hard." She looked back up to Grant. "But I'd love to go out with both of you."

"Good," Grant said.

Maurie didn't miss his pleased expression, and she didn't miss the longing she saw there, either. It made warm tingles travel through her entire body.

"And these are for you, in case you were wondering," Grant said with a wink, holding up the roses.

Maurie laughed and took the bouquet. "Thank you. They're beautiful." She breathed them in, closing her eyes for a moment.

"Does that mean she likes them, Daddy?" Trent said.

"Yes, I believe it does." Grant's voice held amusement.

Maurie opened her eyes, only to be caught up in Grant's intense gaze. Taffy's voice murmured in the background while she chatted with a customer, and Trent might have asked another question, or a dozen. But Maurie felt herself propelled toward the man about whom she hadn't been able to stop thinking for weeks, perhaps years.

She stepped forward, placed her hand on his chest, and lifted up on her toes. And then she pressed her lips against his and kissed him.

Grant didn't hesitate, kissing her back even though they were standing in the middle of her shop surrounded by people. His arms came around her as he pulled her close and deepened the kiss. When he finally drew away, he was grinning, she was blushing, and the customers were clapping.

"Happy Valentine's Day, Maurie," Grant said.

Heather B. Moore is a *USA Today* bestselling author. She writes historical thrillers under the pen name H.B. Moore; her latest are *Lost King* and *Slave Queen*. Under the name Heather B. Moore, she writes romance and women's fiction. She's one of the coauthors of The Newport Ladies Book Club series. Other works include *Heart of the Ocean, The Fortune Café, The Boardwalk Antiques Shop,* the Aliso Creek series, and the Amazon bestselling series A Timeless Romance Anthology.

For book updates, sign up for Heather's email list:
hbmoore.com/contact
Website: HBMoore.com
Facebook: Fans of H. B. Moore
Blog: MyWritersLair.blogspot.com
Twitter: @HeatherBMoore

Hold Your Breath

By Jenny Proctor

One

KAYLA

I DROPPED MY duffel into the entryway and hung my keys on the peg by the door. "Hello? Anyone home?"

"Kayla!" Sixteen-year-old Bridget came running from the direction of the family room, colliding into me before I'd even made it halfway down the hallway. Her hair was wet, piled in a messy topknot and, as usual, smelled faintly of the pool. "I'm glad you're home!"

"Me, too. It's been too long. Where's Mom and Dad?"

"In the family room. We're watching tapes from my last meet. Want to see?"

"Sure I do. Is this the one where you . . ."

"Where I lost? Yeah. I think I've finally figured out why. But seriously. Delaney Fisher is incredibly fast. If I'm going to lose, I'd rather it be to her than anyone else."

I held up a finger. "First of all, second place is not losing. But also, you better not be complacent. You're a Phillips. And Phillips swimmers don't settle."

Bridget rolled her eyes. "You sound like Coach."

I followed my baby sister into the family room. Dad was reclined on the couch, his feet propped on the ottoman. Mom sat at the table under the window, her laptop open in front of her. I leaned over and kissed my dad on the top of his head. "Hey, Daddy."

He turned, surprise evident on his face. Apparently Bridget's chatter hadn't been enough to clue him in on my arrival. "McKayla? When did you get here?"

"Just now. You didn't hear Bridget yell?"

"Sorry. I was studying flip turns. I think you could shave a second or two, Bridg."

Mom crossed the room and wrapped me into a big hug. "I'm glad you're home," she said. "I'd ask you to help get these two talking about something other than swimming, but I have a feeling you'll be no help."

I grinned. "Maybe after we study the flip turns?"

She laughed and turned toward the kitchen, throwing her hands into the air. "Hopeless! The lot of you! I'm getting dinner out of the oven," she called to me over her shoulder. "Did you eat?"

"Not yet. I'm starving."

"Look, right there," my father said to Bridget. "See how you slow your stroke down as you approach? If you speed up instead, you could use that momentum to power through the turn."

"Or to power me straight into the wall," Bridget said, her hands on her hips. She looked at me, her eyebrows scrunched together in mockery of our very enthusiastic father. I grinned, my shoulders shaking in silent laughter. Dad had been the same way with me. At my last swim meet as an official member of the UC Berkeley Swim Team, unable to coach me in person, he'd resorted to sending text messages while I chilled in the ready room before my races. A barrage of last minute pointers and observations. To other athletes it might have seemed annoying, like micromanaging. But Dad's advice was always positive, always encouraging, and frequently dead-on when it came to how I could improve. I'd grown to trust his insight over the years. He'd never failed me yet.

I reached for the remote, rewinding the clip to watch Bridget's turns again. I nodded my head. "He's right, I think. You are losing momentum. You don't need an extra stroke—that probably would get you too close to the wall—but you're holding back. You have to trust your ability to channel your speed into the turn. I'll help. We can go to the pool together."

"Are you going to keep training while you're here?" Dad asked. "Or is this vacation?"

I dropped onto the couch next to him, leaning back into the cushions. "Not a vacation. I probably won't swim quite as hard, or for as long, but I definitely want to be in the water every day."

Dad patted my knee. "I guess with the trials coming up, every swim counts." He stood. "I'm going to see if your mother needs help. Bridg, did you finish your homework?"

"Not yet. I'm working on it."

"No TV 'till you're finished," he said, before disappearing into the kitchen.

Bridget took his spot on the couch and turned sideways to face me, her legs crossed under her. She looked so much like me at her age. Same hair. Dark brown, constantly messy, tamed only by strong rubber bands. Or when we were feeling really patient, *tons* of heat. Same head-to-toe freckles, same deep green eyes. And most importantly, the same love of all things water. We even swam the same events. 200 IM, 200 Free, 200 Fly. It had probably saved our relationship, that I was so much older. There'd been too much of an age difference for us to become truly competitive, though Bridget loved reminding me of the school record she'd broken earlier in her season—*my* record. I still had four on the West High record boards, but Bridget was only a junior. She had plenty of time to catch up.

"So." I pulled a pillow into my lap. "Give me the dirt. How's life?"

She shrugged. "Good. School is good. Swimming is awesome."

"And the boy you like is . . . ?"

She gave me a look of mock exasperation. "What makes you think I currently like a boy?"

"You're *my* little sister, which means you always like a boy. Spill it. What's his name?"

She sighed, her eyes getting all dreamy. "Brett. He swims, too. And he's amazing and wonderful, and I'm pretty sure he's going to ask me to the Valentine's Day Dance. He hasn't yet. But the dance is still two weeks away, and he's hinted at it a few times. I'm pretty sure he's going to."

I smiled. "That's awesome. And good that he's a swimmer, too."

The worst swimming year of my life? My freshman year of college when my very serious boyfriend resented the heck out of my training schedule. I'd tried to keep everyone happy—coaches *and* boyfriend—but I'd failed miserably. My race times had taken the biggest hit.

I'd vowed then and there that no man would ever come between me and the pool.

"How's Coach Davenport?" I asked.

Bridget scrunched her eyebrows. "Um, he retired a year ago?"

"What? Why didn't anyone tell me? I loved him."

"I thought for sure Mom had mentioned it. He and his wife are touring the country in an RV. Or maybe cruising the Caribbean? I don't remember. He's living the high life, though. He sends postcards to the school every once in a while."

"Who replaced him?"

"Coach Hanson. He's young. And really cute. Pretty much the entire girls team is in love with him. He went to West, actually. You might know him."

"Hanson." My heart picked up speed. "Nate Hanson?"

"Yes! You do know him! He teaches freshman English, too."

Did I know Nate Hanson? Silly question. He was only the

biggest, most intense crush of my entire high school experience, which was saying something since we'd only gone to school together for a year. He'd been a senior when I was a freshman, too young for him to have ever been anything but a crush. But somehow he'd managed to set the bar for every other guy I dated all the way through school. Not surprisingly, no one ever managed to measure up.

"I haven't seen him in years, but yeah. We went to school together. We swam together."

"Did you know he made the Olympic team four years ago? Total craziness. He made the team, won his event even, and then like, two weeks later, had this major car crash and smashed up his shoulder." She balled up her fists then flung them open, like exploding fireworks. "Psssh. There went his Olympic career."

"I remember he made the team. I swam those trials, remember?" *Swam* being a relative term. *Thank you, stupid freshman year boyfriend.*

"Oh, that's right. The year you tanked it."

"Thanks, Bridg. Way to be delicate."

"Whatever. You're going to own the pool this year. Who cares about four years ago?"

"So, Coach Hanson." I couldn't get past the fact that my high school dream guy was my sister's swim coach. "What's he like?"

"So hard. Way harder than Davenport ever was. But, he's good. I really like his coaching style."

"And he's still cute, huh?"

She raised her eyebrows. "Still? Does that mean you thought he was cute back in the day?" She raised her hands and made air quotes around the last part of her sentence.

"*Back in the day* makes me sound like I was in high school forty years ago."

"You're avoiding the question."

I chucked the pillow I was holding at her head. "You're terrible."

She flung it back then stood up, racing into the kitchen. "Mom! Did you know Kayla had a crush on my swim coach?"

I followed closely behind her. Only because I knew if she was willing to say as much to Mom, she might also say something to *Nate*. And that was not something I wanted to see happen. "I did not have a crush. We went to high school together. Forever ago. That's all I said."

"*And* that she thought he was cute," Bridget added.

"He is cute," Mom said from behind the stove. "I always thought so."

"You know him, too?" I asked.

"Well, I see him at all of Bridget's meets. But he also came into the clinic for rehab a few years back. After his accident." Mom ran a physical therapy clinic in downtown Oakland. She shook her head. "It's crazy what he went through. And amazing doctors ever managed to put him back together. He was fractured all over."

I dropped onto a bar stool, propping my elbows on the counter, and leaned my chin into my hands. I had a vague memory of his accident. It had been pretty big news among the national swimmers. But embarrassingly enough, I was in my own self-absorbed funk right after the trials. Disappointment in myself had clouded my awareness of others, even when the other in question was my old high school crush. "How did it happen?" I asked Mom.

"What, the accident?"

I nodded.

"Some kid holding a cell phone. Blew through an intersection and t-boned him." She turned to Bridget. "You heard that, right? You better still be putting your phone in the glove box."

"Why do we even still call it a glove box?" my sister asked. "Does anyone actually keep *gloves* in there? We should call it the napkin box. Makes more sense."

"You should call *yours* the cell phone box," Mom said. She dropped the dish towel she was holding and put her hands on her hips. "Bridget," she said in her serious voice. "You're hearing me, yes?"

Bridget crossed the kitchen and took Mom by the shoulders. "I'm hearing you. And I do it. Every time I drive. I promise."

Mom nodded. "Good. McKayla? Do I need to have the same talk with you?"

I squirmed. I was by no means a reckless text and driver. But... yeah. I probably gave the phone a little too much attention. It was sobering, thinking about what had happened to Nate, about how quickly some kid's careless moment had ended his competitive swimming career. "I'm listening. I'll start putting my phone away, too."

"Good. Now let's have dinner. It's been too long since I've had both my girls under one roof."

Two

NATE

I DROPPED MY duffel in the pool office at the clubhouse and pulled off my toeclips. Three minutes to spare. I was making better time every day. At the recommendation of my physical therapist, I'd begun riding my bike from the high school to the club for swim practice. It was only eight miles of easy back roads, so not a serious workout. But it was enough that I was already feeling strength build in my quad—more strength than I'd managed working out in the pool alone. I dug my flip flops out of my bag and slipped them on, then stretched my arms up and leaned over to touch the floor. No pain. It'd been a long time since I'd been able to say that. *No pain.*

"Hey, Coach. How goes it?" Tyler, the lifeguard on duty, swung around in the desk chair.

"Good. How's the water?"

"A cool 89 degrees."

"Ugh. You're killing me, Tyler. That's like swimming through pudding."

"It's the water aerobics brigade that's paying for the pool, bro. You gotta do what you gotta do."

"I feel you." I ran my fingers through my hair, a lame attempt to undo my helmet hair. I pulled my whistle, stopwatch and clipboard out of my bag. "Catch you later, man."

I pushed through the door that led to the pool. Usually by the time practice started, I had a few swimmers already warming up. But today the four lanes we used for practice were still empty. Instead, a crowd had gathered around the end of the farthest lane. I walked over, curious.

Sebastian, a senior and my team captain, sat on the edge of the starting block, his watch in his hand. I nudged his shoulder. "What's going on?"

He glanced up. "Oh, hey, Coach. Check out this girl's split." He held up his watch. "And she's been swimming that same speed for going on 300 meters."

"Who is she?"

"No one knows. She's been swimming since we showed up."

I turned my attention to the swimmer, looking for anything I might recognize. I didn't know who she was, but right off I did recognize one thing. Her swim cap bore the flag and emblem of the US National team.

"All right, guys," I said. "That's enough watching. In the water. 600 meter warm up. Let's go."

"Dude," Sebastian said as he stood. "We gotta find out who she is."

"Who *who* is?" Bridget, one of my juniors, crossed the deck and peered into the water. Sebastian motioned with his head to the swimmer, who was completing a flip turn at the other end of the pool. Bridget squinted, studying the swimmer for half a beat before she smiled wide. "That's my sister. She's going to the Olympics this summer."

Her name flashed into my brain in an instant. Bridget Phillips. *Kayla* Phillips. I'd always known, somewhere in the back of my mind, that Bridget's older sister was also a swimmer. And a talented one. But I'd never before connected the Kayla from my high school swim team, of national team stats and lists of Olympic hopefuls, to Bridget.

"Why didn't you tell me your sister was Kayla Phillips?"

Bridget shrugged. "I guess I assumed you knew. Davenport used to ask me about her all the time."

We watched as Kayla finished another lap. Nearly all my swimmers had made it into the pool, save Bridget. "Come on," I told her. "In the water. You're behind on your warm up."

"Good thing I'm faster than the rest of these yo-yos," she said with a grin. She backed away from me and pulled on her swim cap. "You know, just in case you're wondering, Kayla's single."

I shot her my teacher *you just said what?* eyebrows.

"I'm just saying." She held her hands up in a gesture of surrender. "Maybe it isn't relevant information, but if it is . . . she's in town for two weeks. And she's very unattached."

I crossed my arms. "Water. *Now.*"

Kayla continued to swim for the rest of my hour-long practice. I was wrapped up in timing splits, analyzing strokes, and shouting work outs, but I kept one eye on her the entire time. I didn't want her to get away before we'd had the chance to talk. I remembered a little about high school Kayla. She'd been a freshman my senior year, so she'd always been a little too young for me to pay her much attention. But I'd still noticed.

I remembered one swim meet near the end of my senior season. The bus ride home had been long. And for whatever reason, I'd ended up sitting with her. We'd talked the entire time. If she hadn't been fourteen, I would have asked her out at the end of the night. I'd felt that . . . whatever it is you feel that makes you say, *yeah. More of this, please.*

Now, we weren't in high school anymore. And Bridget's parting words were running through my brain on constant repeat.

Very unattached.

While the team worked on relay starts, I snuck into the office to grab a water bottle out of the mini fridge. I checked my phone, using the downtime to pull up Kayla's national team profile. Recent UC Berkeley grad. Public Relations major. First place finishes in three events at the last US Open. With stats like that, her place on the Olympic team was all but guaranteed. I dropped the phone back into my bag, suddenly aware that a woman I hadn't seen or spoken to in years had been consuming my thoughts for nearly an hour. For no other reason than that she was *in* my pool, had an impressive swim career, and her sister had mentioned she was single.

I needed to get out more.

Back on the deck, I immediately noticed the still water in the far lane. Kayla was gone. Momentarily discouraged, I blew my whistle, calling my swimmers in. Then I saw her, lowering herself into the hot tub. I watched, willing her to look my way and make eye contact, but she kept her back to me.

"Coach?" Bridget said from the water. "We're all here."

"Right. Sorry. Great practice, guys. We're in the pool late tomorrow, so remember dry land practice right after school in the weight room. Then back here at 8 p.m."

"What time is the meet on Saturday?" someone asked from the back of the group.

"11 a.m.," I said. "But we're traveling, so meet at the school at 9:30, and not a second later."

I watched until all but the last few stragglers had filed into the locker rooms, then walked towards Kayla. She'd moved to the edge, only her feet still dangling in the water. I kicked off my flip flops and sat down across from her, lowering my feet into the steaming hot tub. "You gave my swimmers quite a show out there."

She looked up and smiled. "Sorry. I hope I didn't interfere with practice. That wasn't my intent."

"Nah, it's fine," I said. "The club makes us keep the far lane open for members, celebrity guests, and the occasional California dignitary. We're used to ignoring them."

"I'm not sure I fit into any of those categories."

"Maybe they've amended their policy to include Olympic athletes."

She squeezed water out of the ends of her hair then leaned back onto her hands. "Don't get ahead of yourself. I'm not one of those yet."

"Are you kidding? I've seen your times. You're killing it this season. I don't think anyone will touch you at the trials."

She held my gaze. "I didn't think you'd remember me."

I chuckled. "Oh, I remember."

She looked at her hands, as if I'd made her feel uncomfortable.

"But I wondered the same thing," I quickly added. "If you'd know who I was."

She huffed out a laugh. "Was it all that long ago that we were in high school? Plus, Bridget told me you were her coach. This is your first year?"

I ran a hand through my hair. "Yeah. Just trying to figure it out as I go, I guess."

"Oh, Bridget says you're great. Harder than Davenport, but that's good for swimmers like Bridg."

"Good old Davenport. He was a great coach."

"You know, I saw you swim at the trials four years ago," she said. "I was there."

"Really? Did you swim? I feel like I would have noticed seeing your name."

She shook her head, still not making eye contact. "I didn't do well. Didn't advance to any finals. It . . . wasn't good."

"Oh."

"How *is* Bridget doing?" she asked, apparently anxious to change the subject.

"She's great. Best swimmer on the team. I expect she'll take state this year, at least in the IM."

"There's only one flip turn in the IM. That's why. Her turns slow her down."

"Yeah, I've noticed. It's on my list of things to work on with her."

"She holds back. Like she's afraid of the wall or something. I think I could help her, if you don't mind me coaching her a little."

I held up my hands. "By all means. You've got the skill set. I don't mind."

"You're talking like I'm capable of something you aren't. You really *are* an Olympic athlete," she said. "I haven't made it yet."

My jaw tensed, the same knot forming in my gut that showed up whenever I thought about the Olympics that I *didn't* swim in.

Kayla must have sensed my discomfort. "Sorry. That was . . . I wasn't thinking."

"It's fine," I told her. "It wasn't your fault."

"Right. I, um . . ." She stood up. "I should get going."

I tried not to stare as she stepped out of the water, but her long legs and toned arms and freckle-covered shoulders were tough to ignore. *Eyes up, dude. Eyes. Up.* I swallowed. She gave me a small smile then turned to walk away.

"Kayla."

She looked back, and I panicked. I had no idea what I wanted to say to her. "I, um, it's good to see you."

She smiled again, a real one this time. "Yeah. You, too."

Once she was out of sight, I leaned back onto the concrete deck and covered my face with my hands. *I, um, it's good to see you.*

Definitely not my best work.

Three

KAYLA

"I WAS RIDICULOUS." I paced outside my house, not wanting to take my phone conversation inside with Mom and Bridget in hearing range.

"It doesn't sound like it was *that* bad," Ranee said. Though her opinion didn't hold much water. As my oldest friend, she was obligated to always find the positive.

"I brought up what was probably the worst event in the history of his entire life. What was I trying to prove?"

"Nothing. You were making conversation," Ranee said. "It's what people do. Besides, I'm not sure why it even matters. You're not interested in dating him, so who cares? You're only in town for a couple of weeks. You probably won't even see him again."

"I'll see him Saturday at Bridget's swim meet."

"Oh. Right. You don't have to talk to him, though, do you?"

'No. I guess I don't, but . . ." I hesitated. Ranee was right. I didn't want to date Nate. At least the practical side of me didn't. After my epically awful swim at the last Olympic trials, there was no way I was setting myself up for the same kind of potential distraction just because I was attracted to a guy. But this was Nate we were talking about. Nate, the star of every high school daydream I'd ever had. Was it so surprising I wanted him to find me attractive?

"That is a very heavy *but*," Ranee said. "Tell me you aren't reconsidering your stance."

"No. Of course I'm not."

"Because you barely have four months to the trials, Kayla. Four. That's a blink of time."

"I know."

"But?"

"If you could just see him. He's even more gorgeous now than he was in high school. And listening to him coach the team and give them pointers and encourage them and . . . Seriously. It was maybe the sexiest thing I've ever seen."

"Oh, boy. This does *not* sound good."

"Don't say that. It's only an observation. Besides, what could really happen in two weeks?"

"Didn't your parents get engaged in two weeks?"

"That's a totally ridiculous example. They are outliers. Crazy, unheard of outliers."

"Hmm. Fine. Just be good, all right? Don't let him get under your swim cap."

I laughed. "Under my what?"

"I'm just trying to speak your language."

"I love you, Ranee."

"Back at you, babe. And I'm going to see you next weekend, right?"

"I've saved my Saturday night for you. Unless you have other Valentine's Day plans." I shivered. My hair was still wet from my swim, and the cool night air was getting to me.

"You know me. Men lined up for miles to take me out."

Ranee's boyfriend would be on the other side of the country for a business conference on Valentine's Day. Sucky for *them*, but otherwise fantastic. Because it meant Ranee could ditch Seattle and come see me.

"Men should be lined up," I told her. "Tell Adam I said he's a lucky man and a complete fool for leaving you. No, wait. Don't tell him that. I don't want him to change his mind and cancel his trip."

"No trip cancelling. I promise. His boss is calling the shots on this one. Okay. I gotta go. Keep me updated, yeah?"

"Of course. But there won't be anything to update you on. Because nothing is going on."

Nothing.

The look Nate had given me when he mentioned remembering me. The way my heart had literally hammered inside my chest when he sat down across from me.

Okay. Maybe there had been *something* there.

It had been circumstance, I reasoned. *Old* feelings. Childish high school infatuation that didn't warrant a second thought. Except I was already on to third or fourth thoughts. I grumbled at the driveway and stomped onto the front porch, channeling my frustrations into the ground beneath me. Of all the things to deal with. *Why? Why Nate? Why now?*

Later that week, I stopped in the foyer on my way out and studied my reflection for a quick second before grabbing my keys off the hook by the door. I spent so much time in the water, I hardly recognized myself with dry hair and a little make up. I leaned forward and studied my reflection, suddenly wondering if I'd tried too hard. All I was doing was driving to the club to pick up Bridget from practice. I probably wouldn't even need to get out of the car. If Ranee were around, she would have called me out the second I got out my blow dryer. I could hear her voice in my head. "You're trying to impress him. Admit it. You know you are."

So, fine. Maybe I was. But it didn't mean anything.

Which is why it didn't make any sense that I was a nervous wreck waiting for Bridget. She'd texted just after practice ended, saying she was going to shower and she hoped I had a good book with me. I was thoroughly annoyed for the 2.6 seconds that passed before I saw Nate walking out of the clubhouse, a duffel bag flung over his shoulder and a bike helmet in his hands.

I opened my car door and climbed out before realizing I needed a *reason* to be getting out of the car. I walked to my trunk, knowing I was directly in Nate's line of sight, but did my best to avoid eye contact. Because I didn't get out to see him. I got out to get something out of my trunk. A . . . banana peel? Set of weighted wrist bands? Tennis shoes with missing laces? A magazine! I grabbed it and closed the trunk with a satisfied grunt.

"Find anything good?"

I spun around. Nate stood a few paces away from my car.

I held up the magazine. "Just getting something to read. Bridget said she may be a while."

"Doesn't she usually drive to practice?"

"Yeah. But her car is in the shop. Some weird airbag recall thing that needs to be fixed."

He nodded. "Gotcha." He peered at the magazine I still held in my hands. "So, J. Crew, huh? That's good reading material?"

Crap. I smiled. I could play this off. "Absolutely. Their product descriptions are riveting."

"I'm sure they are."

I rolled my eyes. "Whatever. I'm in the market for a new scarf. Maybe there's something in here."

His eyes twinkled, his smile creating deep creases in the sides of his face. "I'm glad I ran into you."

I froze, my heart picking up speed. "Yeah? Why is that?"

"Well, I was thinking it might be awkward if I had to ask your little sister to ask you out for me."

Oh my word oh my word oh my word. "You're asking me out?"

"Dinner tomorrow night?"

"Dinner." I realized I was repeating everything he said, but my brain was still five steps behind. I needed at least a few more seconds to process. Nate asking me out was just so . . . unprecedented. I'd *imagined* the scenario a million different times, but that had been so long ago. I never actually thought it would happen.

"It's the meal that comes after lunch, but before bedtime? I know you're only in town a couple of weeks, but . . ." He shrugged. "It might be fun."

I closed my eyes and took a steadying breath. I'd hoped to see him. Even hoped to flirt a little. Make up for my insensitivity when we'd talked that first day at the pool. But he'd just asked me out. No pretense. No games. Just, "Hey, let's have dinner." It felt refreshingly . . . grown up.

It was the worst kind of test. There wasn't a *right* answer, just two wrong ones. I couldn't say yes. The timing of getting tangled up in a guy, even temporarily, was awful, and I couldn't afford the distraction. But I didn't want to say no, either. This was *Nate* we were talking about. That's all the reason I'd ever needed. My shoulders dropped, my eyes locked on the catalog in my hands.

"I think," he said, "we just officially crossed into awkward pause territory."

I met his gaze. "I'm sorry. You just caught me by surprise."

"A good surprise?"

So this was it. My moment of decision. "I'm only going to be in town a couple weeks, Nate."

He nodded. "I think I already said that."

"And I've just got so much going on right now; I don't think it would be a good idea."

"Oh."

"It's not you, though. I swear." I shifted my weight from one foot to the other, wishing I wasn't still holding the stupid J. Crew catalog. "I feel like I have to focus on my training right now."

He fiddled with the straps of his bag. "I guess that's a reason I can't argue with."

"I'm sorry. If the circumstances were different . . ."

He pulled on his bike helmet, fastening it under his chin. His slightly scruffy, sexy dimpled chin. "It's really okay. I get it."

He didn't get it. He sounded hurt, maybe even a little embarrassed. I wanted to scream. Grab him by the shoulders and shake him. Did he have any idea how much I'd always wanted this very moment to happen?

"Can I call you in August?" I blurted out.

He raised his eyebrows. "August as in, post-Olympics?"

I wrinkled my nose. "It's kind of a long time away, huh?"

He shook his head and smiled, and took a few backward steps across the parking lot. "I'll be around in August. We'll see what happens."

I watched him as he unlocked his bike from the rack just in front of the club. The night before, Bridget had told me he rode his bike from the high school to practice every afternoon, and then back to the high school to get his car. It only added to his appeal. He pulled out a pair of toeclips from his duffle and slipped them on, then shoved his flip-flops into his bag and pulled it over his head so it hung on him cross-body style.

As I watched him ride away, I almost called after him. I had just said *no* to a date with Nate Hanson. What kind of a lunatic was I? I climbed back into my car and leaned my head against the steering wheel. Part of me wanted to cry. It had felt awful, saying no. Like I was betraying my old self. But somewhere inside, my new grown up self also felt a tiny spark of victory. Like I was in control. Stronger than my emotions. Committed to something bigger.

And that was a good a thing.

My resolve hardened.

It was the right decision. The best decision.

The kind of decision a champion would make.

Four

NATE

I'D ALWAYS WANTED to go away to college, so it had been hilarious to my Oakland born and bred parents that I wound up at Stanford, less than an hour away from home. But in the six months that immediately followed my accident, after I'd returned to Oakland to recover, the short distance between my life at college and my *home* life had saved me. My parents had been great when it came to all the medical stuff, but my Stanford friends had kept me human.

Four years later, not everybody had stuck around the area. But there was still enough of the gang left to warrant getting together every once in a while. Chase, my college roommate and best friend from high school. His little sister, Natalie, who'd also gone to Stanford. Bryson. Trey. James and his girlfriend, Rebecca. It was a good group.

Friday night was a pretty typical gathering. My house. The grill going. James and Rebecca in the kitchen making a dinner. But then Natalie showed up. *With Kayla.* Across the living room, Kayla and I made eye contact, and she immediately blushed, then looked back at the door. She whispered something to Natalie, but Natalie waved her hand dismissively and dragged Kayla farther into the house. Once she was settled on the couch, I crossed the room and sat on the ottoman, offering her a drink.

She took it. "Thanks."

"You know," I said with a grin, "as determined as you were to *not* go out with me, showing up at my house might not have been the smartest decision."

She rolled her eyes. "I had no idea we were coming to your house."

"No?"

"No! I ran into Natalie this afternoon, which was a total fluke, because I haven't seen her since high school. She thought it would be nice to catch up and invited me out, but only to hang out with nameless friends. I swear I didn't know."

I smiled. She was cute when she was defensive. "Whether you're glad to be here or not, I'm glad to see you."

She dropped her gaze. "Thanks."

"How was your swim today?" I'd seen her finishing up as my team started their last practice of the week.

"Good, I think. It's hard to feel in the groove training on my own, but I'm hitting my distance and my times, so I can't complain."

I leaned back, my hands resting on the ottoman behind me. "Your fly looked great."

She nodded. "Thanks. It's my weakest stroke in the IM. It's been my focus the past few months."

"I'm sure you'll kill it."

She perked up. "What about you? Are you ever in the water anymore?"

Just then, Rebecca appeared in the archway between the living room and dining room. "Dinner's on, guys. Let's eat."

I was grateful for the distraction. I wasn't quite ready to talk about my swimming yet. Because, there was some. More than therapy swimming. More than just working with my team. Every morning before school, I was in the water by 5 a.m. At first I'd told myself it was just for recuperation. I'd never imagined I might compete again. But then I'd started getting faster. *And faster.*

Still, I hadn't told anyone. I was a long way off from where I'd been before my accident. I was older now. With a full-time job and an almost full-time swim team. There was no way I could ever put in the training hours I'd need to, especially without a coach or team to keep me on target. But that didn't mean I hadn't thought about it.

I stood up and offered Kayla a hand. My couch tended to swallow people. "Are you hungry?" I asked her.

She hesitated an extra beat before accepting my help. "Yeah."

Her hand felt warm in mine. A current of... *something* shot up my arm and settled somewhere in my chest. I liked her. Really liked her. I held on until she looked at me, and then let her go, my thumb brushing across the back of her knuckles.

"Kayla," Natalie called from the dining room. "Come tell Trey about that time our junior year. Do you remember? The party with the bathtub full of ice?"

All night long, I tried not to be the creepy guy staring at her. But it was hard not to. Everything she said. The way she laughed. The way she moved. I was hooked. We made eye contact a few times during dinner. Maybe more times than just a few. But she always smiled, which was encouraging. Or so I hoped. It was possible she was just being nice.

After dinner, I carried a stack of plates into the kitchen, while everyone else moved out to the deck.

Chase followed me in. He leaned against the counter and folded his arms across his chest. "Dude, what's up with you and the new girl?"

"Kayla? She went to high school with us. She's not new."

"She did? How come I don't remember her?"

"She was three years behind us."

"You've been staring at each other all night."

I shrugged. "I like her."

"Have you asked her out?"

"Earlier this week. She said no."

"I'd have never guessed with the way she's been looking at you."

I carried a couple of empty bottles to the recycle bin in the pantry. "It's complicated. She's only in town for a couple weeks. Plus, she's a swimmer. One of the best. She's training for the summer Olympics."

He whistled. "That good, huh? What's that got to do with you, though? I'm pretty sure Olympic athletes are allowed to date."

"It's not an Olympic rule, it's hers. She's focused on her goals, which I totally respect. I've been there." A thought entered my mind. *What if I were training, too?* I pushed the question away. *Training* made what I was doing sound official. I was only swimming. Just swimming.

Chase shook his head. "I don't buy it. Her words might have told you no, but her eyes have been saying something different all night." He glanced over his shoulder through the kitchen window. "Looks like she's standing all alone out there, man. Go talk to her."

James had built a fire in the fire pit where everyone had gathered around. Everyone but Kayla, who stood off to the side, taking in the view of the distant city lights and the water beyond. I stopped right beside her, pulling on the jacket I'd grabbed on my way outside. "It's nice, isn't it?"

She smiled. "This is a great house."

"I can't take credit for it. My parents have owned it forever as a rental. They've let me take over the lease."

"That was nice of them."

"Well, you know, with my high paying job in education," I

teased, "I can afford to live just about anywhere. But since my parents needed someone to look after the place, I figured I'd do them a solid."

She smiled at my joke. "I think it's great that you teach."

"Yeah?"

Kayla turned to face me. "Was it . . ." She hesitated.

I nudged her shoulder, urging her on. "Was it . . .?"

"Sorry. I feel like every time we're together I bring this up."

"What, the accident? It's fine. I don't mind talking about it."

"I guess I just wonder if it was hard to transition into teaching. I mean, I have a degree in public relations. I figure I'll use it one day. But I'm so focused on swimming right now, having an actual career seems like an entirely different life, you know?"

"I don't know. Michael Phelps is worth millions. I doubt he'll ever use his degree."

"Ha. Yeah. But that's hardly a fair comparison." She held up her hands like they were two sides of a scale. "Michael Phelps?" One hand went up. "The rest of humanity." The other hand went down.

"I don't know if you're being too generous to Michael, or too hard on the rest of us." I reached out and took her hands, moving them so one was only slightly higher than the other. "That's better. Except, I'd put you on this side." I squeezed the hand that was higher until she smiled and pulled away.

"You're a flirt," she said.

"Not with everyone."

She laughed and shook her head. "I'll definitely give you points for persistence."

"Do you still want me to answer your question?"

"You mean seriously, this time?" She smirked. "Yes, please."

"It wasn't tough to start teaching. I was out of commission for so long, it felt great to be doing anything. And I like what I do. It's not the thrill of competition, but it pays the bills."

"Do you miss swimming?"

"Of course I do. All the time." Suddenly I wanted to tell her. That I'd been swimming. Working. That I'd even entertained thoughts of a comeback. I hadn't felt tempted to tell anyone else. Not even Chase or my parents knew how I was feeling. The thought of confessing to Kayla, an elite athlete that swam and trained with the nation's best, felt foolish. And yet, it seemed right, too. Maybe more than anyone she'd understand how much would be at stake if I took the leap.

"Are you ever in the water these days?" she asked for the second time that night.

I inhaled and nodded. "I've been swimming every morning before school, actually. Training, I guess." There. I'd admitted it.

Her eyes went wide. "Are you serious? You're thinking of competing again?"

"It's still early. I'd have a lot to come back from, if I decided to make it official."

"Yeah, but . . . Nate, I don't know that I've ever seen anyone swim the way you do."

"The way I *did*."

"If you were to come back . . . it would be amazing."

"It's just an idea. I don't even know if I want to, or if I could ever be ready."

She was buzzing. Excitement dancing in her eyes. "What do your doctors say?"

I shrugged. "I'm good. Bones are healed. At this point, it's more a matter of building up my strength and seeing how far I can go."

"And getting your head back in the game."

"Yeah, that." She *did* understand. Muscle mattered, sure. But it could only get me so far if I wasn't in the right head space. Letting go of the fear. Ignoring the need to breathe, to stop, to slow down. Finding that zone was almost more important.

"Let's go to the pool tomorrow," she said.

"What?"

"Come swim with me. I'm there alone every day, and I'm so bored. Train with me."

"Intriguing invitation, but I've got a meet tomorrow."

"Crap. Me, too. I mean, I'm coming to watch Bridg swim so I'll be there, too. What about after?"

"I don't know," I teased. "Saturday night. That feels a little like a date."

"*Not* a date." She pointed a finger at my chest. "Not for a single second."

"I'll make a deal with you. You tell me the real reason why you won't have dinner with me, and I'll agree to swim with you."

She folded her arms. "Promise?"

I nodded. "I promise."

She sighed and turned to the side, leaning against the metal porch railing. "My freshman year at Berkeley I had a really serious boyfriend. Too serious. I lost my focus. My training suffered, and because of it I bombed the Olympic trials. After that, I vowed I was done. No dating until my career was back on track."

"You haven't dated since your freshman year in college?"

She scoffed. "Don't mock. You've lived this life. You know how little free time there is."

"I have lived that life," I agreed. "And look where it got me."

She closed her eyes. "I'm sorry, Nate. Geez, why do I keep bringing that up?"

"Don't apologize." I took a step forward. "I wasn't trying to make you feel bad. I'm just saying, suffering an accident like I did taught me a few things about life. I realize I run the risk of this sounding self-serving, but can I offer you some advice?"

She nodded. "Okay."

"Swimming was everything. My entire world. Then in a blink, it wasn't anymore. But it didn't take long for me to realize, even without the swimming, I still had a life. I had my family. I started teaching. I'm not saying making the Olympic team shouldn't be the most important thing in your life right now. If I had your stats and rank, it would be for me. But I *am* saying life outside the pool isn't a bad thing. Maybe the problem your freshman year wasn't that you had a boyfriend. It was just that you had the wrong one."

She pursed her lips, a smile playing around the corners of her mouth. "I will consider your advice."

"Yeah?"

"Yes. But tomorrow night is still not a date."

I grinned. "Whatever you say."

"Nate, don't make me get serious with you, now." *Man.* Now she was flirting and it was killing me.

"Meet me at the club at 6:30?"

"6:30," she repeated.

"Hey, Nate," Bryson called from the fire pit. "Where's your cooler?"

"I'll be right there," I said. I looked back at Kayla and whispered, "It's totally a date."

She crossed her arms, and cocked her hip, but didn't stop smiling. "You are insufferable."

"Hey! That's a bonus point word in my English class. Poetry quotes get you double."

She laughed. "I'll remember that."

I motioned with my head. "Come on. Sit by the fire?"

"Fine." Her shoulders dropped in playful resignation. "But only because I'm cold."

"Whatever it takes, Phillips," I said. "Whatever it takes."

Five

KAYLA

Bridget burst into the living room. "Kayla! Where are you? Are you here?"

My parents and I had gotten home from the swim meet an hour earlier than she had. She'd insisted on riding the bus with the rest of her team. And by rest of her team, I meant Brett.

"I'm in here." I put down the book I was pretending to read. Something to occupy my thoughts until I met Nate at the pool. I held up my hand as she came into the room. A congratulatory high five was definitely in order. "Way to kill it, baby sister. Great meet."

"Thank you very much. The girl I beat? In the IM? She holds her school's record."

"Which you smoked by two seconds."

She grinned. "Yes, I did."

"You're awesome."

"And only a few seconds away from beating *your* time, now. Are you getting nervous yet?"

I rolled my eyes. "It's a little more than a few."

She plopped onto the sofa across from me. "Are you ready to talk about my very exciting news?"

"Of course."

"Where's Mom? I want her to hear, too."

"She and Dad went to the store."

"Boo. Okay, fine. But don't tell her before I can."

"I won't say a word. What's up?"

She smiled, her eyes wide, her whole body coiling up with excitement. "Brett asked me to the dance."

"Yay! I'm so glad!"

She pulled a pillow onto her lap and squealed, hugging it tightly to her chest. "I know! I'm so excited. I found this dress at the boutique on the corner. I've been visiting it for weeks, but now I actually have a reason to buy it! It's this deep red—perfect, because, Valentine's Day—with this shimmery skirt and, oh, I'm so excited. Did I already say that? I'm so, so excited."

"Brett—he's the one that swam the 500, right? Tall. With super broad shoulders?"

"Yeah." She sighed and leaned back into the couch cushions. "That's him."

"I'm happy for you, Bridg." I stood up, tossing my book onto the couch. "I gotta go. Mom said for you not to go out again before she gets home. You shouldn't have to wait long."

"What? I just got here. Where are you going?"

"To the pool."

She sat up a little straighter. "Seriously? You're training on a Saturday night? You already swam once today."

She was right, but I hadn't gotten in a full workout. There'd only been an hour and a half after the pool opened before we'd had to leave for her meet. Besides . . .

"This is different," I told her. "I'm not swimming alone."

Bridget scrunched her eyebrows for a second, then her jaw dropped. "Are you meeting Coach Hanson?"

I didn't answer; only smiled as I headed down the hall. She ran after me, following me into what had once been my bedroom but was now a yoga studio with a pull-down murphy bed for guests. Mom had waited twenty whole minutes after I moved out to start the makeover. Good thing I knew she loved me.

"You are!" Bridget said. "You *are* meeting him. Oh, I knew it! I knew you'd be great for each other."

"Slow down. We're only swimming. It's not a date."

"Hmm. You're going to want it to be, as soon as you see him without a shirt on."

"Bridget! Gross. He's your teacher."

"He's not my teacher. He teaches freshman English."

"Fine. He's your coach. Either way, shame on you."

"Whatever. I'm admiring from a distance. Totally allowed. He has this scar down his arm and side. From his accident. It's crazy, but also kind of sexy."

I held my hands up to my ears. "Blah! Stop. I do not want to hear this from you." I pulled my swim bag out of the closet and dug through it, looking for my practice suit. "Where is my . . . ?"

"The one you wore this morning is still hanging in the bathroom."

"I know. I want the other one, though. The blue one."

"Ohh. Good choice. It'll make your eyes look more green."

"Yes. So important, since you can't see my eyes through my goggles." I went to my suitcase and dug through it as well. "Ha! Found it." I tossed the suit into my bag and zipped it up.

Bridget bounced on the edge of my bed. "Tell Coach I said hi," she requested, her voice all sing-songy and stupid. Crazy girl. Some days it felt like she was more twenty-five than seventeen, as focused and driven as she could be. But sitting there on the bed, her eyes all sparkly, her head full of Brett and dances and crazy notions about love, she was one hundred percent teenager.

I pulled my bag onto my shoulder. "You're a nut. See you later."

When I arrived at the pool, Nate was already in the water. I stashed my stuff under a deck chair and took my cap and goggles to the far lane where he was swimming. I sat on the pool edge and lowered my feet into the water while I watched him. His stroke was great—long and clean, and seemingly effortless. My mind flashed back to high school, to the countless times I'd admired him in much the same way. In the same pool, even.

I blushed just thinking about the earnestness of my crush. I'd followed him around like a lost puppy for an entire year. At least during swim season. I'd told myself he'd had no idea what I was up to, that he'd believed all my weird, random reasons for being wherever he was. But in retrospect, it was obvious he had to have known. The entire team had known. That he had never made fun of me or joked about it or made me feel silly only deepened the respect I had for him *now,* eight years later. He could have teased me, and he hadn't. That said a great deal about his character.

Nate reached the end of the pool and stood up, water dripping off his face and onto his shoulders. He lifted his goggles onto his forehead and ran his fingers through his hair, flinging water all over me.

"Hi." He smiled.

"Hi." My eyes were immediately drawn to the scar that snaked around the curve of his left shoulder and down toward his bicep.

He followed my gaze. "Impressive, right?" He lifted his arm and rotated his shoulder, as if to prove it did, actually, still work.

"Was that from surgery?"

He shook his head and touched the scar. "This was from a laceration. It's ugly, but it wasn't as serious as the broken bones." He touched his arm a little lower down. "My arm was broken here, and then down here." He touched his forearm. "My shoulder blade was jacked up, too. Broken in several places."

"I didn't even know you could break a shoulder blade."

"I didn't either. Not until it happened."

"It's amazing that you're here and put back together and swimming again." I lowered myself into the water. It was warm. Too warm, really, but it was better than nothing.

"Yeah. I had some good doctors. And good physical therapy. I actually saw your mom a few times."

"Yeah, she told me." I splashed water onto my arms, trying not to stare at the damage done to Nate's body. Although in general, scar or not, it was hard not to stare. He looked good. Almost too good. Like his old high school self, only more grown up. And definitely more ripped.

We were alone in the pool, save one old guy who was lap swimming in the center lane. Suddenly, I was hyperaware of the closeness of our bodies. Of the heat rising from his exercise-flushed skin; the beads of water clinging to his eyelashes.

He moved an inch closer, a smile playing at his lips. "You okay? Your cheeks are all pink, and you haven't even started swimming yet."

"Whatever." I eased toward the lane rope, realizing too late it was probably weird that I'd dropped into *his* lane in the first place. We had nearly the whole pool. Did we really need to share a lane? "Don't be getting any ideas. It's hot in here. That's all."

"I'll take your word for it. Ready to work?"

I pushed over the rope into my own lane and pulled on my swim cap. "I'm going to warm up with 1000 meters, then we can start with 200 repeats. Does that work? Let's say, 15. The first five on the 2:20 mark, the next five on 2:10, and the last five on the 2. After that, I need some sprint work."

He whistled. "You aren't holding back for me, are you?"

My eyebrows shot up. "Do you want me to?"

"No." He grinned. "Let's do it."

He blew me away.

He wasn't just in good shape, he was in *incredible* shape. Swimming as well, if not better than most of the Berkeley guys I'd trained with. We hit 7000 meters before the workout was finished, and he hung with me lap for lap. A truth made much more significant by the fact that while I'd been working out with

Olympic level athletes for months, he'd been squeezing his training into 90 minute workouts before a full day of school. I was impressed.

We leaned against the pool edge, our tired limbs hanging loose in the water. "You've got to compete, Nate."

He shook his head. "I still don't know if I'm ready."

"Of course you're ready. Your times are amazing. You're obviously strong. Your stroke looks great."

"It's not just about that. It's been so long since I've been in that head space, you know? Competition is intense."

"Whatever. It's like riding a bike. Lots of swimmers make comebacks after time away. You can totally do this." I faced him, excitement filling me with more energy than I should have had. "There are a few Pro Swim Series meets left. You could hit the qualifying times—you probably did tonight, in a 25-meter pool that's twelve degrees too warm. Seriously, Nate. Swimming like you're swimming, you could qualify for the trials. I could make some calls. Do you want me to make some calls?"

"Hey." He reached for my shoulders. "Slow down. I know the meet schedule. I've called my old swim club; my coach at Stanford. I've done all the research already."

I tried to focus on his words instead of the warmth of his fingers against my skin. "Then what's holding you back?"

He sighed and dropped his arms—leaving behind an emptiness I immediately felt. He ran his hands across his hair and leaned back into the water so he was immersed up to his shoulders. He finally stood up, looking at me straight on. "Fear?"

I was impressed he was willing to admit it. But . . . "That isn't a reason not to do it."

He gave me a hard look. "You really think so?"

"Yeah, I do."

He moved closer, my heart instantly picking up speed. "That we shouldn't *not* do something just because we're afraid?"

I swallowed. "Right."

He propped his hands against the pool, one on either side of where I leaned against the pool edge, so I was encircled in his arms. Not quite touching, but almost.

He leaned forward. "Then *you* shouldn't back away from this."

He kissed me slowly, one hand caressing the curve of my cheek. I stopped thinking; every fear, thought, reason, worry disappeared into the heavy, humid air around us. I leaned in, kissing him back, harder, longer, aware of nothing but the feel of him under my touch, the taste of him on my lips, the pounding of my heartbeat pulsating through my body. Only when my fingers found the jagged scar on his shoulder did I pause long enough to take a breath. I eased away but kept my hand there, my fingers resting lightly on rough skin.

"Don't worry." He leaned his forehead against mine. "It doesn't hurt anymore."

"I know. I just . . . I'm sorry you had to go through that." I ran my fingers up the length of his scar, where it arched across his shoulder, then traced it back down again until my hand rested at the top of his bicep. "Sorry. Was that . . . I don't know what I'm doing."

He cleared his throat. "It feels to me like you know *exactly* what you're doing."

I gave him a playful push, my hands re-settling on his chest. "You know what I mean."

His arms slid to the small of my back, nothing but water in between us there. "I know you said you don't want to date anyone, and I can respect that. But I don't want you to be afraid of me."

"I'm not afraid. But it's complicated. You know that."

"I know it doesn't have to be a big deal. I promise not to put crazy pressure on you. And I'll absolutely respect your training schedule. We can keep things easy. Hang out. Have fun."

It was such a nice idea, but he was missing one fundamental point. He was *Nate.* In the formative years of my life, he'd taken up way too much room in my heart for me to keep things easy and shallow now. I'd kissed him one time, and it already felt like I was in the deep end.

I shook my head. "It's not that easy."

"Why not?"

"Because . . . Nate, do you remember my freshman year?"

He scratched his chin. "My senior year."

I nodded. "I had such a big crush on you."

"Yeah. I remember."

I groaned. "You're supposed to tell me you never knew. It would be so much less embarrassing that way."

"You shouldn't be embarrassed. I thought it was . . . sweet."

"Right. Sweet. Great word. Puppies are sweet, too. And little girls in pigtails."

"I didn't think . . . I mean, I did. You were young, and I was *very* aware of that. I remember thinking more than once that if you'd just been a little older, things might have been different."

My jaw hung open. "Are you serious?"

"Um, were you here when I kissed you just now? Why are you so surprised?"

"I'm . . . I don't know. I guess I just felt so invisible that year. All I really wanted was for you to see me. It's crazy now to wrap my head around the possibility that you actually did."

"I promise, I saw you. I think maybe it's what makes this," he motioned between us, "so easy now."

Easy?

It all felt surreal.

Nate. *Nate!* It was surreal, but also crushing. The very fact that it felt so amazing and easy, was what made us being together such a problem. "That's just it, Nate. We'd be too complicated for a no stress, no pressure, having fun kind of relationship. It was more than just a crush for me. It was huge. Big enough that through the rest of high school it pretty much defined every other experience I had with guys. I know it was a long time ago. And I'm not a teenager anymore, and I should be able to separate myself from those feelings now, but . . . I'm pretty sure with you, the chances of me falling hard and fast just like before are pretty high. And then what? I'll be right back where I was four years ago, too distracted to focus on the biggest thing I've ever tried to accomplish in my swimming career. I can't risk it."

"Wow."

My words played back through my brain and I winced. I'd all but made a declaration of love. At least, future love. "Sorry." I pressed my forehead into my hand. "I probably sound crazy."

"Nope." He tilted my chin up and kissed me again, softly this time, lingering only a moment before pulling away. "I get it."

"So you just kissed me again?"

He smiled. "That was totally selfish. But I figured if I'm going to watch you walk out of here without me, I should probably kiss you while I still can."

I huffed. "Make it hard on me, why don't you."

He took a step back, bending his knees so his shoulders dropped into the water. "Better?"

Not a fair question. So not fair. How could anything ever be better with him farther away?

He leaned onto the lane rope, hooking his arms over it and stretched his legs out.

I looked past him across the pool. We were totally alone now. The overhead lights reflected on the water, bouncing on the ripples made by Nate's movements.

"Not better," I finally said. "But necessary."

He nodded. "I know." His voice was sad but kind. "And I admire your dedication. Promise you'll call me after you win all those gold medals?"

I pushed off the wall and crossed the lane so I could wrap my arms around his neck and kiss him one last time. "I promise."

Six

NATE

Telling Kayla I was good with her walking away and actually letting her go were two entirely different things. I couldn't stop thinking about her. Halfway through school on Monday, I was useless to my students. Preoccupied. Distracted. Everything I needed to keep up with in constant battle with the compulsion to call her. I hadn't been so consumed by a woman in . . . ever. During my planning period after lunch, I paced back and forth in front of my desk biting my thumbnail—a nervous habit resurfacing from my youth.

A knock sounded behind me. "Hey, Coach. You wanted to see me?"

I turned. "Bridget. Yes. Thanks for stopping by."

I walked to my desk and pulled a clipboard from the top drawer. "I just wanted to let you know I've worked out the events for Thursday's meet. You're swimming the 200 Free, the IM and the 100 Fly."

She gave me a quizzical look. "Okay?"

I looked back at the list. "Oh, and the anchor leg of the 4x100 Relay."

"So, pretty much what I always swim."

"Right. Of course. But, you know, I didn't want to leave you wondering."

"Is that all you needed?" She still looked confused.

I dropped the clipboard onto my desk and shoved my hands into my pockets.

"Because," she said, "in the two years I've been on your swim team, you've never confirmed events with anyone before we're on the bus, on the way to the meet."

Busted.

"Coach Hanson? If you wanted to ask me about Kayla, it's really okay. I don't mind."

I breathed a sigh of relief. Probably should have just been honest with her from the start. "How is she?"

"Well, let's see. Last night I caught her digging through my room trying to find a copy of my meet schedule."

"Why does she need your meet schedule?"

"I *think* she was hoping it maybe had your phone number on it somewhere. That's my best guess. She wasn't really forthcoming with information once I started pelting her with questions."

"She wants my phone number?" Why hadn't we exchanged numbers already? It's like we'd missed some fundamental step in our communication. We'd had a date, technically, if you could call our swim session a date. But I still had no way to reach her without involving her sister.

Bridget rolled her eyes and crossed to my desk. She picked up a pen and scribbled a phone number onto a yellow sticky note. "Here. Send her a text or something. Maybe then she'll stop talking about you so much."

"Thanks, Bridget."

"No problem." She turned to leave, and then spun back around. "Um, maybe don't tell her I said she was talking about you so much?"

I grinned. "Maybe don't tell her I called you to my classroom to fish for her phone number?"

She laughed. "Deal."

I closed the door behind Bridget and sat down at my desk. I had twenty minutes before my last class. Plenty of time to write up a text.

And delete it.

And type a new one.

And delete it, too.

Finally, I keyed out a quick message and hit send before I could overthink it.

Don't be mad at Bridget for giving me your number.

Her response came through immediately. *Funny. Bridget just texted me the same request. I'm not mad. It's nice to hear from you.*

I smiled. *Glad to hear it.*

Confession? she texted.

Sure.

I can't stop thinking about Saturday night.

Those were good words. Very, very good words. *Me neither. Care to reconsider your decision about having dinner with me?*

Nope. I am resolute in my commitment to refrain. Not excited about that commitment. But still not wavering.

I grumbled. I had to admire her discipline, but those words weren't quite as fun. *Fair enough,* I texted back.

Maybe we could swim together, though. In the name of training.

Of course.

Seriously. I work harder when I have someone challenging me.

Bridget isn't available? I almost felt guilty for goading her. Almost.

Not as long as Brett is on her swim team. I doubt she'd skip practicing with him to see Hamilton on Broadway. Definitely not just to practice with me.

I knew something was going on with those two.

She's very excited about the dance this weekend. He just asked her to go.

Good for him. I texted. *I have to go, too, you know. Teacher duties.*

Painful. But maybe cute, too? Lots of young love blossoming around you?

I scoffed. *Some. Mostly just drama.* I had a sudden and intense desire to have her there with me, and I almost told her so. But she'd been clear.

Are you swimming in the morning?

Yep. Meet me there? 5 a.m.

Only on one condition.

Uh oh. Okay.

Just swimming, she texted. *No kissing.*

Way to hit me where it hurts, Phillips.

Deal?

Fine. But you can't stop me from thinking about kissing you.

A concession I'm willing to make.

I grinned. *See you tomorrow.*

Can't wait.

Those last two words were the best I'd read all day.

Seven

KAYLA

5 A.M. WORKOUTS had never been this fun. Three days in a row, I woke before my alarm and beat Nate to the pool. I told myself it was just because I'd missed working out with other swimmers, but who was I kidding? Not me. And by the way he looked at me, not Nate either.

Thursday morning I took a break and timed him. We'd had a rough idea of where he was coming in, but we needed something more concrete. His times were impressive. More than impressive. When he finished his last 200 free, I showed him the stopwatch app on my phone.

"What's it say?" he asked, his breathing labored and short. "I can't see that far."

"You just swam three seconds slower than the US record."

He shook his head. "It's short course. It's not a fair representation."

He was arguing that the extra flip turn required when swimming in a 25-meter pool versus 50 meters had made him faster. And he had a solid point. Short course times always had an edge. But I shook my head. "It is a fair representation. I'm comparing it to short course times. You're only three seconds off the short course national record. And four seconds off the world record. Do you realize what that means, Nate? You start training full time, and you're there. You are ready for this."

He didn't say anything. Just stood there, leaning against the side of the pool, his head resting on his folded arms.

Finally, he pushed up and hoisted himself out of the water. "I've got to get to school."

"Nate, wait."

He turned back. "Thank you for helping me this morning," he said. "I just can't be late, okay? First period is presenting their monologues, and I need to be there on time."

I nodded. "Okay." Except, it wasn't really okay. It felt like he'd just thrown up an impossibly giant wall between us. Maybe I'd pushed friendly encouragement into, well, just *pushing*.

I understood that it was tough. There were two different sides to his life now: before the accident and after. He'd had to make a living doing something else besides swimming, which totally made sense. And he loved being a teacher and coach, which he'd have to give up, at least temporarily, if he were to pursue another Olympics. But it killed me to think of him missing his chance to get back in. He was ready. He was more than good enough. Was it scary? Sure. Risky? Absolutely. But I was convinced it would be totally worth it.

I resisted the urge to text him throughout the day, wanting to give him space or time or whatever it was he needed. I even played it cool through Bridget's afternoon swim meet. Staying in the stands, focusing on the races instead of trying to catch Nate's eye. When my phone dinged just after dinner, I lunged for it so fast Bridget started to laugh.

"Tell Coach I said hi," she called, as I headed for my bedroom.

I shut the door and dropped onto my bed before reading the text.

I think I screwed up this morning.

My heart melted a little. *You didn't. It's a lot to think through. I get it.*

Will you come with me to the dance on Friday night? It's Valentine's Day, after all. I don't want to go without you.

I stared at his text. Read it over and over. I wanted to go. Of course I wanted to go. But a part of me was also annoyed he was still pushing. Though, it wasn't as if I'd been exactly fair in how I'd handled things. I'd told him no to dating, and then had done everything I could to still see him. We'd been texting every day since I told him I wasn't interested in dating. Talk about sending mixed messages.

Another text dinged through. *I know I probably annoyed you by asking you again. But hear me out?*

I huffed. How did he know me so well? *I'm listening.*

I watched the tiny dots bounce at the bottom of my phone screen, telling me he was typing. It took a while, so I wasn't surprised when a long message popped up.

Here's the thing. You're not the same person you were four years ago. You're older. Wiser. More dedicated. The past six months, you've set more records and won more races than ever before. I don't think there's anything that could derail you. I certainly don't want to. But I would like to cheer you on/buy you dinner/celebrate your victories. You're telling me I should take the risk and start swimming again, and you're right. I should. I guess I'm hoping you'll be willing to take a risk, too.

I couldn't stop smiling. *Are you telling me you'll start racing again, if I'm open to dating?*

You mean dancing. As in high school Valentine's Day dancing.

Ha! That's quite the ultimatum.

It was meant to be more of an invitation than an ultimatum. I'm holding my breath and jumping in, Kayla. Come, too?

His persistence was impressive, but not overwhelming. It was charming, even endearing. But my own fears and doubts still felt so close. I'd been repeating my "no dating" mantra for so long, would agreeing to something different now be a betrayal of everything I'd worked so hard for? But Nate was right, too. Maybe I was a different person than the Kayla who'd made such a mess of things before.

I need to think about it, I texted back.

Take your time, he responded. *But not too much. The dance is on Saturday.* He signed off with a winking emoji.

I dropped my phone beside me on the bed and collapsed onto my back. I thought back to my relationship with Jay, my not so supportive college boyfriend. We'd had great chemistry, and a lot to talk about the first few months, but as time passed, I'd started to see a darker side—an intensity that started to overpower everything else. In retrospect, it was easy to recognize his jealousy, his desire to control parts of my life that didn't have anything to do with him. It made me sick just to think about it. To conjure up how good he'd been at making me feel terrible about myself.

In contrast, Nate seemed so different. More open and honest. Completely transparent in the way he talked to me and told me what he wanted. I believed him when he told me he would support me. As a swimmer himself, he understood better than anyone the commitment I'd made. I thought forward to what it might mean if he started competing again. Maybe we'd be swimming at the Olympics together. I longed for it so badly, I almost texted him right there on the spot.

I was in.

So very *in.*

But Saturday was Valentine's Day. And I could do better than a text message. I grabbed my phone and called Ranee. She answered on the first ring.

"Don't be mad," I said, after saying hello. "But there's been a change of plans. Want to come a day early and help me buy a dress?"

Eight

NATE

HALF WAY THROUGH Saturday night's dance, I'd all but given up hope. I leaned against the wall, close to the water fountain and watched as couples danced under a sea of paper hearts and glittery streamers. Almost like a reflex, I looked for my swimmers, picking them out of the crowd. Were they behaving themselves? Acting responsibly? I'd been clear about how many laps they'd run at Monday's practice if I caught any of them drinking. So far, the ones attending the dance hadn't given me reason to worry. Bridget and Brett were maybe kissing a little too frequently, but I figured that fell outside my responsibilities as coach so I tried my best to ignore them.

I pulled out my phone to check for new notifications. Nothing. Not a call or text. Not even a shout out on Twitter. I'd given Kayla time to mull over my invitation, but she'd surprised me by not responding at all. It didn't seem like her. To leave me hanging with no answer.

I'd texted her earlier that afternoon with a simple query. *Are you in?* Her lack of response was probably all the answer I needed. I sighed and shoved my phone back into my pocket. It was time to let her go.

"What a way to spend a Valentine's Day, right?" Mike Shepherd leaned up against the wall beside me. Shep taught world history and coached the basketball team, and was generally pretty optimistic. Even about school dances.

"What's got you down, Shep?" I asked.

"Ah, I don't know. I forgot to do something for Angie for Valentine's Day. And I forgot to tell her I had to be here tonight, so, yeah. She's not too happy with me right now."

I grimaced. "Ouch. You have a recovery plan yet?"

"I'll figure it out, I guess. Take her out tomorrow, maybe. What about you? You got anybody special to go and see?"

I ran a hand across my chin and shrugged. "I thought maybe I . . ." I froze. Kayla stood at the door to the gym, her eyes scanning the room. "Sorry, Shep. I gotta go."

When I was ten or so paces away, she saw me, a huge smile spreading out across her face.

I stopped right in front of her. "Hi."

"Hi."

She looked amazing. But then it's not like that was hard for Kayla, a woman who managed to make a swim cap look good. All dressed up, with the hair and the dress and the heels, it was a lot to take in.

"I'm sorry I ignored your text earlier," she said. "I just . . . I had this idea to surprise you. Some big Valentine's Day gesture."

"Yeah?"

"But then I remembered that you're a faculty member chaperoning a dance full of your students and athletes, and it suddenly felt silly to think I could just waltz in here and find you without, I don't know, making a scene."

I grinned. "A reasonable worry."

"I mean, my little sister is *right* over there."

I held out my hand. "Want to go for a walk?"

Kayla nodded.

We skirted around the edge of the room still holding hands, past Shep, who gave me an approving thumbs up and cut into the hallway. We weren't far from my classroom, so that seemed like a reasonable destination.

"Man," she said. "It's crazy to be back here. Was it weird for you at first?"

"A little. I'll tell you the weirdest thing is working with teachers who used to be *my* teachers. You know Ms. Greenley is still here?"

"Is she really? She's been teaching forever."

We stopped at my classroom door, and she ran her hands across the plaque that bore my name. "You like teaching?" she asked.

"Yeah. I really love it."

"What are you going to do?"

"About?"

"Training. Will you keep teaching?"

I blew out a weary sigh. I'd been tossing around that same question all weekend. There's no way I could get the hours I needed in the water while still teaching full time. But the thought of leaving my students didn't feel great either.

"I don't think I can," I said. "Not if I'm really going to do this. I was thinking maybe I'll stick around to the end of swim season. We only have a few more weeks. Then I'll see if the school will let me take leave through the rest of the school year."

She reached her hands up, resting them on my shoulders. "You're going to be amazing. You know that, right?" She kissed me softly.

"Right now, I'm pretty sure I'll believe anything you tell me."

"You should believe it. It's true."

I kissed her one more time. "Happy Valentine's Day, Kayla."

She smiled. "Happy Valentine's Day to you, too."

Six Months Later

KAYLA

I SAT IN the stands, my hands gripped tightly around the arm rests. Nate stood in front of the starting block in lane 4. He was the top seeded swimmer in the final heat of the men's 200 Free, and, if he swam like I believed he could, he had the potential to take the Olympic record with his win. I wouldn't swim my final event until the following night. For now all my nerves were for him.

He stretched his arms, paying particular attention to his left shoulder. I closed my eyes. He'd be fine, I told myself. He'd been swimming like never before. He was ready for this.

I didn't expect him to look my way. He was too focused for that. But I almost wished he would. I wanted him to know how much I believed in him. That I loved him, and no matter how he finished, I'd never been prouder of how hard he'd worked and how far he'd come.

The buzz around his comeback had been huge. It had been a little uncomfortable at first, all the media attention, especially when people realized the two of us were a couple. Once high school teammates; now both on the Olympic team. It was a pretty compelling story. But Nate did his best to channel the attention into awareness, using every opportunity he could to talk about safe driving and the potential consequences of texting behind the wheel. We both preferred that be the focus, more than our love story.

Bridget put an arm around my shoulders and gave me a squeeze. "How are you holding up?"

"I feel like I'm going to be sick. It's worse than when I'm swimming."

"He's going to win, Kayla. Don't worry. You're both going home with medals."

I nodded. "He's got this. I know he does."

Nate stretched his arms over his head one last time and pulled his goggles into position. This was it. I said a quick prayer that all would be well; that he would swim his very best and be satisfied with his performance.

A minute and forty-two seconds later, tears were streaming down my face as I cheered, Nate's gold medal victory finally secured. After the medal ceremony, instead of completing the press circuit designed for athletes to pose for pictures and answer questions, Nate broke ranks and came into the stands, climbing until we stood face to face, only a guard rail between us.

"Hi," he whispered.

I laughed. "You're crazy."

"I gotta go," he said. "Just wanted to say I love you." He kissed me, cheers erupting from the crowd around us, then made his way back down to the pool deck.

"I love you, too," I shouted after him, laughter bubbling up inside of me. I was proud of our wins, his and mine. But more importantly, I was so happy it was an experience we'd had together.

He'd been right all along. He was definitely a risk worth taking.

Jenny Proctor was born in the mountains of Western North Carolina, a place where she still resides and considers the loveliest on earth. She and her husband stay busy keeping up with six children and a growing assortment of pets. She loves to hike with her family and spend time outdoors, but she also adores lounging around her home, reading great books or watching great movies and, when she's lucky, eating delicious food she didn't have to prepare herself. Jenny's recent novels include *Love at First Note* (2016) and *Wrong for You* (May 2017).

    Website: www.jennyproctor.com
    Twitter: @writerjennyp
    Facebook: Author Jenny Proctor
    Instagram handle: jennysp123

The Ultimate Bachelor Challenge

By Annette Lyon

One

"We'll head over to the cafeteria for breakfast at nine," Sam said to the four of her roommates who were gathered in their apartment's common room. She opened her bullet journal to the page where she'd planned the annual Valentine's Day marathon, to take place all day tomorrow. "Don't worry about showering and putting yourself together for the day. Just roll out of bed. Half the fun is walking to the cafeteria in pajamas and then hanging out here all day, swooning over the heroes in the movies we pick."

Beth hugged a throw pillow. "Could we start earlier than nine?"

Oh, how little she knew. Sam had lived through many Valentine's Day marathons and had honed the event year by year until it was practically an art form. After tomorrow, Beth would never again look at the holiday the same.

Sam adjusted her position on the couch, excited to explain. "See, we need our sleep if we're going to do the marathon right. Sure, we'll be sitting around all day, but that's surprisingly tiring if you're not well rested. So everyone, set your alarms for five minutes to nine. That's when we roll out of bed, shove our slippers on, and go eat. We'll need a decent breakfast, or we'll start flagging around one or two in the afternoon, and that would be unfortunate."

"Makes sense," Beth said with a nod. She began playing with the pillow's fringe.

Sam consulted her planning page. "Okay, start thinking about what you'll provide for treats. Here's a sign-up sheet so you can see what others are bringing. We want variety. And remember, we're not stopping for lunch."

Tara took the paper and clipboard from Sam's outstretched hand. "I already bought chips and salsa," she said, writing that down.

A scoff from MollyAnne came from the love seat. "As if we're trying to be healthy."

"Oh no, no, no," Tara said, shaking her head. "It's not that." She handed the clipboard to Beth, who rested it on the pillow in her lap.

For their freshman and sophomore years, Sam, Tara, and Alyssa had roomed together. Sam had taught them the principles behind her traditional marathon, and the two of them were now almost as good at evangelizing the event as its founder. Sam first held a Valentine's Day marathon in high school when she didn't have a boyfriend or even a date, and the tradition had carried into college. This year, Alyssa wasn't at the planning meeting, and she wouldn't be attending, either. She now had a fiancé, so she'd be spending the day with him.

"Just listen to Tara," Sam said. "Trust me; we aren't trying to be healthy."

With a nod of acknowledgment, Tara explained. "If you eat nothing but sugar, you'll end up sick of it, stop eating, and with a headache. You need something salty or savory to break up the sugar. That's how Sam and I eat those massive sundaes at the creamery—we alternate eating ice cream and caramel with fries."

"Which we add extra salt to," Sam said.

"Oh . . . Wow . . ." Whitney said, her first contribution to the conversation. "I always wondered why you ordered fries with sundaes."

MollyAnne's mouth opened slightly as if she hadn't realized

she was in the presence of Olympic-caliber junk foodies. "Okay, I think I understand. The savory-sweet thing is why we're ordering pizza for dinner, right?"

"In part, yes," Sam said. "Also because once the marathon starts, we don't stop except for bathroom breaks between shows."

"And without an official lunch, we'll need dinner," Tara added. "So we may as well have it brought to us, right?" She held out a hand, knuckles out. She bumped fists with Sam, who then made a big show of sighing.

"I have one piece of sad news, though," she said, pretending to study the journal page. Instead, she was doodling flowers and hearts to hide the excitement building inside her. "I will probably miss dinner." She bit the corner of one lip as heat spread up her neck and into her face until her face had probably gone as pink as cotton candy.

A chorus of "What?" and "Why not" came from MollyAnne, Beth, and Whitney.

"Um . . ." Sam hedged. Nothing was official, but all signs pointed one direction. And she didn't want to suddenly disappear if, well . . .

Tara took over the explanation. "There's a good chance that Sam . . ." She dragged out the words to increase the suspense. ". . .may soon be in Alyssa's shoes."

"What? Engaged? That's fantastic!" Whitney squealed.

"Congratulations!" Beth and MollyAnne said at the same time.

The roommates hopped off the couches, love seat, and floor, and group hugged as they congratulated Sam. She encouraged them to sit down again, and hedged. "Thanks—really. But it's not official. Steve—"

"He's in town?" Whitney interrupted.

"Maybe," Tara said.

"I don't know anything for sure," Sam said. Forget cotton candy. Sam's face had to look more like a fire engine. "Steve said he couldn't fly back for a visit until April, but earlier today, he texted saying that he needed to talk about something important that has to do with Valentine's Day..." She shrugged. "He could be planning a surprise visit, but I don't dare get my hopes up that the theater company would give him that much time off."

Steve was performing with the Royal Shakespeare Company in London for a year, so he and Sam maintained their relationship as best they could over the phone and through email. Christmas break was the only time she'd seen him since he'd left in August. But so far, they'd made it as a long-distance couple. One semester was behind them, and this one was well underway.

Because of the time difference, they usually texted and Snapchatted, but he'd seemed awfully determined about calling and actually talking to her on Valentine's Day. Maybe he'd found a way to visit, even if just for the weekend. And the important thing to discuss? It didn't take a mathematician to figure out what that might mean, and she was a math major.

She'd be more than happy to miss part of the marathon and pass the hostess torch to Tara if it meant receiving an engagement ring. Sam settled into her spot on the couch, her notebook in hand. "I don't know when he'll be calling, or anything else for sure. Let's plan the day as if I'll be here the whole time. And if I end up leaving early, you'll know why."

Squeals of excitement rippled through the room again. Sam let her friends' happiness wash over her and her beating heart. Being apart from Steve had been harder than she'd expected, but it would be over soon. *And it'll all be worth it.*

"Back to business," she said with her most authoritative voice. "Let's talk movies."

Tara clasped her hands. "Jane Austen is a must. The question is which one?"

"How is that even a question?" Beth said. "*Pride and Prejudice* screams 'Valentine's Day.' I mean seriously. We can't *not* watch it."

"But we watched it last year," Tara countered.

"Because it's a classic," Beth said. "And I wasn't here."

MollyAnne groaned. "Can we watch one of the shorter versions? I don't want six hours taken up by one movie. How about the Kiera Knightley one?"

"You can't be serious." Whitney's look of utter disbelief and disdain suggested that MollyAnne had spoken blasphemy.

Sam sat there with her notebook, smiling at how emphatic her friends were about their movies. Smart women with strong opinions who were all romantics at heart. That's what the marathon was all about.

Tara raised both hands as if trying to broker a peace. "Let's leave *Pride and Prejudice* as a big maybe, okay? Remember, there are other Jane Austen movies—*Emma, Persuasion, Sense and Sensibility*. Besides, we'll have all day *and* all night. Maybe we can do more than one Austen." The others relaxed a bit, murmuring some level of acceptance for tabling a final decision. Tara turned to Beth. "Just remember that we could watch two or three movies in the time it would take to watch Jennifer Ehle and Colin Firth."

"Exactly," Whitney said. "Like *She's the Man* or *10 Things I Hate About You*. Those are Shakespeare adaptations—"

"But six hours of *Colin Firth*!" Beth interjected desperately, ignoring Whitney's English major Shakespeare plea.

"*Five* hours," said Sam with a laugh as she made notes. "And he's not in all of it."

"The A&E version has six episodes," Beth countered.

"That are each fifty minutes long," Sam explained. "Which makes the whole movie five hours, not six."

MollyAnne lifted an eyebrow at Beth. "I'd think a Colin-Firth-as-Mister-Darcy aficionado would know that."

Beth harrumphed and slouched on the couch, joining Whitney with her arms folded in protest.

Sam jotted down more notes. "I'm including the other Austens that Tara mentioned, plus the two Shakespeare adaptations for you, Whitney. Remember, none of this is final yet. I have to point out, though, that Heath Ledger is in *10 Things I Hate About You*. Just saying."

"If we're talking Heath Ledger, let's add *A Knight's Tale*," Beth said. "Oh, and *Can't Buy Me Love*. But that's Patrick Dempsey." She grinned.

"Nice," Whitney said. "Sam, add *Serendipity*."

Suggestions continued to fly at Sam as fast as she could write. They'd never watch the entire list, of course, but recording everyone's suggestions was the first step in planning the marathon. The list provided backup ideas, which often proved necessary, as preferences inevitably shifted. Sam didn't worry about tonight's disagreements causing problems tomorrow. She'd seen plenty of marathons come and go, and somehow, almost like magic, whenever it was time to start a new movie, everyone could agree on what to watch next.

"*You've Got Mail*," Tara said suddenly. "I haven't seen that in forever. And that other one with Tom Hanks. Written by the same woman. Shoot. What was it?"

"I should remember," Sam said. "It's one of my parents' favorites. I'll check IMDB." She reached for her phone on the couch's armrest, but instead of launching the app, noticed an unread message. "Steve texted," she said quietly.

"What does it say?" Tara asked, scooting closer.

With a laugh, Sam pulled the phone out of view from the others. "Let me read it first."

I have something to tell you. And something to ask you. Can we connect in the morning, say around nine? I need to see your face.

Good thing she was already sitting; Sam nearly passed out before remembering to breathe. *He might not be coming. He could just want to FaceTime from London.*

"What is it?" MollyAnne said.

"Tell us," Beth added.

"Come on," Whitney said, not to be left out of the conversation.

"He has something to tell me. And something to . . ." Sam swallowed and licked her lips. "Something to *ask* me."

She waited out the exclamations of excitement before looking up from her phone and going on. "He wants to see me in the morning at nine." Hearing the words leave her mouth, she felt blood drain from her face. "Holy crap. I can't do breakfast in pajamas. I have to be showered and looking hot by nine. And I haven't done laundry in a week. What was I thinking? I don't have anything to wear." Sam stood and paced the small room from the door to the kitchenette and back again, gripping her phone for dear life.

"You were purposely *not* getting your hopes up," Tara said. "Remember?"

"Right," Sam said, combing her hair with her free hand.

Tara went on. "You said that if you washed your favorite outfits, you'd jinx Valentine's, and he wouldn't come for sure."

"I'm an idiot," Sam said. "Now I have nothing cute to wear." She paced some more, thinking aloud to process her thoughts and make an alternate plan. The marathon had flown right out of her head. "I have to do laundry—now. I'll wear my red maxi skirt with that top you gave me, Tara. They look so good together. I need to wash both. And my good bra. I hope there's enough time for it to air dry . . ." The corner of her thumbnail slipped between her teeth, and she gnawed it—an old habit from childhood that returned whenever she felt nervous. Except that when she was three, the habit was sucking her thumb instead.

Tara stood and reached for Sam's shoulders, stopping her frenetic pacing. Tara nodded toward Sam's bullet journal, which lay abandoned on the couch. "I'll finish marathon prep. You've taught me well, Master Jedi. As your Padawan, I'll make you proud. I'll even remember to play Wynn Rock's YouTube channel between movies."

"Excellent," Beth said. "That way, we'll still have eye candy on the screen."

"And it'll be a hot guy who's real," Whitney filled in. "Not some character from a movie."

"And someone we already know is a decent human being," MollyAnne finished.

They'd essentially recited Sam's top reasons for keeping Wynn Rock videos playing in the background as she did dishes and homework. She must have seen each of the videos a hundred times, sometimes watching, always listening to Conner Wynn, whether he was on an outdoor adventure or giving an impassioned opinion on conserving nature, saving energy, or helping a charity. He really was the kind of person the world could use more of. Plus, as her friends had said, he was awfully easy on the eyes.

Sam dropped her hand and looked around the room. "You guys won't hate me if I skip out on you tomorrow? I don't know how long I'll be gone with Steve. I could miss the entire—"

"What is there to be mad about?" Beth asked, talking over her. "Getting proposed to? Spending time with your fiancé, who has been out of the country for the better part of the last six months? Are you kidding? Of course we won't be mad!"

Whitney made a shooing gesture with both hands. "Go. We'll be fine. Remember, we have Tara to take care of us, and you've trained her well."

MollyAnne leaned forward, chin resting on her palm. "But we do expect to hear every little detail after the fact, or *that* will make us mad. Deal?"

An un-containable grin spread across Sam's face. "Deal," she said. "You guys, I can't even . . ."

"Go!" they all said.

"Okay, I'll start a couple of loads of laundry in the basement. I won't be gone long. We can keep planning in just a few minutes."

Tara physically dragged her into their shared room, where they stuffed Sam's laundry bag with the essentials—her red maxi skirt, along with any other darks she could find to wash with it. After all, she couldn't very well wash just her skirt in a full load; that was wasteful of water, detergent, and electricity. She'd never be able to look Conner Wynn in the face again—or, she supposed, the screen. After adding some of Tara's jeans and Sam's red university sweatshirt into the top, the mesh bag ended up pretty full. A quick look in her dresser drawer, however, produced two quarters. She'd totally forgotten to pick up another roll.

"Here," Tara said, placing a full roll of quarters into her hand. "Pay me back later."

"You're the best." Sam gave Tara a quick hug and grabbed her room key, but before she could leave, MollyAnne appeared in the bedroom door.

"Bad news, ladies." She held out a piece of paper. "Katie just dropped this off."

What was their RA doing passing out fliers an hour before midnight? Tara took the paper and groaned, holding it out to Sam.

Laundry room is closed for the weekend due to a frozen pipe bursting. Sorry for the inconvenience. Use the laundromat on Acorn Street until further notice.

Sam slumped onto the end of her bed. "Now what?"

"You go to the laundromat on Acorn," Tara said. She held the paper over her shoulder for MollyAnne to take.

"I think you're forgetting a few small details," Sam said. "Acorn is four blocks away. It's winter. It's late. And I don't have a functional car."

"So?"

"So I can't walk dark, icy city streets by myself at this hour." Sam hoped to have enough money saved in another month to either pay for a new transmission on her old beater car or buy a new-to-her used car. Until then . . .

Tara went to her desk and returned a second later with something she clapped into Sam's hand—car keys. "Take mine."

Sam's fingers curved around both the keys and the roll of quarters. Her eyes grew misty. As excited as she was to be with Steve, she'd miss rooming with Tara. She stepped forward and gave her a big hug. "You're the best, you know that?"

"Pretty much," Tara said, chuckling. She pulled away, looking a little emotional, too. "I learned from the actual best, though." She tilted her head toward the door. "Now go wash that skirt."

Two

Connor checked his phone yet again. Midnight was fast approaching, which meant that his social media rival, Trevor Knowles, would be posting the first challenge in his latest attempt to crown himself king of YouTube and Instagram.

For six months now, Connor had sidestepped Trevor's attempts at driving competition between them. They didn't have that much overlap in audience anyway. Connor made a comfortable living; he didn't need to stroke his own ego by beating an arrogant chauvinist like Trevor Knowles. The guy dedicated his feed to showing what a great bachelor life he had: showing off his washboard abs, trips to sunny beaches, and more women—"babes" in Trevor-speak—than he knew what to do with.

But this time, Connor had finally caved, because Trevor's latest contest idea involved raising money for charity. The winner picked a charity that the loser had to donate five thousand dollars to. Connor had no idea what charity Trevor had in mind—if the guy had thought that far ahead, which he doubted. Connor had already picked the charity for Trevor to donate to: the local women's shelter. The guy spent so much time objectifying women that the least Connor could do was make him help women like his mother—strong women who needed help fleeing abuse.

Trevor would be posting the first task of the challenge a few minutes before midnight. Wanting to watch the video alone, Connor stepped onto the porch of the old house he'd rented with some roommates near campus. The glow of the porch light spilled golden onto unblemished snow.

He checked his phone. Sure enough, he'd been tagged in a new post. For what had to be the hundredth time that day, Connor considered pulling out of the contest. It hadn't started yet. Any hubbub over his canceling would settle down soon enough. *His* audience wasn't the one clamoring for the competition. He'd happily give five grand to Trevor's charity of choice. He only hoped it wouldn't be something like a foundation that bought costumes for needy role-playing gamers or something equally pointless.

His thumb hovered over the icon. In his gut, he knew he'd go through with the challenge. He'd made a commitment, and he didn't renege on a promise. Plus, he really did want to raise money for the local battered women's shelter. He planned to match Trevor's donation, making it ten thousand total. And Connor could encourage his audience to donate as well.

He remembered all too well living in a shelter as a kid, after his mother had taken him and his brother and fled from his dad with little more than the clothes on their backs. She'd passed away three years ago from breast cancer. That was another charity he'd considered. In the end, though, he knew that he literally owed his life to that shelter and to the volunteers who'd helped his mother stand on her own two feet again after she'd taken him and his little brother there. A few years later, his father was convicted of killing a girlfriend and would spend the rest of his life in prison. Connor had no doubt that if his mother hadn't acted, she would have been the woman he killed, and Connor and his brother would have been split up in foster care—if not dead.

You're stalling, he thought. He pulled his focus to his phone. He needed to watch the video introducing the contest, which

Trevor had dubbed, "The Ultimate Bachelor Challenge," because supposedly it would prove which of them was the "real" man.

But before Connor could tap the icon, he heard the sound of spinning car wheels, followed by a door slamming and a voice saying, "Crap. Crap, crap, crap!"

Wondering if someone needed help, he stepped off the porch and walked toward the street. Two houses down, an old sedan had run into a bank of snow left by a snowplow. He knew from experience that the snow was likely several feet thick and about as hard as concrete. That car was definitely stuck. The car beeped and flashed its lights as it was locked. Soon after, the figure of a woman appeared, lugging a laundry bag over one shoulder. She slowly picked her way along the icy road. He glanced to his left, toward the laundromat down the hill. That's where she had to be headed. But at midnight? In the winter? Alone?

"Hey, you okay?" Connor called, hoping to help.

She let out a high-pitched yelp, clearly startled by his presence. She slipped, dropping the bag and catching her balance on a mailbox. Her boots went in opposite directions as she held on and regained her footing. She didn't respond to him except for glancing his way with wide, worried eyes.

Crap, he thought, echoing her own exclamation. He hadn't meant to scare her. *Mom taught you better than that.*

He retreated slowly and headed for the house so she'd know he wasn't some creep who followed random women in the middle of the night. Once inside, he closed the door, turned out the living room lights, and stood at the edge of the living room window so he could make sure she was okay. The woman—a university student, he guessed, based on her age and the direction she'd come from—picked up the bag, still holding onto the mailbox, then carefully let go and walked, one tiny, quick step at a time, as if trying to hurry but knowing that bigger steps would mean another fall.

Before she disappeared down the slope of the hill, she paused and looked over her shoulder at the house. Connor moved into the shadows of the living room, hoping she hadn't seen him, or she might be spooked after all.

Good guys, he remembered his mother telling him and his brother, Jacob, could help ease women's fears by consciously *not* appearing threatening. She'd given examples like walking on the other side of the street so a woman didn't need to worry whether a man was following her.

Mom would smack me on the forehead if she could see me now.

The young woman passed beneath a street lamp. Her hair seemed to glow from a streetlamp breaking through her hair, lighting it into a deep copper flame. He'd always been partial to redheads. He smiled at that, wishing they could have met under other circumstances. He couldn't exactly chase her down now and ask her out. She'd probably call 911 or pull a can of pepper spray. But as she disappeared into the darkness, he noticed something bright red in the snow—very different from the gorgeous shade of her hair. Something had fallen out of her laundry bag.

He slipped out the door and hurried over to the blob in the road—a University of Utah sweatshirt. He picked it up and shook off the powdery snow, rescuing it from getting soaked. The edge of the collar was worn in spots, as were the cuffs on the sleeves. The white logo had faded somewhat. The shirt had obviously been worn and well-loved. She'd miss it.

He turned in the direction she'd walked. *I could catch her and return it.*

To his credit, he restrained the instinct to yell to her. She'd likely slip and fall again, maybe hurting herself—and then she'd call the cops on him. Maybe he could leave it on the hood of her car. No. It'd end up sopping wet—maybe stolen.

Slinging the sweatshirt over one shoulder, he headed for the house. He'd figure out what to do with it later. First, though, he needed to bite the bullet by finding out the first task of The Ultimate Bachelor Challenge. Whatever it was, he had to beat Trevor. As soon as Connor got inside and clicked the door shut behind him, his phone squawked with the barnyard noises he'd assigned to Trevor's number. Connor reluctantly checked the text.

Challenge #1 is live. May the best man win.

Connor wished he'd insisted on more ground rules, including having an impartial third party select the challenges. But Trevor had insisted publicly that his assistant, Johnny, would create the challenges in secret, and that Trevor wouldn't know them until each one was announced live. Tired of arguing with Trevor, and glad he'd agreed to the charity donation aspect, Connor had relented.

On the up side, the challenges would significantly increase Connor's audience, which, he hoped, might turn into increased donations for the shelter. Yet he dreaded the possibility of the tasks reflecting Trevor's personality, like taking selfies kissing strange women. Rather, *chicks* or *babes*.

To keep my integrity, I'll have to be creative, he thought.

His phone mooed, clucked, and baa-ed again with a second text from Trevor.

Chicken? A fitting text, considering the barnyard noises that accompanied it. Another text followed.

You backing out?

Connor quickly typed a reply before Trevor could turn his taunting to social media. *Game on. Prepare to lose.*

He sent the text and then panicked—what if the first task was something horrible that he couldn't bear to do?

Here goes nothing. Connor played the video.

Trevor wore his trademark fedora. "Hey, there! It's Trevor

Knowles from The Trevor Dudes. Right now it's *just* past midnight, so it's officially Valentine's Day. And you know what that means . . ." He let an air horn rip in one hand and threw confetti with the other. "It's time for The Ultimate Bachelor Challenge! That's right, Fellow Trevor Dudes! For the next twenty-four hours, I'll be facing off virtually with Connor Wynn, the guy you *might* know as the host of Wynn Rocks. The two of us will be posting updates right here on Instagram and on YouTube. Be sure to follow the official Ultimate Bachelor hashtag so you don't miss a thing!"

He made a hashtag symbol with his fingers.

"A new task will be announced every two hours, right here on my feed. So keep your eyes peeled on the even hours: the next task will go live at two o'clock, then four o'clock, and so on. Each successfully completed task earns the bachelor two hundred points. But the *first* bachelor to post proof of completion earns an additional hundred points. At the end, we'll tally up likes, shares, thumbs-up, follows, and all of that, throw the numbers into a fancy algorithm, and we'll know the winner." He nodded and rubbed his hands together eagerly. "Simple, right? My good friend Johnny here came up with the tasks. They're known only to him. I haven't seen any of them. Right, Johnny?"

The camera rotated to the left, where Johnny waved and called, "That's right. Hey, Trevor Dudes!"

The feed panned to Trevor. "Today will be full of surprises for both me and Connor. Scout's honor." He held up two fingers, reconsidered, added a third, and then waved his hand dismissively. "Aw, forget it. I don't know the salute. Is that even what they call it? Who cares? I was never a Boy Scout!" He laughed, and Johnny joined in from off camera. "Seriously, though, let's get down to business and announce challenge number one!" He held his right hand out, and from off-screen, Johnny handed him a white board. Trevor read the red marker, nodded approvingly, then showed the text to the camera as he read it aloud.

"Take a selfie wearing a strange woman's piece of clothing. Owner of the item must be in the shot."

He gave a thumbs up. "This should be an especially interesting challenge for the middle of the night." He leaned forward and grew more serious. "Now remember, Connor, it has to be an article of clothing from a *strange* woman." With one finger, he tracked the word on the board, almost as if he were a kindergarten teacher. "That doesn't mean some weird chick, right Johnny?"

"Nope." Johnny appeared in the frame. "Finding a freaky chick like a streetwalker isn't the point—although that *would* be interesting, and it would count." He and Trevor laughed and high-fived.

"So it just has to be something owned by a woman we don't already know?" Trevor clarified.

"Right," Johnny said, nodding at the camera and then leaving the frame again.

Trevor turned to the camera, and when he spoke, Connor felt as if his nemesis were speaking to him right there in the living room. "Someone we don't know. No borrowing your mom's high heels or your sister's maternity dress. And no putting on something for sale at a store like at a Walmart because it's open late. It has to a piece of clothing that belongs to a real chick you didn't meet until tonight." Trevor lowered the white board and grinned mischievously. "Let's see what Team Trevor Dudes and Team Wynn Rocks come up with. Ready, Connor? I am. Let The Ultimate Bachelor Challenge begin!"

The video ended with the electric guitar riff Trevor used at the end of all his videos, along with his bright yellow logo of a fist punching forward, as if it were hitting the viewer. The guy was nothing if not lacking in class. Connor glanced at the stats. The video was only a few minutes old, but it already had more than a thousand views and almost a hundred comments.

Connor let out a mouthful of air. Where was he supposed to

find a woman he didn't know, who would willingly let him put on something of hers *and* post a selfie of the two of them? He grabbed the sweatshirt off his shoulder, meaning to toss it onto the couch, but then the obvious solution hit him. He looked out the window at the spot where the woman had clung to the mailbox for dear life. What if he got a picture of himself wearing it at the laundromat before returning it to her? He might complete the first task before Trevor. A boost of energy went through him.

But how to approach her and ask for the picture? He could hear his mother's voice in his ear now. *You're going to frighten the poor dear to death.*

What if he showed up to do his own laundry? A guy with a laundry basket wouldn't be as threatening, right? He doubted that she'd seen him, so walking into the laundromat shouldn't scare her. He wouldn't put the sweatshirt on until after getting her permission, of course.

This could work.

Plan set, he went to his room and gathered his laundry. Soon he had the basket, a bottle of detergent, and the sweatshirt all loaded into his car, and he was driving down the hill to the laundromat.

Valentine's Day and the stupid Ultimate Bachelor Challenge might start off on a very good note after all.

Three

SAM PUSHED HER way through the laundromat door and hefted her bag on top of the nearest washer.

No one was inside. Washers and dryers lined the perimeter, and a double-wide row ran down the middle of the room. One washer was mid-cycle, with a basket on top, filled with folded tops and cardigans—definitely a woman's laundry. After Tara's car took a nosedive into the snow, and having to walk the rest of the way in the dark, Sam had been on edge. Hearing some guy call out to her hadn't exactly helped her nerves. But now, in the warmth and solitude of the laundromat, she relaxed.

She planned to start two loads and read a novel on her phone until they were done. She'd call a taxi or Uber to her apartment. It was only five blocks, and part of her argued that paying for such a short ride would be silly. But she'd been spooked enough on the way here, and walking *up* the icy hill even later into the night would mess with her head even more. She'd enlist her roommates to help dig out the car, maybe during a break between movies. Hopefully the car didn't have any damage.

She crossed to the double row of machines and dumped her mesh bag on top, then proceeded to sort her dirty clothes into two machines—whites in the left, colors in the right. One of these days, she'd separate her clothes more, into both lights and darks, whites and delicates. But not until she owned her own machine and didn't need to be aware of exactly when her loads were done or risk having her laundry stolen. And when she didn't have to make sure she had enough quarters.

Just as she started the colored load, which included her beloved maxi skirt, the bells on the door rang behind her, followed by the squeak of a wet sneaker on the linoleum. Sam's head came up, but otherwise she froze, and her fingers dug into the holes of the mesh laundry bag, though she wanted to bite her thumbnail. Who had come in at this hour? Hopefully the owner of the pink cardigan.

Please be another woman, Sam thought as she slowly folded her bag, trying to act casual. Too bad she hadn't thought of using the machines on the other side of island; that would've given her a perfect view of the door. And too bad Steve wasn't with her right now to play the part of bodyguard. Then again, if he was in town—which he probably was—they wouldn't be hanging out in a dingy laundry room. There was a reason she would be showering, straightening her hair, doing full makeup, and wearing her best outfit before she saw him again. She definitely wouldn't be getting engaged wearing sweats and a t-shirt, and sporting a messy bun.

The person walked to her right and set a laundry basket on a washer on the side wall. From the corner of her eye, Sam confirmed that it was indeed a man. From the corner of her eye, all she could see was his back, so she couldn't tell much besides the fact that he had to be over six feet and probably in his twenties. That also described about eighty percent of the men who lived in the area.

He might be entirely harmless, but she'd still create some distance between them and discourage conversation. After all, these were Ted Bundy's old stomping grounds, and being a friendly person is what got all of his victims into trouble. She heard about the serial killer every time she went home; her parents worried over her and regularly reminded her to stay safe, and that even nice-looking guys could be dangerous. Maybe their parents' paranoia had affected her more than she'd realized.

Sam turned around and hopped up to sit on a washer and held her phone to her ear, pretending to be on a call. "Oh, Steve, you're so sweet," she said in her most maple-syrupy voice. Anyone hearing her would have to assume that she was actually talking to her boyfriend. She pretended to listen to a response, twirled a lock of hair and tossed it over one shoulder, then laughed. "I'm going to hold you to that, you know."

The guy, now off to her left, glanced her direction, then resumed loading a washer with jeans and t-shirts. She couldn't avoid noticing his build. He probably played some kind of sport. But he was shorter than she'd guessed at first glimpse. He might be barely six feet, if that. He took off his coat and tossed it onto a dryer, revealing a t-shirt stretched over his torso. Was it possible to have a six pack on your back? Because every inch of the guy seemed ripped. What kind of sport created that kind of physique?

Good thing none of her roommates had joined her. Tara would have gasped, or even said something embarrassing, like, "Ooh, I'd like him for dessert."

Her parents' warnings cranked up her nerves. She was a small-framed, five-foot-one, as her mother often reminded her. Even with a self-defense class under her belt—something her dad had insisted on—someone that ripped could pretty much do anything he wanted to her without breaking a sweat.

He closed the washer door, and as he reached for his detergent bottle, he looked over, throwing her a hint of a smile and nod as a hello. Her nerves relaxed a bit. Except that her mother would argue that putting a girl at ease was exactly the kind of thing a creeper would do. Sam shook her head and ordered herself to stop thinking like that.

With the detergent poured in, he started the washer, then tossed a faded Utes sweatshirt to one side. He must have forgotten to toss it in with the rest, though it probably belonged to his girlfriend; it was much too small for him.

Sam said a fake good-bye and pretended to hang up, then brought the novel up on her phone. Sitting cross-legged on the washer—still mostly facing the guy—she tried to read, but mostly swiped pages without comprehending the words. Instead, her gaze kept returning to him. She hadn't yet gotten a good look at his face, but a few glimpses said he was definitely cute. Not that it mattered; she had a serious boyfriend.

Based on the sweatshirt, he was probably a university student—or at least a girl he knew was. He seemed a little older than the typical college student, so maybe he was in grad school. She kept pretending to read, and even made a real effort to, but even if her college degree had depended on it, she couldn't have described the first thing about the story.

With his one machine running, the guy turned around and leaned against it, looking at his phone, too. Sam's attention kept returning to the discarded sweatshirt, still visible behind him. Strange that he'd brought it but not washed it.

Unless . . .

Wait. Where's mine? She looked around but found nothing in the empty mesh bag. She remembered putting the sweatshirt into it—but didn't remember putting it into the washer with the load of colors. Had she put it in with the *whites*? She hoped not; the red shirt would turn her socks and underwear pink. But no, she hadn't seen the sweatshirt at all since she'd stuffed it into the laundry bag in her room.

It had probably fallen out on the way there. She'd try to find it in the morning when it was light, but knew the chances were slim of locating it. She'd worn that shirt at almost every meaningful college experience since her first home football game. She considered it a lucky charm, in a way, often wearing it while studying for tests—along with her pink bunny slippers, which clashed with the red hilariously. She could replace the shirt, but a new one wouldn't be the same.

I get to talk to Steve soon, she thought to lighten her mood. *And he has something to ask me.* Sam tried to read again.

"Um, miss?" Laundry guy's voice seemed amplified in the room filled with metal machines.

Sam looked up at him. He looked oddly familiar, but she couldn't place him. Maybe they'd crossed paths on campus. She didn't answer, exactly, just made a noise that might have sounded a bit like, "Hmm?" or maybe, "Me?"

He picked up the sweatshirt and held it out. "This may sound like a weird question, but . . . is this yours?"

"Uh, I don't—" She meant to return her attention to the book, but the faded elbows caught her eye. Hers were worn in a specific way, and the sleeve hanging in front of her looked just like hers.

He looked closer at something on the collar. "Maybe not. Someone wrote *Sam* here." He turned the shirt front to back, looking at it again, then at her.

The movement revealed a dark spot to the right of the white U—the hint of a stain from a food fight. Alyssa had lobbed a wooden spoon covered in melted chocolate right at her.

No one was ever supposed to see Tara's faded handwriting, done with a black Sharpie. She'd written everyone's names into their shirts to avoid any mix-ups. Sam had protested that they were adults, not kindergarteners, and could find their own clothing, but more than once, having their names written inside the collars had been convenient. Now, though, having an attractive guy see it made her feel about six years old. Her cheeks felt warm as she held out her hand for her sweatshirt.

"Yep. Sam. That's me," she said. "Technically, it's Samantha. I answer to Sammie and Sam, too. One of my roommates wrote that. It was out of my hands. But you know, try winning an argument with Tara, and you'll lose every time." She stopped talking, aware that she'd blabbed a long, meandering reply. Her cheeks blushed hotter. She decided to blame the warmth of the room.

He grinned. "So this *is* yours."

"Yeah." She hadn't lost her school sweatshirt after all. But how did this guy find it—*and* her? Had he followed her here?

Mom would so freak out.

She could hear her mother's warning as clear as day. *No, Salt Lake isn't Chicago, but it is the place where a serial killer got away with killing a lot of young women, because they were too trusting of a normal-looking guy.*

But this guy was so not normal. He was something out of a movie or a magazine. She felt a twinge of guilt for noticing, but quelled it with the rationalization that she could set him up with one of her roommates. One big point in his favor: he didn't hold himself like so many guys she'd met whose every word and movement oozed a complete awareness of their good looks. Ironically, that was something she found *unattractive* more than almost anything else. She tended to gravitate toward guys who didn't live in a gym, and who would otherwise be categorized as average. Someone, she realized, a lot like Steve.

"Hey, are you okay?" laundry guy asked.

That was what the man had asked when she slipped on the road. Wait. This *was* the same guy. Had he really come to do laundry? He took a step closer and tossed the beat-up sweatshirt onto the machine beside her.

Confused at the understanding gesture, she reached for the shirt and held it to her chest. He seemed like such a nice guy, but then again, she had to know . . .

"Did you follow me here?" she asked, looking at the chocolate stain instead of him.

"I live just up the road, and . . ." He drew his hand down his stubble. "My name's Connor, by the way."

"You didn't answer my question. Did you follow me?"

"Technically?" He raked one hand though his hair, mussing it, and nodded sheepishly. "Sort of." He held up a hand and took a step away as if he knew his answer would freak her out. "You were carrying a laundry bag, so I figured you were heading here, and when you dropped that"—he gestured toward the sweatshirt—"I wanted to be sure you didn't lose it."

She tilted her head, unconvinced.

"Plus, I have my own laundry to do, as you can see. And nothing going on tonight except . . ." Connor cleared his throat. "Well, anyway, sorry to interrupt your evening. I'll leave you alone." He returned to his machines, hopped onto one of them as she had onto hers earlier, ignoring the folding chairs in the corners, and pulled out his phone.

For the next half hour or so, neither spoke. Connor seemed engrossed with his phone, scrolling through posts or comments, tapping here and there, reading short things—maybe posted comments or tweets. Hard to tell at that distance, but he was certainly reacting to whatever he found online—and not in a good way. His posture rounded slightly. He sighed more than once and began worrying his lower lip with a thumb and forefinger. He looked upset.

Her heart softened toward the guy; he seemed genuinely frustrated over something. It took her a few minutes to muster up the courage to break the silence, but finally she asked, "Hey, are *you okay?*"

He looked up, clearly surprised at the question. He looked at his phone screen and bit his lip again before answering. "Okay, so I really did want to return your sweatshirt—honest. And I assumed you were headed here because of the laundry bag. But . . . I had another reason for coming here besides laundry."

Sam's brow furrowed. Her mother's voice threatened to break through and ratchet up her nerves again, but she fought back the reaction. "So . . . why did you want to find me?" Something about him felt familiar and safe—something she could never explain to her worried parents—but for some reason, she wasn't nervous. She simply waited for Connor's explanation.

He licked his lips. "This will sound really weird, but I have a favor to ask. If it makes you feel the least bit uncomfortable, I'll leave, and you'll never see me again. But I swear I'm not a stalker or anything." Again he raked his fingers through his already-mussed hair. His expression looked half hopeful, half filled with dread, as if she held his future in her hands.

But Sam grinned. The sudden shift from her feeling insecure and uncomfortable to sensing *him* feeling the same way calmed any lingering worries she might have had. He looked vulnerable, and if she could help him, she would.

"What if I say you need to leave? What happens to your laundry?" She couldn't stop smiling. The shift in tension from her to him put her so much at ease that she found humor in the situation.

He patted the chugging washer and shrugged. "Then I'll hope my clothes are still here in the morning. Even better, I'll send my roommate Ben to pick them up. That way, you can be sure you never have to lay eyes on me again."

"Oh, but that would be unfortunate," she said, then closed her mouth. Did that come out sounding as if she was attracted to him? Because she totally was. In an odd way, she almost felt as if he were an old friend—just one she couldn't quite remember.

"But maybe you'll see Ben," he said. "He's shorter than I am, but much better looking. At least, that's what *he* says the ladies say. That may be changing, though. After his last breakup, he swore he wouldn't shave until he kissed another girl, and he's starting to look like the missing *Duck Dynasty* brother."

At the image his words painted, Sam couldn't help but laugh out loud. She snorted and covered her nose, embarrassed.

Connor smiled, clearly pleased with her reaction. "If you tell me to get lost and my clothes get stolen because Ben is too slow, then tomorrow I go clothes shopping." He put on a mock-serious expression. "And I hate clothes shopping. But it'll be worth the sacrifice if you'll do this one small favor for me."

Her curiosity mounting, Sam hopped off the washer and walked toward him, arms folded. "Okay, what's the favor? Tell me what it is, and then I'll decide whether to send you packing. And shopping."

"It's kind of dumb—and believe me, *not* my idea." And he sounded entirely serious, which piqued her interest even more. "But it's for a good cause."

She stood right in front of him. "Try me." If the favor was really silly, it would make an even better story to tell Tara. No matter what it ended up being, it would *not* be a story her parents would ever hear about.

He pointed to her sweatshirt, which she'd left on a washer. "Could I put that on and . . ."

"And . . . what?" Sam asked, looking at the faded—way too small—sweatshirt.

"And take a selfie . . . with you . . . while I'm wearing it?"

"Um, I guess so . . ." Sam said, confused. "Can I ask why?"

He hemmed and hawed. "It's for a bet with a—I don't know what you'd call Trevor, but he's not a friend." He set his hands on his knees and tried again. "I'm supposed to wear an article of clothing that belongs to a woman I didn't know before tonight."

"Guys are weird, but the favor could have been so much weirder," she said, confused and amused at the same time. "Would you rather wear something more obviously feminine? I mean, if the bet is more along the lines of Caitlyn Jenner—"

"No, no, nothing like that," he said, waving both hands. "At least, that wasn't in the rules. It's the first in a series of dumb challenges to raise money for a charity. If I win, anyway."

"Okay." Sam lifted one shoulder and let it drop in agreement. She grabbed the sweatshirt and tossed it to him. "Knock yourself out. But *do* try to avoid stretching it out." She grinned, hoping it was clear that she was kidding.

He didn't laugh. Instead, he rubbed his palms on his jeans. "Actually, there's more."

"Are we talking several favors now?" That's not what he'd suggested, but Sam didn't mind. She had nothing better to do while waiting for her favorite outfit.

"I need to post the selfie online."

Steve. How would he react to seeing her with another guy—and that guy wearing her sweatshirt? Then again, what were the chances he'd see some random picture on a college student's feed?

"See," Connor went on, "for it to count, you need to be in the picture with me."

"For it to count . . . for the bet," Sam clarified. A tiny bell of recognition went off in her head, but it was faint enough that she couldn't grasp it before it vanished.

"It's kind of a, um . . . *public* challenge . . . thing." He cringed.

Anything posted online never went away, but it wasn't as if she were agreeing to do something lewd, illegal, or offensive. Nothing that would hurt a future job interview. Taking a selfie with some random guy wearing a too-tight university sweatshirt—where was the harm?

Sam tilted her head again. "How public are we talking?"

"I probably should have led with that part." He blew out a breath and shoved both hands through his hair. "Here's the deal. Are you at all familiar with The Trevor Dudes or another channel called—"

"Wynn Rocks." Her hands flew to her mouth. Sam's eyes widened so much, they must have made up half her face. "Oh my gosh. You're—you're—Connor—"

"Wynn. I take it you're familiar with my channel." He got off his washer and held out a hand. "And you're Samantha . . ."

She stared at his hand as if a ghost had appeared before her. "You're Connor Wynn. *The* Connor Wynn."

Four

No wonder she'd felt as if she knew him. She *did* know him—so much about him—even though they'd never met. How had she not recognized Connor Wynn right away—his face *or* his voice? She played his videos all the time, but only in her apartment. At a laundromat, the context had been all wrong to put the pieces together.

Who would have ever thought she'd run into the Connor Wynn of Wynn Rocks in the middle of the night? Because of his videos and locations of many of his outdoor adventures, she knew he lived in the Rocky Mountains—but not a few blocks from her.

"The selfie is the first task of The Ultimate Bachelor Challenge," Sam said, the conversation becoming clear in an instant.

"So . . . you *are* familiar with . . . all of it."

"Um, yeah." She wasn't about to mention *how* familiar.

She turned around and raked her fingers through her own hair as he had. "Oh, wow. This is crazy. Tara will die. Utterly and completely die."

"Look, never mind. I totally understand. I mean, millions of people will see it, and—"

Sam spun around. "No, I'll do it. Trevor is a slimy jerk. He *can't* win." She tossed Connor the sweatshirt. "If wearing that helps take him down, do it."

"Really? Thank you." Connor's worried expression softened into relief. "You have no idea—or, actually, maybe you do."

She extended her right hand as he had a minute before. "Sam McKinley. If you're going to wear my clothing, I figure you should probably know my full name."

He shook her hand warmly. "A pleasure."

A delicious thrill went up her arm. "I can hardly believe you're *the* Connor Wynn. I mean, you and Trevor have millions of followers between you. Heck, *you* have millions of fans of your own."

"Which brings me to . . . Are you sure you want to be part of this?"

Sam pulled up Instagram on her phone and searched for the contest hashtag. "Trevor hasn't posted anything yet. Let's put up a selfie so you win the first task. I'd love to make someone like Trevor help a women's shelter."

"Wow. You're really familiar with my stuff."

"Of course," Sam said. "I also know that Trevor hasn't announced his charity, which seems a bit sketchy if you ask me." She pointed at the sweatshirt. "Put it on."

Connor hesitated, as if waiting for her to withdraw her assurance. When she didn't, he set his phone aside and opened up the bottom of the shirt.

"Don't stretch it out," she said. He froze, arms inside the sleeves, and hair poking through the collar. The sight of him stuck half in, half out, got her laughing. "I'm kidding," she said between giggles. "Really. But I don't know how you'll fit."

She helped tug the opening over his face and then pulled the bottom edge as far down his chest as it would go, which wasn't far. His arms stuck out at his sides, the sleeves barely reaching his elbows. "Technically, you're wearing it," she said through more laughter. "Selfie time. My camera or yours?"

"Mine," he said.

She turned to face the camera and eased in close enough for them both to fit in the frame, which meant her back pressing against his chest. She wished she'd had on makeup and something a whole lot cuter than yoga pants and a ponytail. But hey, she'd met Connor Wynn. Who cared what she looked like? She'd be cute later for Steve.

Connor adjusted the camera angle, then took several pictures of them with a variety of poses and expressions—everything from the classic teen duck face to horror then laughter. When their mini photo session was over, he held his phone out so they could both see the images. They picked their three favorites, quickly made them into a collage, and posted it.

After he'd officially claimed the win, they high-fived. Sam texted Tara, telling her to check the Wynn Rocks Instagram feed ASAP.

Connor cued some music on his phone, blasted the volume as high as it would go, then put the phone in a plastic cup he found in a window sill, creating an effective speaker. She didn't recognize the artists, but she and Connor danced around like little kids for three tracks.

For the moment, she forgot that it was the wee small hours of Valentine's Day, and that in a few hours her boyfriend would arrive for a visit. Then a metallic vibration echoed through the music, and Sam realized her phone was ringing, vibrating on top of a washer. Probably Tara or MollyAnne freaking out over Connor's post.

But when she grabbed her phone, the screen showed Steve's face—he was making a FaceTime call.

Gripping the phone, she walked to the other end of the room, muttering, "Crap. Crap-crap-crap-crap." Steve wasn't supposed to see her like this. He wasn't supposed to see her until she was at least showered and preferably primped for a Valentine's date. And possibly more.

"You going to answer that?" Connor asked. "At this hour, it's probably something important."

"Um, yeah." Somehow Sam's trembling thumb found the answer button. She cleared her throat as she put the phone to her ear before remembering that it was FaceTime. She tried to smooth out some frizzy wisps of hair, which only stuck out again. Nothing she could do about that now.

"Hey," she said cheerfully.

"Why hello, Miss McKinley," Steve said.

"Is . . . everything okay?" Sam asked.

Did she sound breezy, as she intended? Or did her voice come off strained, which was what she actually felt? Her eyes darted Connor's direction. She hadn't mentioned Steve to him. She hadn't said anything about being single, either, but now the whole sweatshirt thing felt a little flirty. She hadn't exactly hidden her excitement about meeting him; he probably assumed she didn't have a boyfriend. How, exactly, did she handle a conversation with Steve in front of Connor?

I guess we're about to find out.

"Everything's fine," Steve said. "Great, actually. Why?"

"I didn't expect to hear from you for a few more hours, that's all."

He checked something on the desk beside him. "But it's nine o'clock. I said I'd—oh, wait . . ." He rolled his eyes at himself. "I apologize. I was so excited that I completely spaced the time difference. It's what, two in the morning there? I'm surprised you answered. Where are you, anyway? That doesn't look like your apartment."

"I'm just doing laundry. And of course I'd answer, no matter when you called." Sam stopped herself before adding anything about how a girlfriend always answers the phone when her boyfriend calls. For some reason she couldn't identify, she didn't want to say *boyfriend* in front of Connor.

When Steve texted that he wanted to see her face, she'd hoped he meant in person, not over the phone. The excitement she'd felt earlier whooshed out of her like air from a balloon. Steve was clearly *not* in town, but she didn't want her disappointment to be too obvious. Steve might still be planning to pop the golden question.

"So what's up?" she asked. "What did you need to talk to me about?"

"Well . . ." Steve took a deep breath. "Remember what you said over Christmas break?"

She searched her memory but couldn't pinpoint any one particularly meaningful conversation. "Remind me."

"You said that you admired how I didn't care what others thought of my passions, and that you were proud of how I chased after them, even when other people thought they were silly."

"Oh, of course. I still think so. You know that."

Steve had two older brothers who fit the "manly" mold a lot better than he did. One had been an all-star football player in high school and now played on a college team. The other was about to graduate from law school and already had a job lined up at a big firm, a position that would likely lead to a partnership. And then there was Steve—the singer, the dancer, the thespian.

Even with the push for girls in STEM fields, Sam understood what it was like to be a round peg trying to fit into a square hole. Even though she'd always aced her math classes, she regularly had guys trying to mansplain advanced calculations—problems she often ended up tutoring *them* on later in the semester. She'd chosen a predominantly male field, so of course she'd support Steve's passion in an area that wasn't traditionally masculine.

"I really took your words to heart," Steve went on.

"I'm glad. You're incredibly talented. Before long, the whole world will know your name, you'll have a star on the Hollywood Walk of Fame, and I'll be able to point to movie posters and say I knew you when."

That is, unless she was walking the red carpet with him.

Steve looked to his right for a second, smiled sheepishly, then looked at the camera again. "Remember how I said I have something to tell you? I have some news. And a question for you."

"Yeah?" Sam's heart sped up, and she tried not to let her hopes rise, too.

He gestured to someone out of frame to come closer, and a moment later another man appeared—Steve's roommate, maybe? Her brow furrowed in confusion.

"This is Garrett," Steve said. "He's from Liverpool. We met rehearsing *A Midsummer Night's Dream*."

"Hi," Sam said with a bewildered wave. "Nice to meet you, Garrett."

"I've heard so many wonderful things about you," Garrett said in a smooth British accent.

Steve and Garrett scooted closer to each other. Two spots of pink bloomed on Steve's cheeks, and he seemed flustered. "He's my... um... you see... we..."

Garrett broke in. "We're engaged," he said simply.

The world seemed to come to a screeching halt. Stunned into numbness, Sam didn't know how her arm was still extended, holding her phone, and why she hadn't dropped it. She couldn't feel her body or move her hand or say a word. It took Connor's approach, combined with his concerned expression, to break her trance.

She blinked several times before managing, "Wh—what?"

"I know it's unexpected," Steve said. "Although you've known me so long that I'm sure you're aware that I'm, well, not like other men."

"No, no you're not." Suddenly, old conversations and experiences held entirely different meanings. Like how Steve always critiqued *People* magazine's choice of Sexiest Man Alive and gave alternate—heated—opinions about who should have been selected instead. She used to think that his teenage obsession with

D. H. Lawrence, Oscar Wilde, and Marcel Proust meant he loved deep, high-brow literature. Back then, the fact that they were all gay authors was nothing but a strange coincidence.

A flood of other moments, both small and large, came to mind, one after the other, as if she were watching her life play out with an entirely different script, and bright, neon highlights on things she'd never noticed.

How did I not put the pieces together?

"Sam, I should have been more forthcoming with you, especially when I was home over Christmas. But the truth is, I'm not . . . I'm not . . ." His voice trailed off weakly.

"You're not straight," she finished. He didn't even have the courage to say the words himself.

Garrett put his arm around Steve. "And we're getting married."

As if the first landmine hadn't been enough, Sam felt as if a grenade had exploded beside her. "O—oh."

Did she say the word? Or did only a strangled noise escape her throat? Either way, she wanted to hang up, crawl into a hole, and cry her eyes out.

I was so blind.

She'd gotten snarky questions about Steve and his orientation, and she'd always defended him, saying that of course he was straight. Not being built like a linebacker didn't automatically make someone gay, she argued, and neither did a love of the arts. She and Steve had chemistry . . . or she'd thought they had. They didn't make out all the time or anything, but he'd always been affectionate. In private. He hated PDA. Or so he claimed.

"You are my best friend in the world," Steve said. "I hope you know that."

She felt herself nod. He'd said that before, but she hadn't realized what it meant.

"My question is for my best friend. If you need to think

about it before answering, just say the word. And I'll understand if you say no." Now that Sam had completely lost her voice, he seemed to have found his. "I'd like you to be my best man—or best woman, I suppose. You really are my best friend. You're the one who helped me find the path to being true to myself, even if you didn't realize it."

"I don't know, Steve..."

"Just think about it for a while. The wedding isn't until spring, and I have enough miles that I could cover your plane ticket."

That was his big question? It did involve an engagement, just not hers.

At some point, the call ended. Had it dropped, or had she disconnected it? Had Steve? She wasn't sure. Maybe Connor had, because somehow he now held her phone. Maybe her stunned fingers had lost their hold, and Connor caught it before it hit the floor. She felt as if she were in an alternate dimension, standing a step apart from reality, in a dimension where sights and sounds were muffled and confusing.

"Sam?" Connor said gently. He slipped the phone into her palm and wrapped her fingers around it. His touch was warm and strong—solid and real. It brought her back to the moment.

She tried to breathe normally, feeling as if she'd just returned from a bizarre dream, only to realize that she'd really woken up from a fantasy and now faced the real world. She looked down, where Connor's hand was still wrapped around hers.

With her world shifted off its axis, she might have fallen over. For the moment, the only thing that felt solid was Connor's hand encompassing hers. The rest of her seemed to be sinking into emotional quicksand.

Don't let go, she silently begged of Connor.

"Sam?" Connor said hesitantly.

She blinked and looked up at him. "Yeah?" Her voice sounded far away.

"Do you want to go out for a bite? I know a place that serves breakfast all night. My treat."

"Breakfast?" Sam said absently.

"They make the best pancakes and bacon around."

"Bacon sounds good." Her tone sounded hollow. She shook her head a couple of times, trying to rid her mind of the image of Steve and Garrett, of what their revelation meant for her. How everything she'd thought about her past and future had been upended. She didn't know if she could trust her own judgment about anything anymore. Maybe she didn't really like math, and had entered the program because of all the pressure on girls to enter STEM fields. Everything she thought she knew had shattered into millions of pieces around her like so many ice crystals trampled underfoot. She'd been so blind. So stupid.

Moving forward, how could she ever trust herself enough around men? Maybe she should plan on being single for life. That might be safer.

Other people had warned her that Steve was gay, but she'd always assumed they were too caught up in stereotypes, that they didn't know the real Steve. Turned out that *she* hadn't known him. She felt so unsure of anything that she almost wondered if gravity was still real.

"I can't go back to my apartment," she said in almost a whisper. How could she face her roommates, crashing the marathon with the most un-Valentine-like news ever? She'd kill any happy mood and attract pity. She couldn't bear her friends' pity.

"Is that a 'no' on breakfast?" Connor tilted his head and squinted slightly.

"No." She shook her head. "I mean, no, it isn't a no. I mean, yes, I'd love some food. Thank you. That's . . . really nice of you to do for someone you don't even know."

Was she smiling? She meant to be, but she still felt as if she were moving through a thick fog. How could she know if her face was smiling the way she thought it was, when she hadn't even known her boyfriend was in the closet?

Connor helped her into her coat then held the laundromat door open for her. With one hand on the small of her back, he led her through it. "I'll text Ben to come down in twenty minutes to switch our loads."

"Thanks." Sam hadn't even thought about her clothes until he'd mentioned them. She wouldn't care if her red maxi got stolen. Not anymore.

Five

As they walked to Connor's car, Sam's entire body trembled. The confident woman he'd talked with earlier seemed to have withdrawn into a fragile shadow of herself. He unlocked the car with the fob, opened the passenger-side door, and helped Sam in to make sure she wouldn't slip on the icy parking lot.

The walk around to the driver's side didn't take long, but it was enough time to decide to cheer Sam up. Connor climbed in, put the car into gear, and pulled out of the parking lot. That Steve guy would have called tonight and broken her heart whether or not Connor had been at the laundromat.

I'm glad I was there. That kind of thing would be tough to bear alone.

She wouldn't have had anyone around to take her out for pancakes and bacon, for starters. Their breath fogged up the windows, so he directed air to defrost the windshield.

Sam absently tapped her phone, which lit up her face. She was probably checking social media and email, or maybe playing a mindless game. He could relate to distracting himself with his phone. If ever there was a time a person needed a distraction, it would be Samantha right now.

"The diner isn't far," he said, breaking the silence. When she didn't reply, he added, "But we can go somewhere else. It doesn't have to be breakfast. I'm sure we can find a Village Inn or something where we can order pie or hamburgers or whatever else you're craving." His glance slid to her and back to the road.

She still didn't answer. He tried again. "Unless you *do* want breakfast food..."

What was she thinking and feeling? Was he making things worse by talking? Maybe he should offer to take her to her apartment. Or, more likely, he should dig her car out of that snow bank at the side of the road and *then* see her safely home.

She finally looked up. "It's past two."

He tried to puzzle out her train of thought and the relevance to the time—and failed. Her tone offered no explanation either. "What?"

"The next task is live." She held out her phone, where a video was loading. "The timestamp on his selfie is ten minutes after ours."

"That's . . . great." But under the circumstances, Connor didn't really care. If he lost the challenge, he'd donate the money to the shelter himself. For now, he needed to make sure Sam was okay.

But why did she suddenly care about The Ultimate Bachelor Challenge? She hardly knew him. She had to be in shock after being dumped in the worst way. Connor pulled to the side of the road, shifted to park, and rotated in his seat so he almost faced her. Before he could talk, she did.

"You scored an extra hundred points for posting first, right?"

Connor looked at her phone. "Yeah, but none of that matters right now when you're—"

"Please, no. Stop." Sam put a hand up, almost touching her fingertips to his lips. She shook her head several times, and when she spoke again, her voice wavered. "Right now, more than anything else, I need to be distracted. Helping Connor of Wynn Rocks beat the snot out of that pig Trevor Knowles is the best distraction I could possibly dream up. So . . . please . . . just . . ." She swallowed hard. "Can we not talk about . . . that?"

The screen's glow bathed her features in soft light, making her look even prettier. She still had her hand up in a "stop" gesture, so close he could have leaned forward *just* a little and kissed her fingertips. At the thought, he found himself leaning forward, but fortunately regained his sanity and stopped himself before making contact. The last thing a woman needed after a bad breakup was a strange man hitting on her. Even if she was familiar with him from his online presence. And even if he wanted to comfort her. Even if he found her maddeningly smart and funny and gorgeous...

Now *he* was the one who needed a distraction. He cleared his throat, putting the side of his fist to his mouth as he coughed as an excuse not to touch her porcelain-like skin that would have looked like marble if not for the sprinkling of freckles across her nose and the little mole on the side of her chin that looked like the beauty marks old starlets used to paint on.

He cleared his throat. "What's the next task?" Had she heard his voice squeak? He felt as if he were back in eighth grade, going through puberty again.

"Let's find out." Holding the phone between them, Sam leaned in. To his delight—and dismay—she drew so close that their arms touched and he could smell her perfume.

So much for being distracted by something else.

This video was much shorter than the last; Trevor did little more than read the second task from Johnny's whiteboard. "Task number two is for a video instead of a still shot, and it must be at least five seconds long. Ready? Here it is: Be kissed by a girl whose name begins with the letter M." He chuckled and fist-bumped Johnny. "Nice one. This will be fun. Right, Connor? Remember, it must be five full seconds." He winked, and the video ended.

"Ugh," Sam grunted. "His ego oozes through the Internet."

"A lot of women—or, I guess I should use Trevor's terminology and call them *chicks*—"

"Or *babes*," Sam interjected.

"Oh, of course—babes," Connor corrected with a knowing smile. "A lot of them fawn over Trevor. Why?"

"I don't get it," Sam said. "Any self-respecting woman would see through him a mile away." Sam clicked her phone off and rotated to face Connor. He felt the lack of her touch, like the sudden loss of a warm comforter in winter. Except now she was looking right at him. He could lose himself in her eyes. Were they blue? In the dimness of the car, he couldn't be sure. But by the street lamp's glow, they seemed paler than the eyes of most redheads he'd known.

"Are your eyes blue?" he said. *Lame segue, Fabio,* he thought. She'd think he was feeding her a line. Too bad he couldn't rewind the last five seconds for a do-over.

"They are," she said, her face lighting up. "Pale blue. Not many people notice. But red hair and blue eyes is supposed to be one of the rarest combinations in the world."

"You're—I mean they're—gorgeous." Yet again he wished for a five-second time-travel machine.

Sam didn't look annoyed or offended. She didn't roll her eyes, viewing his words as a "line." She simply lowered her chin, her eyes crinkling with pleasure. She looked flattered, though he couldn't see her eyes anymore. Even better, she smiled. She seemed genuinely *happy*. A serious coup after Steve's apocalyptic call.

Connor couldn't help but be glad that something *he'd* said had created that reaction in her, and at an otherwise miserable time. He wanted to create that expression again, make her even happier. The urge was what he imagined an addict must feel, yearning for another hit of an intoxicating drug. Similar to what he felt while skydiving or rappelling or base jumping. His mind raced with how to make her smile like that again.

With her face lowered, the streetlamp highlighted her long

lashes fanning across the tops of her cheeks. "So," she said, dragging out the word. "Where are you going to find someone to kiss whose name starts with M?"

Right. The stupid Ultimate Bachelor Challenge. Trust Trevor to ruin what could have been a great moment. Connor barely bit back an exclamation—one he didn't want to say around Sam.

"Right. That." He stared out the windshield, then looked at her. "I don't suppose your middle name is Maria or Maggie or—wait a minute." He shifted the car into gear and pulled onto the road.

Sam looked at him quizzically. "Let me guess, you remembered an old flame living nearby named, oh, Monique?"

"Not exactly." He'd have to watch the video again to be sure he wouldn't lose on a technicality, but he didn't think that Johnny had been specific enough to rule out Maddie. As he'd suspected, he needed to be creative to complete the challenges. The more he considered the plan, the better he felt.

"You're grinning like the Cheshire Cat," Sam said. She shifted positions and gripped the arm rests. "That can't be good. Please don't tell me you're stooping to his level."

"Nope." His cheeks almost hurt from grinning. Trevor wouldn't ruin this night. Not if Connor could help it.

A few minutes later, he pulled into the cracked driveway of his rental house. "Home sweet home," he said, killing the engine. He reached to open his door, but Sam's arm shot out and stopped him. He happily turned to her, enjoying the warmth of her touch through his shirt.

"Wait, are you married?" she asked.

He almost laughed at that, but at her serious tone, he refrained. "No."

"Do you live with a woman, then? A girlfriend? Is it a sister? A cousin? Who's in there that you're going to kiss?" Her pretty eyes were pinched, with a worry line across her brow.

He wanted to reach over with his thumb and smooth out the wrinkle. "No one like that. Come on. This will be quick. And then I'll take you out for breakfast."

"O . . . kay . . ." she said, sounding skeptical as she opened her door.

Rather than prolonging the suspense, Connor hurried to the porch and threw open the front door. "Maddie," he called. "Come here, Maddie!"

"She'd better be a step-sister who will kiss you on the cheek," Sam said, elbowing him in the ribs.

Connor laughed but called again. "Maddie? Come on! Where's my Maddie Mad Dog?"

"What do you mean *yours*?" came another male voice. Its owner appeared a second later, scratching his beard.

"You must be Ben," Sam said. "I'm Samantha."

"Let me guess, the beard gave it away?" he asked. "Or is it my devastatingly good looks?"

"Devastating *something*," Connor said, punching his roommate in the shoulder. "You look like a mess."

"What do you expect when you wake me up in the middle of the night?"

Sam broke in. "Connor wasn't entirely honest. You do *not* look like a missing brother from *Duck Dynasty*."

Ben leveled a stare at Connor. "I'm not sure whether to be flattered that you assume I can grow a beard that long, or offended that you think I look like I have a rat's nest growing from my face."

"Where's Maddie?" Connor asked, ignoring the comment and trying to peer past Ben.

"She's my dog," Ben said. "Remember?" He whistled over one shoulder, and at the sound, the Golden Retriever's claws erupted into a stream of clicking on the laminate floor, followed by Maddie trotting into view.

Connor fished in his pocket for his phone and held it out to Sam. "Would you take the video?"

"I'm going back to bed," Ben said with a tired wave. "You found yourself a weird guy, Samantha. Hope you know that."

"Not *weird.* I'd use a different word," Sam said, bringing up the camera on Connor's phone.

He'd lowered to one knee to prepare for Maddie's "kiss," but he suddenly straightened and stared her down. "And what word would that be?"

The porch light made her face glow gold. She blushed and avoided eye contact, now turning his phone over and over in her hands. "You have the beginnings of a beard, too, you know."

He rubbed the stubble on his jaw. "Yeah?"

She tilted her head one way and then the other and managed, "And I've always thought that five o'clock shadows are kind of . . ."

"If not weird, then . . . what?"

She laughed and shoved his phone into his chest playfully. "Rugged. Masculine." She pressed her lips together before finally saying, "Fine. They're hot. Happy?" Her half joking, half embarrassed tone belied her words, which might have otherwise sounded snippy. She really seemed to think a little scruff was attractive. Connor filed that detail away, inexplicably pleased that Sam thought something about him was "hot."

Nothing about this night had turned out as he'd expected. He'd dreaded the entire challenge, but look at what it had brought him—he'd met an amazing woman he wanted to get to know better. On impulse, he nudged Maddie into the house and closed the door.

"What are you doing?" Sam asked. "Trevor probably had chicks lined up for every letter of the alphabet, just in case. We need Maddie Mad Dog—is that her name?—to kiss your face. We can watch the announcement again before posting, but I'm pretty sure he said nothing about the girl having to be human." Sam stepped closer. There was the hint of her perfume again—vanilla, with a hint of something else, maybe cinnamon. "This task is one more way for him to belittle a woman. We can't let him win."

Connor looked at the door. He could hear Maddie's whimpers from the other side. "Trevor will still say I cheated. You know he will."

"True." Sam sighed and chewed on her nail, trying to come up with another idea. "One of my roommates is MollyAnne. She's never had a boyfriend, so she'd totally freak out, but Trevor didn't say it had to be on the mouth. She could kiss you on the cheek for five seconds."

"Maybe," Connor said, but without any conviction.

"MollyAnne would pass out hearing that the host of Wynn Rocks is coming over to—"

"Wait. I have another idea." He wasn't sure whether to be excited or terrified of it.

"What?" Sam said. "Are you okay? You look a little pale."

Connor decided to ignore the comment and jump into explaining his idea. "When Steve called—"

She stiffened. He immediately regretted having to bring it up. "Yeah?"

"He used your last name."

"He's adopted a bunch of things that he thinks make him sound more British. That's the only reason he sometimes called me Miss McKinley, and—oh!" Her mouth stayed open, and she leaned back the slightest bit but otherwise didn't withdraw—a good sign, he hoped.

Drawn by the heady scent of her perfume, Connor took a tentative step toward her. This time, she didn't lean away. "Trevor didn't say it had to be her *first* name, did he?"

Sam shook her head and stammered, "I—don't—think—so."

Connor drew nearer still. He thought she caught her breath, but he wasn't certain. The thought made his own heart race. With one hand, he cupped her cheek and stroked her jawline with his thumb. She closed her eyes and leaned into his touch.

His rational side yelled at him. *Are you insane? She was just dumped by a guy who broke her heart. She'll hate you for taking advantage of her when she's vulnerable. Besides, why would she want to kiss you? She doesn't even know you.* The thoughts came at him as fast and hard as bullets.

Maybe she'd think he was using her like Trevor used women. He couldn't stand the thought that she'd think that. Just as he resolved to be a gentleman and not pressure her into a rebound situation, she closed part of the gap between them.

With one hand, she reached up and smoothed her hands across the stubble on his cheeks. Before he knew it, she'd threaded her fingers through his hair and was drawing his face toward hers. At last their lips met. In the quiet of the night, he half expected fireworks or shooting stars to accompany the explosions going off inside him.

The only sound was from Maddie Mad Dog, who'd ducked under the curtains by the living room window and was watching. She barked happily at the sight. After a long kiss that still felt too short, they drew apart, but only a hair's breadth from each other.

Her eyes remained closed as he stroked her cheek and took in every curve of her face. He wanted to memorize it all—spend the rest of his life getting to know every part of her features, her mind, the entirety of the woman before him. He leaned in for another kiss and then another.

After the third, Sam whispered in his ear. "We didn't record it."

"I don't care." Connor felt as if a weight had lifted from his shoulders. He didn't care—not about Trevor, not about losing views or subscribers.

She looked at him questioningly. "But—"

"I'm done with the challenge. I'll concede the loss and donate to his charity—and to mine."

Still in his embrace, Sam put both arms around his neck. "You hardly know me, but I know everything about you."

"I tend to overshare on my channel."

"Not at all. I read between the lines of what you do and say. You are a true gentleman, Connor Wynn of Wynn Rocks. And I don't mean just tonight. You've made me a better person, and I want to get to know you better."

For his mother's sake, he hoped he was a gentleman, that he was making a difference. He was trying to be the kind of man she'd be proud of. And to think that those efforts might have led him to a woman like Sam. He couldn't wait to take her on hiking trips and share his adventures with her, get to know her as well as she seemed to know him.

Connor brushed a wisp of hair from her face. "I really don't care about losing to Trevor." He leaned in for another kiss, which she readily returned. Then he smiled against her lips and murmured, "I still win."

"No," Sam said, pressing her forehead to his. "I win."

Annette Lyon is a *USA Today* bestselling author, a four-time recipient of Utah's Best of State medal for fiction, a Whitney Award winner, and a five-time publication award winner from the League of Utah Writers. She's the author of more than a dozen novels, even more novellas, and several nonfiction books. When she's not writing, knitting, or eating chocolate, she can be found mothering and avoiding housework. Annette is a member of the Women's Fiction Writers Association and is represented by Heather Karpas at ICM Partners.

Find her online:
Blog: blog.AnnetteLyon.com
Twitter: @AnnetteLyon
Facebook: Annette Lyon
Instagram: annette.lyon
Pinterest: AnnetteLyon
Newsletter: http://bit.ly/1n3I87y

Deal Breakers

By Heather Tullis

One

COLETTE BUNKER'S HOPES to fly home that evening were being pounded with every icy snowflake that hit the airport window. Standing inside the warm terminal, she watched another airplane taxi toward her through the swirling snow and wondered how long air traffic control would allow planes to land in this February blizzard. Denver had probably not been the smartest place for her to transfer through today, considering the growing strength of the wind and the storm warning alerts coming through her phone. Was there a chance she would continue home to Kansas City before morning?

The doors closed behind the flight heading to L.A.—the flight she had gotten off of less than an hour ago, and now the plane was heading back there again. She kind of wished she was on it—looking out at the snow surrounding the Denver airport made L.A. seem pretty fantastic. She saw the plane pull out and start taxiing down the runway, and then the other plane that had arrived from Wichita pulled into the gate.

By the time people began streaming through the doors into the terminal, the snow had thickened significantly, so Colette could no longer see the end of the runway. This was not a good sign.

A deep male voice came over the loud speaker: "Attention passengers. Due to the rising storm, all incoming flights are being re-routed. Outgoing flights are being canceled or delayed.

Hopefully we'll have more information for you soon. Thank you for your patience as we deal with the weather."

"Perfect. Just what I need." It had been a long week in L.A.—land of the perfect weather. One would think that being somewhere with clear skies and friendly beaches would have made her time in the city fly by, but Colette had spent the whole time wishing she were home with her sister, Sarah, who was suffering from chemo treatments for breast cancer.

It had been terrible timing to be out of town to train a west coast company's accounting department, but since the training had been scheduled for six weeks and her schedule was full for the next couple of months, Colette hadn't been able to get out of it.

She tasted the spearmint gum on her tongue, smelled the baby sitting behind her—apparently someone was due for a diaper change—and heard the chattering of unhappy voices surrounding her. Several people talked about renting a car to finish the drive home, others talked about getting a hotel room. Driving in this storm was definitely not on her to-do list no matter how badly she wanted to be home. The weather might be better once she cleared the valley, but crossing what in good weather was ten hours of open prairie by herself in a storm was not a great idea.

Colette really hoped it didn't come down to that. Maybe the storm would let up in an hour or two, and she would still be able to find a way out of here. Positive thinking—it was what her sister kept repeating—some shaman of a natural doctor kept telling Sarah that positive thinking was half the battle. Though Colette didn't really believe it, she was willing to support Sarah in whatever she needed to make the struggle easier.

"Attention passengers: cancellations are showing up on the schedule for flights that are leaving soon. Please contact a service representative for your airline to receive notifications about your flight."

There was a communal groan from the crowd, and though her flight wasn't scheduled to leave for over an hour, Colette had the funny feeling that a major delay, at least, was in the plans. She glanced at the people coming off the flight in the next gate over and wondered where that plane was supposed to be going next.

She sent a quick text to Sarah to let her know that she wouldn't be arriving on schedule and to call when she was up to it. Next, Colette called the shuttle service she had used to let them know that her flight was likely delayed, but that she would let them know when she had specifics on her return. She looked up as the last of the passengers exited the plane, followed by the pilots.

She glanced back down at her phone, then her brain finally processed what she'd seen, and she looked up again at one of the final passengers.

Oh. My. That was Drew Beck. Her heart sped up while she studied him, not sure if she believed it. He walked in her direction, though his gaze was definitely elsewhere. He was six-foot-one and as lean as she remembered from college, though his face had softened a little. Had it really been more than a decade since she saw him last? His dirty blond hair was spiked up in front, and his brown eyes tracked across the crowd, passing right over her.

A couple seconds clicked by, and then his gaze moved back to focus on her. He stopped in the middle of the walkway, staring at her.

Emotions raced across Drew's face: surprise, recognition, confusion, and then it was all wiped away as if he had no more feeling for her than anyone else in the room. Their gazes held and people streamed around him.

Unable to let it end there without at least trying to bridge the huge gap she had caused between them in college, Colette lifted a hand and waved.

That seemed to break him from his frozen state, and he

walked up to her. "Hi, Colette. I, wow. You're the last person I expected to see today."

Ditto, like a hundred times over. "Yeah. Did you hear about the cancellations?" She didn't know what to say to him, how to act, so she tried treating him like anyone she might have had a glancing acquaintance with in the past—though it had most definitely been more than that.

"Yes, they told us before we even started to get off the plane."

"I've been here about an hour. I have, or rather I *had* a three-hour layover. It sounds like it'll be a lot longer."

He adjusted the gray carry-on over his shoulder. "Uh, yeah. It could be a while."

Though it felt like her heart might explode from racing so hard, Colette sucked up her insecurities and asked, "So, since we're going to be here a while, you want to grab some dinner and catch up?" She needed to ease into a discussion about the past, wondering if he regretted the way things had ended between them as much as she did. Not that she could come right out and ask him that, but she wished she could.

He hesitated, then nodded. "Okay, I could eat." He waited while she slung her purse across her body and grabbed her carry-on's handle.

They walked across the mosaic tile art, hooking a left at the enormous sculpture of a railroad track, a map of the earth, and some tall blue things—she had no idea what the sculptures were supposed to represent—to the junction where several terminals met.

"Are you heading on a trip or going home?" Colette asked after a strained moment.

"Heading out. My brother, Keith, is getting married." Drew shifted to his other foot.

"He's not in Kansas?" His family had lived in the Wichita area practically since the Mayflower landed in America. She'd liked Keith, though he'd been a scrawny high school kid when she'd last seen him.

"No, he and Stacey are in Oregon. I'm supposed to be his best man."

"Oh no, that's awful that you're stuck here. I hope you can get there in time."

"Yeah."

After another strained moment, Colette asked another question, hoping he would thaw enough for a real conversation. "Where are you living?"

"Wichita, I'm teaching high school chemistry. How about you?"

Colette had wondered if he had returned there after school, but hadn't heard. "You won't believe it, but I'm living in a little town outside Kansas City." It was worlds away from Milwaukee where she had grown up.

His surprise melted a little more reserve in his eyes and he leaned in. "Really? What brought you to the sunflower state?"

Relieved that the awkwardness was softening, Colette let her shoulders relax. This was still Drew—she may not know him now, but she had known him once, and he didn't seem that different from before, at least not on the surface. "Two things—first, Sarah, you remember my sister, right?" When Drew nodded that he did, she continued, "Her husband, Bill, started working there, and I wanted to be close to her; Bill helped me get hired at his company, which is where I still work six years later."

"Anything I would have heard of?" They stepped off the escalators and entered the food court. The crowds were thick, since no flights were leaving anytime soon. They looked at the selections—pizza, burgers, Chinese, and Mexican restaurants circled the seating area—there was definitely nothing out of the ordinary. "Tacos?" he asked.

"They're still the best." She couldn't help but remember all of the times they had gone on a late taco run to fuel their studying.

"Another thing that hasn't changed about you," Drew said while they worked down the line of restaurants.

When they stopped at the end of the line at Taco Bell, Colette asked, "What else do you think hasn't changed about me?"

His gaze moved over her features. "I swear you don't look like ten years have passed. Did you time travel or something?"

Colette chuckled, flattered. "You have a faulty memory, but I'll forgive it this time. You might be surprised at some of the things that *have* changed about me."

"Oh, are you married with five kids and vacation every winter in Maui?"

"Maui." She sighed longingly. "Doesn't that sound heavenly? But, no. No marriage, no kids, no Maui. Maybe this spring I'll have to make that one happen, though." If Sarah responded well to her treatments and was able to travel. Maybe Colette could get tickets for the two of them and Bill to enjoy something beautiful after such a hard, miserable winter.

"I'm surprised you haven't married. What happened between you and Nick?" Drew looked over her shoulder rather than at her face, as if he didn't want to see her expression when she responded.

Colette pulled a face, kicking herself for that particular decision for at least the thousandth time. "Nick was the biggest dating mistake I ever made." She stopped short of admitting that she'd realized too late she'd screwed up choosing him over Drew.

"What happened? You were so in love with him once." There was more than a hint of bitterness in his voice.

She bit her lip for a moment then squared her shoulders. "Look, could we table all of that for a little while?"

Drew nodded. "Maybe that would be best. I'm not sure it would make a difference to hash it out at this point anyway."

Colette sighed, searched for the conversational thread before she had derailed it, and grasped onto it again. "I've dated several people since, three of them seriously. One actually made it all the way to an engagement, but thankfully I came to my senses before too late. So it's just me."

"No dogs or cats or anything?" he asked.

"I used to have guppies. Yeah, I know. Laugh all you like, but they were fun. I travel too much now, though." She actually missed coming home to her fish at night and the sound of the bubbler filling the air while she drifted off to sleep.

Drew kept grinning. "You travel for work?"

"More than I'd like sometimes."

They reached the front of the line and each ordered and paid, then slid to the side to wait for their tacos. A few minutes later, Drew found two seats at a bar where they could sit to eat.

"So, what is it you do?" Drew asked when they had each eaten part of their dinner.

"Ah, and this is the part you won't believe. I'm a trainer. I teach classes on how to use my company's accounting software."

The taco he'd been about to bite into hung in the air while he stared. "Wait, like standing up in front of a class and teaching them. As in, public speaking? Mind. Blown."

Colette laughed. It was almost like old times. She had forgotten how much she loved being in Drew's company.

Two

DREW COULDN'T BELIEVE what he was hearing. Or what he was seeing. Colette—the woman he had been head-over-heels for in college—before she dumped him to date someone else. He had cut her off at the time, unable to watch her date the jerk she had picked over him. The break had been necessary for his peace of mind, but he'd come to wish that he hadn't done such a thorough job of it.

He couldn't imagine the girl he had once known standing in front of a class full of people.

"You—*you* teach people? That's absolutely fantastic. I thought you might end up sitting behind a desk where you didn't have to interact with anyone face to face." This was an exaggeration—she was good with people. She just had an issue with stage fright. The poetry class they had taken together fall semester his senior year—her freshman year—had been proof of that. It hadn't helped that they'd had to write their own poem and read it to the class. That had nearly been enough to do him in, and he wasn't afraid of public speaking like she had been. Apparently she'd gotten over it. "How did you start out terrified of talking to groups and end up teaching?"

Though he hadn't been sure if he was happy to see her at first, the anger and frustrations of the past had been melting away as they spoke. He still had plenty of questions, but they had a little time to get their bearings before picking at that sore. For the moment he only wanted to know what had happened with her. What had happened to them—maybe it would help him stop having the same kinds of problems over and over. He always seemed to pick women who were more concerned about something else in their lives than they were about their relationship with him.

Colette tossed back her shoulder-length brown hair, which was smooth and cut in a way that framed her face perfectly. "After the poetry fiasco, Sarah challenged me to overcome my fear of public speaking. I challenged her back to get over her fear of horses, and the next day I looked up my local Toastmaster's group."

"And just like that, you were cured?" he asked, knowing it couldn't possibly have been that easy. Her fear had been real, definitely more than the average person's nervousness.

"Not even. I started out with small things, learning techniques and practicing short readings, and then I eventually graduated up from there. I was still nervous for a long time, but after several years I overcame my terror and here I am, teaching classes practically every week. I admit, I still stumbled over my words the first year that I taught the class, but the practice has made me much more confident. It helps that I've had so much practice now."

He found her every bit as amazing as before. "And how did Sarah do with her challenge?"

Colette chuckled. "It's a work in progress. She *is* doing better with horses, though. Her husband really wants to get some to ride, but he won't do it until she's comfortable around them. We almost got her onto one last summer."

"He must be very patient." That was a quality Drew was trying to improve in himself, so he admired it when he saw it in others.

"He's the best. She's lucky to have him."

"But he's not lucky to have her?"

"Oh no—he's totally lucky to have her. She's practically perfect—other than her weird horse phobia, which isn't that big of a deal, really. She pretty much never complains, no matter how bad things get. They did an excellent job of picking each other."

"It seems that some people get super lucky while others . . . well, not so much."

She looked up and their gazes met. No words were needed—Drew saw understanding in her eyes. He'd missed the connection that they had found so easily.

He broke the silence after a long moment. "How is she, your sister? Besides being scared of horses."

Colette bit her lip. "Sarah was diagnosed with breast cancer about six weeks ago. She had the lumpectomy and has done two rounds of chemo. She had her second treatment this week, when I was in L.A. I hate being away from her while she's sick."

He slid his hand over hers on the table, compassion softening some of the rough edges of their past. "That must be hard for you."

"It is. It doesn't help that her husband has to work all weekend because of a product release. Sarah and I had Valentine's Day plans."

"Really? What did you have on the docket? Something anti-V-dayish?" From what he'd heard, two women together on Valentine's evening usually resulted in some kind of guy bashing.

"Nope. We were going to watch a movie or two with plenty of action, order pizza, and stuff ourselves with cheesecake."

"That's not anti-V-day?"

She crumpled the wrapper from her taco and opened a second one. "No, because it's not about woman power. It won't be a sappy movie. It'll be something with plenty of cars blowing up or other action and really fantastic food. This year we planned to re-watch *I am Not a Serial Killer.*"

Drew laughed in surprise. "Wow, your taste in movies has expanded."

"Thank you, I try." Colette wondered if she actually would get home in time to see that show with her sister. "When do you think the first flights will be going out and where they'll be going?"

He tipped his head. "I don't know, but it probably won't be too much longer. We'll get you back home."

"I know, I'm just impatient."

"So how often do you travel?" He changed the subject, seeing that she needed a change of subject. It was strange how well he remembered the nuances of her expression.

She let out a sigh, but appeared to relax a little. "About half the time. I go out to companies to train people. Or they send people to me, and I work with groups from the home office. It's nice to be able to get out and see a lot of places, but it also gives me time to do laundry and settle in between. How's your family doing?"

They finished their dinner while they talked, the crowds rotating around them while people finished eating and others arrived.

The loudspeaker clicked on, then a female voice said, "Attention all passengers: all flights for the rest of the day have been canceled. We will not be able to have any flights in or out until the snow lets up. Contact your airline for more information, or to reschedule your trip."

That was not the kind of news Drew had been hoping for, though he couldn't complain too loudly about who he'd been stranded with. "Oh man. Keith is not going to be happy about this."

"I knew I should have taken the later flight that routed through Phoenix," Colette agreed.

"We better see if we can get hotel rooms before they're all

gone." The airport floor didn't strike him as the most comfortable place to sleep.

"Too late," the woman beside them volunteered. "My husband has been calling around for the past twenty minutes, and we can't find anything open. Those who do have openings aren't running their shuttles to the airport because of the storm. Even the taxis aren't coming out here anymore."

"Rental cars?" Colette asked, though she looked skeptical.

"Long gone. It sounds like they were all gone within ten minutes of the first word of delays." The woman sighed deeply. "It looks like the rest of us will have a long night in the airport."

"Perfect." Colette frowned.

Though Drew was not happy about it, there was still a chance he could make the wedding on Saturday afternoon. It was only Thursday night, but he might miss the rehearsal dinner and bachelor party on Friday.

"I'm going to make some calls." Colette pulled out her phone. "I know a few people. Maybe I can get a ride out of here."

Drew called Keith to tell him about the weather delay. He turned back to Colette in time to see her hang up. "So, any news?"

"Nope. Looks like we're stuck here."

"All of the locals seem to have been smart enough to clear out already," he said, looking around the food court at the diminished crowd. "I bet everyone's off staking out their chairs for the rest of the wait."

"We probably ought to do that, too." Colette stood and dumped her garbage before returning for her suitcase. "I wonder how long the food court will be open?"

"Or the gift shops."

Their eyes met and they nodded. "We better stock up on a few essentials before they get picked over."

Apparently they weren't the only ones with that idea. The lines at the cash register in the first gift shop they passed held at least a dozen people each. They moved to the next, and Drew noticed the sodas were already getting low. They headed in and split up to gather the necessary items. He snatched up the last two jerky sticks, a package of trail mix, two packages of M&Ms, a large water bottle, and, on a whim, a pack of face cards.

Colette stepped into line behind him, and they compared purchases. She had grabbed the latest cozy mystery by Heather Justesen, a magazine on gardening, a box of crackers and tub of dip, and some gummy worms.

"Gummy worms, huh?"

"Always and forever. M&Ms?" Her eyebrow lifted at him. "No reading material?"

"I have a book in my bag already. When did you get into gardening? And since when do you *not* have a book on you?"

"I have a book, but it's almost finished. I decided to get a backup." She glanced at the garden magazine. "I wanted something different than the book in case my attention span gets short. It was this or a hunting magazine."

"Slim pickings."

The area where they had met was full, but they continued down the terminal and came to one gate that still had a few seats open—and was not too far from the charging station. A mother about their age with three young children he guessed to be between ages seven and three were seated next to them. She was distracting her kids with coloring books and crayons. The youngest one whined in her arms while she tried to interest him in a plastic car.

Drew studied all of the others around them. He would expected major storms in December and January, but the weather was already warming up a little in Kansas.

"You grew up in Milwaukee," he said. "How long do you think this storm will last?"

"This isn't Milwaukee."

"No, but Denver's, you know, the land of the snow. Not entirely unlike Milwaukee in that way. How long do you think we'll be stuck here?"

"Overnight? Three days? Who knows? It could be a while. My phone says it's supposed to keep snowing at least another twelve hours, maybe sixteen. But if the snow lightens up the last few hours of the storm, we could get lucky and get out while it's still the weekend."

Definitely not great news, then. "So you're saying I should ration my M&Ms, just in case."

"Definitely. You can even give them to me for safe keeping if you're afraid you might eat them too quickly." Colette shot him a sunny smile.

"I'm sure they would be very safe in your hands." She might be somewhat addicted to gummy worms, but chocolate was a close second. He didn't plan to chance it.

"The safest." Colette grinned. "So, tell me absolutely everything you've done and everywhere you've gone since we talked last."

"Everything?" That encompassed a lot of topics.

"Yes. If we have three days, then there will be plenty of time for us to discuss every detail of what we've been up to."

"You're on." He told her about finishing his degree at University of California, Riverside, and his student teaching. He didn't mention his lack of a social life after she had chosen Nick instead of him. Instead, he asked a question that had passed through his head several times over the years.

"How long did you stay with Nick before kicking him to the curb?"

Her head swiveled in surprise. "What makes you think I broke up with him, instead of the other way around?"

Their truce was still tentative, so he was careful about his tone, wanting this to be a friendly conversation rather than a big fight. "I knew him better than you did at the time. I knew what a jerk he was, and the kind of person you were. You couldn't be fooled for long. Then again, I was surprised that he had managed to fool you at all."

She nodded, "Three months. Which was honestly about a month longer than things between us should have lasted. I think I was trying to convince myself that I hadn't totally screwed up by picking him over you, but I knew better. Staying with him didn't make it better; it only made me miserable for longer than I needed to be."

It was actually a relief to get it out in the open, even though it made the conversation awkward and uncomfortable again. "That was a rough year. I missed you."

"I missed you, too. I totally screwed up with you, and I'm sorry. But you seem to be doing well now. I mean, you have a good life, right?"

He couldn't argue that point. "I absolutely have a great life. I love teaching, I have great students, and I coach girls' lacrosse every year for the school—practices start next week. Our team is phenomenal, and I'm living in my home town, which definitely makes me happy."

"I'm really glad. I learned a few things from Nick myself. Him making fun of my fear of public speaking was what actually pushed me to join Toastmasters. Sarah knew that he had worn me down, that I needed self-confidence, and that facing my fear was only one way for me to conquer it. That's why she invented the bet, thought I didn't realize it at the time."

They talked about their jobs and family trips, his first year of coaching lacrosse, and her first year of working for her current employer.

When ten o'clock rolled around, they decided they were hungry and decided to take turns with one person ordering for both of them while the other saved their spot.

They flipped a coin, and Colette lost. As she walked off and

Drew stretched out his cramping legs, he wondered if maybe she had actually won, and not the other way around. He needed to move around for a while.

He glanced over at the little girl who was a year or two older than his niece back home. He also had a nephew who was a year younger. He could only imagine how difficult it had been for this mother to manage all three kids for the past few hours. The boys were already sacked out on the floor—he hoped for their mom's sake that they slept well.

"Is she your girlfriend?" the five-ish-year-old girl beside him asked.

"Hannah," her mom said. "Hush, don't pry."

"It's fine," Drew assured her. "No, Colette's not my girlfriend. We used to date a little, a very long time ago."

"How long?" his tiny companion asked.

"Before you or your brothers were born."

"Wow. That was a long time." She nodded her chubby little face. "But you're friends now?"

"Yeah. I think we are." Or at least they were headed that way, which was a nice thing to be able to say again. It had been a long time since he'd been able to consider Colette his friend, though back then he had wanted much more. He'd missed that. He looked out the window and watched the snow swirl and drift and fall. Periodically, he saw a snow truck clearing the tarmac. It was a losing battle, but he supposed it would be easier to clear the runway for real when the snow stopped, if the trucks kept it from accumulating too much first.

"Where are you guys from?" Drew asked the mom a few minutes later.

"New York. We were going to Arizona."

"I bet Arizona is great right about now."

"Yeah, my sister sent a text this afternoon to gloat that her kids were out running on the lawn in their shorts."

"Meanwhile, you're stuck trying to keep your kids entertained in an airport. There's always that one sibling who has to rub things in." That one sibling used to be him, but he'd gotten over himself. Mostly. "I'm Drew."

"Teresa. Where are you headed?"

Drew told her about the wedding in about forty hours and the activities he was probably going to miss. He asked the kids about school and their favorite show. By the time Colette finally returned with their late snack, he was able to introduce the women as if they were old friends.

They snacked on fries and apple wedges, and Drew offered to get something for Teresa if she wanted anything.

"No thanks, I think the kids have had enough to eat tonight, but I might take you up on it in the morning." She yawned, but seemed determined to stay awake.

"I'm going to stretch my legs for a few minutes," Drew told Colette. "I'll be back."

He studied the people around him as he walked through the halls. A lot of travelers had fallen asleep. The airport had brought in cots, but there weren't enough to go around, so there were still quite a few people sacked out on the semi-padded seats or the floor. On the way back he helped an older couple with their bags and filled a water bottle for a kid who couldn't reach the dispenser button. There were a lot of stranded passengers, but other than a few grumbles, most people seemed to be taking it in stride. He wondered how long that would last.

Security guards roamed up and down the terminals keeping an eye on things. Drew greeted one, "Hey, how are things going?"

"As well as we can expect, I guess. Things are quieting down. The restaurants are going to be closing soon for the night, since they can't get new workers in to cover the night shift."

"Good to know. What time will they open again?"

"By breakfast, I'm sure. I've never worked here when everyone has been snowed in." He shrugged.

"Will they have enough food if they can't get deliveries?" It was a joke, mostly, because the food vendors served a lot of people every day here and surely would have plenty to last a couple days.

"It depends on how long this lasts, but I wouldn't worry about it yet."

"Thanks." Despite being admonished to not worry, the conversation left Drew slightly unsettled.

When he returned to their group, he noticed that Teresa had fallen asleep with her children gathered around her in the corner and Colette was on the phone.

"I know, I'm sorry to put you in such a bad position at the last minute. I promise to let you know. Tell her everything's fine. Yes, really. I ran into an old friend. Okay. Talk to you tomorrow. Sorry, Bill."

She looked unhappy when she ended the call.

"Who was that?" Drew tried to act only mildly curious.

"Sarah's husband. He called to see if I was going to be home tomorrow." Colette's brows furrowed. "How was your ramble?"

"It was good to stretch. I talked to a security guard." He pitched his voice low so no one else would be able to hear. He adjusted their things to provide a little extra buffer for Teresa and her kids from everyone else, and to keep all of their things beyond the reach of sticky fingers. While he worked, he told Colette about his conversation with the security guard. "I hope it doesn't become a problem."

"Maybe the snow will slow down soon?" she suggested.

"Maybe." He doubted it. This could be a long wait if the storm didn't let up by noon like they expected.

Three

COLETTE READ FOR a little while after Drew settled on the padded seat beside her, but she was starting to get sleepy.

She turned to find him fully engrossed in his book. It seemed unreal to be with him now, here.

Drew met her gaze.

"Looks like a lot of people are hunkering down for bed. How are you holding up?"

"I'm good for a while yet. You can lean here if you want." He patted his shoulder.

Colette was tempted, even though she didn't want to fall asleep yet—it was too nice to be with him. "I may take you up on that later, but I was thinking maybe we could try a game of Slapjack for now."

A smile stole onto his face. "You know me, I'm always up for a game of Slapjack. Only we have to be quiet enough that we don't wake up the kids." Drew reached into his bag for his pack of cards. They sat cross-legged on the floor facing each other as he started mixing them up and then dealt their hands.

"I haven't played this since college," Colette admitted. Not since she'd last played it with him, actually. It was his favorite game.

"Well, then, be prepared to be creamed."

"You always were a big talker."

"Fine, if I win the first round, you have to share your gummy worms with me."

She feigned shock. "No! Not my gummy worms. Pick something else."

"I don't want anything else. It's gummy or bust. Unless you don't think you can beat me . . ."

This guy—this was the man she had liked so much in college. She loved the competitive look in his eyes. It was worth her gummy worms, she decided. "Okay, you're on."

It didn't take long for her to get right back into the groove, and though he won in the end, it didn't happen nearly as fast as she had expected.

"You earned it," she said when she pulled the gummy worms from her bag.

He waved the candy away. "How about you hold onto them? I'll claim my winnings tomorrow. I don't have any way to keep my half overnight."

Colette yawned. It was almost midnight in Kansas, and it was definitely past her bedtime.

Drew pushed himself back up onto his chair and patted the seat beside him. "Come on up and rest. You know you need to get some sleep."

"If you don't take your gummy worms now, you might not be able to before we get out of here tomorrow." That thought make her surprisingly sad.

"I seriously doubt it'll be that early." His eyes narrowed and he pointed at her. "Don't try eating them all just to keep me from my share."

"How did you guess I was thinking about that?"

"I remember how you are."

Colette chuckled and boosted herself back up beside him, glancing over at Teresa to see how she was handling the kids. The kids were all sleeping soundly. Colette tipped her head against Drew's shoulder. They were facing the windows where snow continued to twist past their view. She thought of the wedding he would be missing if he didn't get out of here tomorrow. "Why do people want to have their anniversary on Valentine's Day?"

"Keith jokes that it's so he only has to remember one day to give his wife a gift, and that it'll save them money, but I'm pretty sure it's because it's supposed to be romantic."

The tone in his voice made her lift her head and scrutinize him. "You don't think Valentine's Day is about romance?"

"No, Valentine's Day is about making people feel guilty if they forget, or crappy because they don't have someone, or awful because their relationship isn't all happy and la-de-da-tiptoe-through-the-tulips. You don't need a special day designated by greeting card companies to be romantic. Romance is remembering the person every day, not just once per year. Romance isn't about the big gestures—that's not to say that big gestures from time to time aren't great. But that's not what makes a romance work. It's the little expressions of love that keeps a marriage working over a lifetime. That's what I see when I look at happy relationships that last."

The breath stopped in Colette's throat. How was it possible that *this* man was still single?

"That's completely right," she said. "Exactly. I'm glad people love Valentine's Day and enjoy it, but I think the holiday can be bad, every bit as much as it can be good."

She tipped her head back to look at him. "You're pretty amazing."

His lips curved slightly and he slid his hand over hers. "I wish you'd figured that out ten years ago."

I did, just a little too late. She opened her mouth to say so, but then remembered the hurt and anger in his expression when things had ended between them, and the discomfort it had caused during their discussion earlier—did she want to dredge that up already?

Then again, maybe discussing the past wouldn't cause problems after all.

"Go to sleep," he said. "It's going to be a long night."

As her eyes drifted closed, she saw the yellow blinking light of the snow plow pass by the window again.

Four

"Mom! I'm hungry!"

The little boy's voice woke Colette from her fitful night's rest. She lifted her head from what turned out to be Drew's lap and looked up at him. He had put his arm up on the back of the chair and propped his head against it. His other hand created a pool of warmth on her waist. His eyelashes fluttered open, exposing brown eyes, and he sucked in a deep breath.

"Good morning, beautiful," she teased him.

"I should be the one to say that. How did you sleep?"

She twisted her head from side to side, working out the kinks in her neck. "Not great. How about you?"

"Better than I expected. Not nearly as well as you did." Drew rubbed his neck and stretched his back.

"I'm sorry, having me take up half your space probably didn't help."

"I didn't mind. Do you want me to see if the restaurants are open?"

"That's probably a good idea. I'll hang here with our things." She would need a bathroom break soon, but at the moment she was doing okay. She brushed the hair back from her face and realized her appearance could probably use a touch-up. She opened her suitcase and pulled out her makeup case. Oh yeah, she was as far from beautiful as she could get. Her mascara was badly smeared and her hair was a mess. Colette pulled out a comb and straightened the hair first, and then cleaned up her face and fixed her makeup.

She put the comb away and, not wanting to wake her sister with a call if she was asleep, sent Sarah a text message asking for an update on how she was feeling. It was frustrating being so far away when her sister was probably sick. Chemo had been extra rough this time. Bill had rearranged his work schedule to be there almost full time while Colette worked, but this delay in her trip home meant she'd left them in the lurch.

Colette watched the snow pelting against the windows. A quick glance at the weather app on her phone indicated it would be at least a few more hours before the storm dissipated. She hoped the weatherman was right that it would end today. She put her phone away and looked back up in time to see Drew returning—empty handed. He shook his head.

"No food?"

"One is open, but chow mein for breakfast is just wrong. Two of the restaurants apparently stayed open after all the others closed and ran out of food a couple hours ago. Most of the restaurants have posted that they'll open again at seven. You can hold out for another hour, right?"

"Yes, I'm glad it's only a delay. I could imagine the revolt if they run out of food before we can leave the airport."

"Tell me about it." He plopped down beside her. "Did you notice the snow outside?"

"Yeah. Did it stop at all last night?"

"Doubtful."

"But I'm hungry!" the little boy said again.

Teresa sighed. "I can't buy you any food until the food court opens again. I'm sorry."

"Hey, do you want some trail mix?" Drew dug into his duffel and pulled out the bag he had bought the previous afternoon. Most of it was still in the package. "I think there's enough to go around."

"You don't have to," Teresa demurred, but Colette could see that she was tired and probably hungry, too.

"He wouldn't offer it if it was going to be a problem." Colette took the package and opened it, pouring some into each of the kids' hands. "How did you guys sleep?"

The kids all answered, though the older boy was less groggy than the rest. Colette shared some trail mix with Teresa, poured a very small amount in her own hand, and then passed what was left back to Drew. Thankfully it had been a rather large bag, so it wasn't entirely empty.

When the oldest boy finished, he said. "I'm still hungry."

"Josh, be nice and tell them thank you. We'll have breakfast later." Teresa turned to Colette with embarrassment. "I'm sorry, you're very kind to share with us."

"You're welcome," Drew reassured her.

Collette focused on the boy. "That wasn't breakfast, it was only a snack to keep your stomach from hurting while we're waiting for the restaurants to open. It won't be too much longer."

"Hey, do you guys like to play Go Fish?" Drew asked, pulling out his pack of cards.

"Yeah," the older boy said. "We both like Go Fish."

"Perfect. Colette and I like it a lot, too. Come sit on the floor with us."

It was a little cramped to squeeze two adult-sized bodies and two kids onto the floor between the rows of chairs, but they managed to get down and play several rounds of the game while they waited for breakfast time.

Colette loved watching Drew interact with the kids, joking with them and distracting them from the fact that they couldn't eat for a while. He was good with kids, even though they were much younger than the teens he taught at school. She wondered if he had experience dealing with small children, or if it was natural.

When people started returning to the terminal area with

bags of food, they finished the game and Drew stood. "How about if I go grab us all some breakfast. Any requests?"

"Pancakes!" the older boy demanded.

"Eggs!" the girl added.

Teresa reached into her purse and pulled out a five-dollar bill. She looked apologetic. "I hadn't planned to buy two meals at the airport."

"No problem," Drew said. "My treat. What about you and the kid there?"

"Oh, I can't." Teresa looked embarrassed.

Colette caught Drew's imploring look. She took the seat beside Teresa. "Look, Drew makes a ton of money at his job—seriously, he's wildly overpaid—and he wants to help you. He won't miss it, and your kids are hungry. You need breakfast, too, if you're going to keep up with them. Let him help you." She hoped he hadn't told Teresa that he taught high school, or her excuse would never fly.

Tears pricked the woman's eyes and she nodded. "Thank you. Eggs, or egg sandwiches, pancakes, whatever you can get. My kids are equal opportunity eaters of breakfast foods."

"Good to know," Colette said. "I'm going to fill my water bottle." She followed Drew away from their things, now that they had gotten to know Teresa enough to trust her to keep an eye on them for a couple minutes.

"I'm loaded, huh?" Drew asked.

"She wouldn't have accepted if she thought you were a starving school teacher. Besides, lunch will be more expensive to buy than breakfast, and I'll handle that one."

Drew stopped and looked at her, fun shining in his eyes. "You are something else. I've missed you, Colette." He touched her face, and then moved away, heading for the food court.

Colette felt her pulse jump at his touch, grinning as she went to fill her water bottle.

If it weren't for Sarah, she would hope the snow never stopped falling.

"Blue or Red?" Colette asked Drew. She leaned back in her seat, her head tipped near his.

"Blue."

"For me, too."

"Venice or London?" Drew asked.

"Ooh... tough one. London."

"Really? I'm all about Venice."

They were seated in the terminal chairs, which were growing increasingly less comfortable, passing the time and watching the snow plows clear the tarmac. *At least the wind has calmed down.* "I admit, Venice is pretty amazing. I had a great time there. Nuts in your chocolate, or toffee?" she asked.

"Toffee. When did you go to Venice?"

"Three years ago I took a two-week cruise of the Mediterranean. It was incredible. I also prefer toffee."

Colette had an armful of sleeping toddler. Teresa had taken the older two kids for a walk around the terminal, to go up and look at the tile mosaics from the second floor railing, and to get some of their wiggles out. Lunch was already past, and the natives were restless. The good news was that the snow had finally stopped, and the plows were actually making some headway. And Colette and Drew were whiling away the time learning more about each other. It might not give them deep insights into each other's souls, but it was interesting.

Though she was glad that they lived in the same region, at least, Kansas City and Wichita were still several hours apart, so managing a relationship would be difficult.

That was if he even *wanted* a relationship with her after this was over. They hadn't talked about that at all. Though she felt they were growing closer with every hour, the specter of their past hung between them like a wedge.

"One kid or two?" she asked.

"Four."

Colette turned to him. "Four? That's a lot of kids."

"Not that many, and I like kids." He grinned over at Teresa's children. "I think one is way too lonely, and two is not enough. With three one might get elbowed out sometimes and feel alone, so I'm all about four."

"I suppose your wife would have some say in the matter."

He grinned. "Yes, my theoretical wife would totally have a say about whether we had four or five kids."

"Five!" Unthinkable.

"See, I knew you would agree, the more the merrier."

Colette poked him in the side. "I'm surprised you're teaching high school instead of kindergarten, if you like little kids that much."

"I like all ages of humans. I'm no respecter of age."

"Good to know. Ageism is totally wrong." She tried to wrap her head around his plans. "Seriously, five? That's a lot of kids."

"It is, and I'm only half serious about that. I wouldn't be against it, but I'd be happy to start with one and see how it goes."

"I'm sure your theoretical future wife will appreciate that."

Another snow plow came into view, pushing a load of snow to their left. "Looks like they're going to actually get the area cleared for take-off before long."

The snow had stopped nearly an hour earlier, and a lot of the heavy snow had finally been cleared. The wind had died back to a more reasonable amount as well. A giant brushing truck followed a plow, headed for one of the runways.

"It'll probably take a while to get everyone who is stranded back in the air," Drew said. "Assuming we're both here, we could watch a movie tonight. I have my tablet, we have free Wi-Fi here, and we can share a pair of earbuds. Maybe get a pizza from downstairs. We could even borrow the movie of your choice with plenty of violence and gore."

"Hey, my movie wasn't really that gory—I said action, not violence. They don't have to be gory to be exciting. And it's all about good triumphing over evil. What's not to love about that?"

He squeezed her hand. "Absolutely nothing."

Teresa returned with the two older kids, who were full of energy and excitement after their run around the upper floor.

"Can we play some more Go Fish?" the boy asked.

"How about if I let you two borrow the cards and you can play together?" Drew offered.

"Okay." The kids sat on the floor and started up a game.

Teresa looked like she was ready to collapse.

"Hey, we've got this for a little while if you want to take a nap," Colette suggested. "I know you have to be exhausted."

"I couldn't possibly."

"I understand why you don't want to take your eyes off your kids, but I know you didn't sleep much last night. I swear, the kids won't go four feet from your side without your approval."

Teresa bit her bottom lip, but finally nodded. She was asleep within two minutes.

"Wow, she was even more tired than I thought," Colette said.

"It's tough being a mom. I watch my sister dealing with her two kids. I'm amazed every day by how much she loves them."

"That's why you're so good with them. You must love having her nearby, to spend time with all of them."

Drew grinned. "I do. Not as much as my mom does, though—she's like Super Grandma, but it's great."

Colette was actually a little jealous of that. Her parents were still in Milwaukee, and other than Christmas when they came to Kansas City, she rarely saw them.

"So tell me more about your job," Drew asked. "What does your schedule look like these days?"

Colette adjusted the boy in her arms a little and settled back to tell him more.

Five

THE AIRLINES STARTED some of the flights again in less than two hours. There were some flurries that afternoon, but the snow removal equipment seemed to handle it fine as they slowly opened more and more runways over the next few hours.

Drew helped Teresa deal with the woman at the ticketing counter to get on the first possible flight going to Phoenix, even though it meant his own connection would probably be full by the time he tried to book it, and he might have to wait until morning to continue to Oregon. Thankfully his brother's wedding wasn't scheduled until the next afternoon. There was still a slight chance Drew could make it for the ceremony. However, keeping Teresa and the kids from waiting here longer than absolutely necessary was more important.

After helping them settle into seats six gates down for a flight that was leaving soon, Drew returned to Colette, who was watching their bags back at their seating area.

"You want to join me in the melee of people jostling for the next available flight?" he asked.

"I already did mine over the phone. I managed to catch the red-eye. If I could have, I would have taken care of your ticket, too. I'm sorry." Colette slid her hand into his, where he had started to think it belonged.

He hated the thought of her leaving and them not seeing each other again, but they hadn't discussed the future yet. He still had six hours with her, though, and he was going to make the most of it. He called in to see about fixing his ticketing, and he managed a flight leaving at seven in the morning. The seating assignment did not please him, but he would make the wedding. He called Keith to let him know, and his brother sounded as relieved as Drew felt.

"Now that's handled, you want to explore the airport with me?" he asked. "We still have a solid five hours until you have to board."

"We might as well."

They stood and headed for the main thoroughfare. They paused to look at sculptures, studied paintings as if they were the greatest of art, and discussed the most ridiculous interpretations possible. They marveled over the huge garden growing in the middle of the airport, sampled smoothies, and tested the chocolates from the candy store. Thankfully, several delivery trucks had made it through that afternoon so the little shops had a lot of their selection back in stock.

Colette bought him some chocolate-covered cinnamon bears. "I know they aren't gummy worms, but I figured you'd like these better."

"You're right." He opened the package while they walked along, Colette dragging her suitcase behind her and his bag slung over one of his shoulders. "You want one?"

"No, I like fruity bears, not spicy ones—even if they are covered in chocolate."

"Right, of course. What was I thinking?"

Colette shook her head. "I have no idea."

Drew grinned over at her. "This has been the best twenty-four hours I've had in a long time."

She tipped her head to study him, her tone more serious than before. "Me, too."

The intensity in her gaze made him acutely aware that their

time was limited. "Well, hey, it isn't over, is it? After all, we still have time to watch a testosterone-laden movie and eat junk food."

"I don't think my system can handle any more junk food."

"Then we'll stop and get some juice or something instead. What do you think of Dr. Pepper?"

Colette lifted her brows, which made Drew laugh. He pulled her into the Jamba Juice he had seen earlier and bought her something loaded with vitamins and minerals.

They found her new terminal and settled down to stream a movie while they waited for her flight, but Drew couldn't seem to let go of her hand.

He'd seen the movie before, which was good, since his mind wouldn't focus on the screen. It kept veering back to Colette.

Halfway through, she paused it. "I'm sorry, it's a great flick, but I'd rather talk to you while I still have the chance."

Drew smiled, glad he wasn't the only one. "That makes two of us." He turned off the tablet and set it on his lap, then snuggled her under his arm. "Where do you see yourself in five years?"

"Is this a job interview?" she asked.

"Something like that."

"Hmmm. Let me think."

Drew couldn't see her expression. Was she leading him on, or did she not have a plan? She'd always had a plan in college.

"I guess I haven't taken the time to think about exactly what I want or where I want to be in five years—shocking, I know—but I've been trying to take things as they come, and I hadn't expected this job to last, but I like it a lot. I'll keep working there for as long as it make sense. I enjoy traveling and meeting new people all the time. On the other hand, I'm not exactly getting any younger, and I'd like to have a family—maybe not *five* kids." She turned to look him in the eye.

Drew laughed. "Would you want to stay home with the kids?"

"I think kids benefit from a parent at home, but I'm not sure I could see myself as a soccer mom. I guess the important thing is that I'm open to it, depending on how things go and the circumstances surrounding whenever my husband and I get to that point. Or maybe I'll be the working parent, and he'll be a stay-at-home dad."

"Are you serious?" He knew it worked for some families but wasn't sure if he would want to take time off work to raise the kids, even if his wife could make enough money for them to easily afford it.

"I don't know, but it's always an option. It's a lot to figure out without any specifics. How about you? What do you see for yourself in five years?"

Drew didn't know. He had thought he did, before this weekend, but after running into her again, he felt like looking at the matter with new eyes. Upon reflection, he supposed that it wasn't a fair question—they hadn't even figured out what they wanted, or didn't want, from each other. Had it really only been a day since they had found each other again?

His head was so full of Colette that he couldn't think straight. She had broken his heart once before—was he ready to put his heart on the line again for her? "I want a family and a wife who wants to build a life, not one who's looking for separate lives, but using the same name. I'm not saying spouses can't have their own interests, but I want to make sure we're on the same wavelength and headed in the same direction."

He realized why he had really brought up the whole discussion. He'd been brushing off echoes of the anxiety that had filled him in college when he told Colette how he felt about her, even though she had been dating Nick. No, *because* she had just started dating Nick. Normally, he was deliberate and thought things through—except, apparently, where she was concerned.

"I've been thinking that I wasn't sure what I wanted, because

I've been more than a little mixed up since seeing you yesterday. The truth is that it's not complex, it's actually very simple. I still want the future I see when I look at you; when I look to the future, I think of you and me. But you broke my heart, Colette. It messed me up, so I need you to be sure that you want to pursue something with me, wherever it might lead. That it's not just the excitement of seeing each other again keeping us together."

Colette opened her lips to say something more, then closed them again. "I don't think we've known each other enough to be sure of what either of us really wants." She looked at him for a long moment before pursuing what had been lingering behind her eyes. "I really wish I hadn't been such an idiot when it came to you in college. And I wish you hadn't turned your back on me. I understand why you did—or I tried to understand, anyway."

Drew brushed the hair back from her face. "Me, too. More than ever. But I couldn't stand to be your second choice when things imploded with Nick, and I was afraid you'd turn to me only because there was no one else there, and it wouldn't mean what I wanted it to mean."

"You could never be second best."

The muscle of his arm contracted under her touch as he held back his immediate response to pick his words more carefully. "That's nice of you to say, but we both know better. You turned your back on me the moment someone more interesting came along."

Colette shook her head. "That wasn't it at all."

"It looked that way from where I was standing."

"Maybe if you had stuck around a little longer instead of cutting me off, you would have learned the truth. You didn't leave me a chance to explain or reconsider—you were just *gone*. The one time I tracked you down, you refused to listen. You weren't the only one who was hurt, Drew. I needed you, and you wouldn't listen. You knew I didn't have anyone else, but it didn't matter."

Drew stood, surprised that he was worked up about it after

so long; he had told himself he was over it, but apparently not. He needed a few minutes of space to process so he could finish the conversation calmly. "I need a minute."

"Of course you do," she muttered under her breath.

"What is that supposed to mean?"

"You figure it out."

He stalked down the next terminal, considering her words. Had cutting her off all those years ago been wrong? Besides the fact that it had obviously left her no one to turn to when things had ended with Nick, had it hurt himself, too?

By the time he made it back to Colette's parting gate fifteen minutes later, he was calmer and ready to have an actual conversation. They were running out of time, and he wanted to get through this problem before it was too late. Otherwise this could end up in the pile of regrets he already lived with.

"It was hard watching you fawn over Nick," he said when he reached her again. "I didn't know how to deal with it, and I reacted badly."

The look of irritation in her eyes hadn't subsided while he'd calmed down. "It was hard being torn between you two. I didn't think you saw me as anything but a friend until after I started dating him." She lifted a palm to stop his retort. "Yes, we did things together, but it wasn't like you ever told me that you liked me. Was I supposed to read your mind? Whenever you were uncomfortable about a topic—especially when it was about dating in any form, past or present, you would duck out of the conversation or change the subject.

"Nick was persuasive, actually making me feel guilty when I hesitated to make it exclusive. Deciding to date him was stupid. I know it now, but I didn't see it at first. Then you suddenly decided to kiss me, out of the blue . . ."

It had been a stupid move. Maybe if he had done it a couple months sooner . . . "It didn't feel at all out of the blue to me. I wanted to show you how I felt, but I wasn't great with words then." Not that he was feeling like a linguistic giant at the moment.

"You *were* great with words," she corrected. "You totally aced the poetry reading."

"That's different. They may have been my words, but they didn't come from my heart; I wasn't putting anything on the line. I risked something with you, and you rejected what I offered. I was humiliated, so I couldn't face you again."

"I was new to the area, I didn't get along with my roommates, and you abandoned me. And as soon as you were out of the picture, there was Nick, tearing my confidence to shreds."

Drew kept his mouth shut so he wouldn't respond without thinking it through first. He had promised himself that he was going to listen this time, consider what she said, and face it. Today.

"You don't have anything else to say?" she asked.

"Give me a minute. We obviously remember the past differently. I thought that I made it clear that I liked you. I spent practically every free minute with you." Had it all been his fault—well, mostly been his fault, for not saying something sooner? It wasn't like he forced her to go out with Nick—that was on her. But the rest of it, had he been so bad at showing her what he felt? Or had she been bad at reading the signs? Or both? He had known Nick was a jerk, but he hadn't seen him with another girl enough to know he would tear her down like that.

"I can't be sure about how I was really acting, but I admit that I was scared to talk to you about us. You weren't like any of the other girls I had spent time with, and you were too young for the way you made me feel."

"I wasn't that young."

He smiled, remembering the unusually innocent eighteen-year-old. "Yeah, you were."

Colette took his hand, her gaze searching his. "How do you feel now?"

He had been trying to figure that out since the previous day. This could be his last chance, and he didn't want to lose her again. "I think we could actually make this work. Seeing you again has shown me that I'm not really over you." He felt like his stomach was going to turn inside out and his heart was being slammed repeatedly by a lacrosse stick.

"Wow." Her response was as dry as fading autumn leaves. "I feel positively blown away by all the love."

"I told you I'm not very romantic."

"No, you didn't. You said you don't believe Valentine's Day is about real romance." She paused and took in two deep breaths before finishing. "I think you're probably a real romantic at heart. I thought so in college. I liked you then. A lot, but I was an idiot who gave up on getting your attention in that way just as Nick showed up, showering me with attention. It turns out that I still like you. A lot. I'm not sure if what I feel is a remnant of leftover feelings, or if it's something we can actually build on."

Drew was glad to at least have the truth—he figured he could work with that, one way or the other. "Then maybe it's a good thing I have a wedding to go to, and you have a sister to sit and watch adrenaline-filled movies with." He picked up her hand and held it loosely. "If you decide that you really want to see what's between us, let me know."

Colette nodded, wetting her lips and drawing his attention. "Okay, but I'll need your number for that." She pulled her cell phone from her pocket with her free hand.

Drew typed in his phone number, address and email—just to be thorough. He didn't want any excuse for her to not be able to reach him. He took down her information as well, fully intending to use it.

They called the first boarding for her flight, and Drew looked up, surprised at the time. Where had it gone? He wasn't ready.

Colette didn't leave him a few minutes later when they called out that they were boarding zone two—her zone of the plane. She did, however, finally stand.

Drew joined her, taking her hand in his.

"Promise you're not going to forget me as soon as I'm out of sight?" she asked.

"I promise."

The woman at the counter announced, "Boarding all zones for flight number 346 to Kansas City."

"Okay." Colette's gaze studied his face.

Drew glanced up and saw there were only a handful of people still in line to board.

He thought of the last time he had said goodbye to her, and of the awkward kiss he'd given her—at twenty-two he should have been a lot better at it, but she'd made him feel like he was fourteen all over again. He felt an echo of that while he studied her face, trying to memorize it before he leaned down and gently pressed her lips with his. If this was all he ever got, then he would take it while he still could.

Colette's arms came up around his waist and pulled him closer. The softness of her fingertips brushed against the nape of his neck, and he forgot momentarily about the crowds of people around them.

"Last call for flight number 346 to Kansas City."

Drew pulled back, though he didn't want to. "Go, before you miss the flight."

"I'll call you," she said, grabbing the handle of her suitcase and adjusting the purse over her shoulder.

"I'll be waiting."

She was the last one to enter the ramp. In the instant before they closed the door, Drew could have sworn he saw her looking back at him.

Her plane hadn't even disconnected from the gangplank before he sent her a text message asking her to dinner the next weekend.

Six

THE CROWDS AT the airport after Colette left seemed considerably thinner. Drew was almost sure it wasn't only because she was no longer there. Shortly after her plane touched down in Kansas City, she texted back that she was definitely up for dinner Saturday.

He slept a few hours using his duffel bag for a pillow, then grabbed a bite to eat from the food court before returning to his terminal to wait for his new flight. He felt grimy and rumpled and before they started boarding his plane, he sent his brother a text that he needed a shower first thing when he arrived.

Keith popped back that Drew could have anything he wanted, and that someone would be waiting for him at the airport.

Before the plane finished climbing to cruising altitude, Drew was asleep again. The chair was more comfortable than anything the airport had provided—not that the terminal chairs were much of a standard to beat—plus, he wasn't worried about someone walking off with his stuff or one of the kids. He didn't awaken until the captain announced that they would be landing in ten minutes.

"How long were you at that airport?" the old man beside him asked.

"A day and half."

"Wow, I don't envy you. That must have been horrible."

It would have been without Colette, but Drew didn't explain that to his neighbor, choosing to give the easy answer that it could have been worse.

Flynn, one of his cousins, was waiting by the time Drew reached the baggage claim area. "You arrived alive," Flynn greeted. "You look a little worse for wear, though."

"I feel it, too. I want a regular meal, a solid twenty minutes in the shower and three hours in a soft bed. Or maybe ten." He still felt groggy from the long nap.

"Can you settle for two out of three? The bed will have to wait." Flynn took the duffel from him as they moved to the baggage claim area.

"I'll take what I can get. Keith said the rehearsal went well. How was the bachelor party?" Drew did his best to focus on his cousin and the wedding ahead, instead of letting his mind wander back to sitting on the airport floor playing Slapjack with Colette.

The shower was heaven, a bowl of Frosted Flakes never tasted so good, and the weather was beautiful. It was times like these when Drew seriously considered moving to Oregon, the way his brother was always coaxing him to.

He felt his phone buzz in his pocket when he had donned his rented tux. He pulled it out to see a note from Colette.

I hope you made it safely to Oregon. Sarah is doing much better today. I miss you already.

Drew grinned. **I'm here, showered, had a proper breakfast of cold cereal, and am dressed for the wedding. I think I might even be able to stay awake for the ceremony. Maybe.**

Colette: I wouldn't be unhappy with a picture of you in that tux. I hope your brother has a lovely wedding.

Drew: I'll be sure to send the picture. Thanks. Take care, I better get moving or someone is going to come up to find out why I'm not down there doing my job of best man.

Colette: TTYL

Considering that a good sign, Drew slid his phone back in his pocket and headed down the stairs to the room where Keith was getting ready for the ceremony.

"Wow, you look human. Flynn said you were pretty rough-looking when he picked you up." Keith greeted him with a hug. "I'm glad you made it on time."

"Me, too." Drew hugged him back. "I still feel pretty ragged, but at least I don't smell like it anymore. You ready for this?"

"Totally. This woman is amazing. Wait until you meet her."

Drew was glad that even on his wedding day, Keith was still sure about his choice. He hoped to experience the same thing someday.

Seven

A DECENT NIGHT'S sleep in her own bed, a healthy breakfast, and some exercise had rejuvenated Colette, but she couldn't help looking at her watch and wondering what Drew was up to, how the wedding was going, and if he was struggling to keep his eyes open.

After another long shower, Colette made a shopping list, rotated her laundry, and went out to run her errands. For the next two weeks she'd be at home, training people who would be flying in to her office. She was glad to be in a familiar place and to have a chance to think through her feelings for Drew.

Spending two amazing days—okay, one and a half—with someone she was sure she could love gave her a better perspective on life. Everything in her snug little apartment seemed drabber. The week stretched out before her, and the time she had to get through before she could possibly see Drew again, seemed never-ending. Darn three-hour distance between their cities.

She received a text message from Sarah at three. **The movies and cheesecake are waiting for whenever you get here.**

Colette shot back that she would be arriving soon, and then she stopped for a bunch of roses and to pick up the pizza she had pre-ordered. It wouldn't be the most romantic Valentine's ever, but considering the evening she had spent with Drew before boarding her re-scheduled flight, she didn't feel deprived.

"Happy Valentine's Day!" she called to Sarah as she entered the house.

"You seem awfully chipper for someone who spent almost two days in an airport." Sarah greeted her at the door and wrapped her in a hug.

"What's not to be happy about? Did you get the movie?"

"Sorry, it was already rented, but I did pick up the first three *Rush Hour*s."

"That will have to do." And it would fulfill Colette's quota for explosions and suspense beautifully.

Sarah chatted away, obviously feeling much better a few days post-chemo.

They watched the first movie, eating their way through half the pizza, then paused between movies to put the food away and get out the cheesecake Sarah had ordered from an amazing local bakery.

"Why do you keep checking your phone?" Sarah asked, pausing the second movie. She looked worn out from the party, despite relaxing on the sofa most of the time.

"I don't. I've only done it a few times." Colette slid the device into her pocket. The wedding would be over, the dinner at least in full swing if not finished, and she hadn't heard from Drew since that morning.

"You've looked at it at least ten times during this movie, and you're not responding to text messages, so what's going on?"

When Colette had contacted Sarah from the airport in Denver, she had vaguely mentioned running into an old college friend, but Drew's name had never come up. She craved advice. "Drew. College Drew. He's the one I ran into in Denver."

"Whoa, you spent all that time with hunky Drew? And you didn't mention it before?" She set the remote on the table beside her. "How was it?"

Colette slumped further into her comfy chair. "So good. Better than I remembered from college; better than any relationship I've ever had. Of course, it was like a day, not really long enough to know anything, but still."

"What's he up to?"

Starting at the beginning of their encounter, Colette filled her sister in on the salient details of her time at the airport and about Drew's life.

"So, you two swapped phone numbers, and what's going to happen now?"

Their kiss before she'd left should have answered that question, but there were still a lot of questions. Distance and busy, fairly rigid schedules were not their friends. Even if they ended up making it work and decided they needed to live closer, who would move? Would he be willing to move to Crystal Creek so they could really get serious, or would she have to quit her job and move closer to him? "I don't know what's going to happen next. We decided to take some time to get to know each other. Wichita is pretty far away."

"I always thought you should have chosen him instead of the jerk." Sarah had never been reticent about her feelings for Nick.

Colette smiled, though it wasn't really funny. "I wish I had figured that out a lot sooner."

"So is Drew going to call you?"

"We have a date Saturday, but I hoped he'd find time to text me this evening. He's probably busy with the wedding stuff."

Colette leaned back in her seat and looked at Sarah. She was pale and tired easily these days, and it was probably past her bedtime, but she hadn't said anything about needing to turn in. "So what's your plan?"

"We'll date, we'll call and message and see where things go. I really want things to work."

"It probably wouldn't hurt to figure out if leaving your job would be a deal breaker—if your relationship reaches that point. Knowing your deal breakers up front can help you both figure out what you can work around, and what you can't."

That was a good idea. "I knew you were the wise sister."

"Being married can be really fantastic, but it can also be really hard. If you know what you can and can't live with, it will make it easier to work out the rest."

Colette was tempted to say that there were no deal breakers, because spending time with Drew had been great. But until she gave herself a little time to breathe and figure out how she really felt when the first flush of love wasn't tainting every thought, she wouldn't be able to make a real evaluation. Maybe a little distance wouldn't be a horrible thing after all.

Eight

DREW: HAPPY V-DAY. How was your movie and junk food at Sarah's?

Colette: It was fun, and thought provoking. She told me to think about my deal-breakers and what would stop this relationship from being viable. I've never thought about it that way before.

Drew: She's a wise woman.

He hadn't been thinking about it that way, either. In addition to her figuring out what she wanted, it would probably be good for him to do the same. What would he *not* be willing to give up to be with her? His brain was fuzzy from lack of sleep the past few days. He had left the wedding reception early, with Keith's blessing, to return to his hotel room. The party had been great, and he'd enjoyed seeing cousins and friends who had made the long trip into Portland, but he had reached the end of his reserves.

Colette: It seems odd to me that I could spend so little time with you—just a weekend—and miss you anyway, but I do.

Drew: Me too. Everything I used to feel seemed to flood back when I saw you.

Colette: Same here. I could chat for hours, but you're probably exhausted.

Drew: Unfortunately, yes. I'll talk to you tomorrow. My eyes are already drifting closed.

Colette: Sweet dreams!
Drew: You too.

He ended the texts, already thinking about talking to her in the morning.

Nine

"Great work, Colette." Colette's boss stopped her Wednesday on the way out of the day's training. She had ten students from across the country in town for the week, learning about the company's software.

"Thanks, Bob." It had been a long few days. She'd been able to stay on task at work, but during breaks and every evening, she had been thinking about Drew, IMing him, chatting with him on the phone or via text. She thought about their time together, a possible future, and what she really wanted. She couldn't wait until Saturday, when she'd have another chance to see him.

Then they would have to figure out how the heck to make a relationship work.

"I've been talking about you to the higher ups," Bob continued. "There's an opening in the Chicago office. More travel overseas, higher pay, and more room for advancement."

It was what she had been working for only a week earlier, but looking at it now, she wasn't sure she wanted it anymore. Well, part of her wanted it, but the rest of her . . . not if it meant that she couldn't have Drew. "That's great. Thanks for letting me know."

Sarah referred to it as realizing what her deal breakers were, but the only thing Colette could think was that if she took the promotion she wouldn't be able to see Drew—pretty much ever—and she wasn't ready to make that decision yet.

Colette made some polite social talk with her boss, then set things up for the next day's class—it was a four-day training, so she could cut out of the office early Friday to go see Drew.

Jen

DREW TOLD HIS lacrosse team to clean up and hit the showers. It had been a crazy few days of tryouts, but he had his team picked out and would send the emails notifying the girls after he got home that night. Then he could put it all aside to focus on his Saturday date with Colette.

Jason, his assistant coach caught his eye and nodded toward the door. "Anyone you know? She's definitely too young to be one of their moms."

He turned to find Colette at the door to the gym. She was half in, half out of the room, as though she wasn't sure if she would be welcome. "Yeah, I know her. Talk to you later." She was almost a whole day early—and in the wrong city—did that mean she had decided to let him down in person?

Colette started to speak before he reached her. "I know I changed our plans, but I hit my forty hours for the week at noon, so I cut out early to come down. I know you probably have things going on, but I hoped we could grab dinner together. And if you intended a quiet evening with your lesson plans, there's no reason we can't work in the same room. I have lesson plans to make, too." She bit her lip, as though nervous he would turn her away.

He was only partially relieved. He had been saving up his nerves for seeing her the next day, so they all seemed to attack him at once. "I'd love that. Come see my room. I need to pick up a couple things from my desk anyway." He held out a hand to her, and she slid hers into it. Utter perfection.

Drew asked about her class that week and how Sarah was doing as he turned through the empty halls to his classroom. He unlocked the door and ushered her in. "This is my other domain."

Colette stepped into the classroom, looking around her at the equipment in the adjacent lab and the huge poster of the periodic table of elements. "You're really a chemistry teacher." She said this as if she hadn't believed it before.

"Yeah. Did you think I was making that up?"

"No, it just seems odd, even though I know it shouldn't. You always did want to be a teacher. You're probably great at it." Colette walked over, her no-nonsense, navy blue business suit ending in a skirt that fell an inch or two above her knees.

Her legs were something he hadn't seen the previous weekend thanks to her long pants. She had great legs—always had. He tore his gaze away and focused again on her face, the curiosity playing over her features. Though he hadn't expected her, and did have things to work on, he was really glad to see her. "I didn't realize I was so irresistible that you'd have to drive down a day early to see me."

She grinned. "Well, you are. I figured if you were busy, I'd spend a little time driving around the city to get a feel for it, to decide how I would feel about being here a lot more if things go well for us."

"Oh?" He set his clipboard on the desk and crossed to her, sliding his hands onto her waist. "I really hope you start spending a lot more time here."

Colette brushed her hands along his arms and up to his shoulders. "I've been thinking this over all week, considering my deal breakers, and what I didn't think I could live with before, but know now that I can. I told you about Sarah's cancer."

"Yes."

"Well, she needs me now. A lot."

"Right, of course." But that wouldn't last forever, right? "So you need to stay in Crystal Creek."

"No, wait." She set a hand on his arm when he turned away, drawing his attention back to herself. "You and I talked about figuring out our deal breakers. For the next little while, I need to be there for her. That doesn't mean that we can't date, but it does means that her needs are going to have to be considered if we decide we need to move this relationship into a single city anytime soon, instead of us living hours apart. I know you have work here, and I'm not sure what my boss will say if I ask to work from here instead of Kansas City. But I might have to change jobs."

"Is that also a deal breaker?" Drew studied her face while his insides tossed and turned with each sentence. He had thought about moving to the Kansas City area. Seeing her again, he knew he would do it if she wanted him to.

"Nope. It's the funniest thing, because I thought I would have a long list of things I wanted, that I needed if we were going to make this work. But I realized last night that I really don't. Other than being near Sarah for as long as she needs me, I'm all open to explore this. Whatever this is between us, even if it eventually means changing careers. How about you?"

Drew smiled, peace settling inside him. He brushed a lock of hair back from her cheek. How did she get such soft skin? He ran his thumb over her bottom lip—he had once obsessed over this mouth. He thought it would be very easy to start obsessing again. "Colette, when it comes to being with you, there are no deal breakers for me. If you want me to move, I can do it. There's nothing I wouldn't do or change to grab another chance of having you be mine." He nuzzled her cheek, before finding her mouth with his.

Rockets went off.

Or maybe that was something in his lab. He'd check that later.

Heather Tullis has been reading romance for as long as she can remember and has been publishing in the genre since 2009. She has written more than two dozen books. When she's not dreaming up new stories to write, or helping out with her community garden, she enjoys playing with her dogs and cat, cake decorating, trying new jewelry designs, and hanging out with her husband.

Learn more about Heather at her website and sign up for her newsletter: HeatherTullis.com

Facebook fan page: Heather Tullis Books

Hey, Helen!

BY SARAH M. EDEN

One

Hey, Helen!

My landlord says that I shouldn't be grilling chicken in the hallway, something about a "fire hazard." What do you think?
—Chicken Chet

Was this truly what passed for advice-column questions these days? Helen Blakely had been in the syndicated column business for three years, and she'd spent more time rolling her eyes than answering inquiries.

She zipped up her hoodie against the late January breeze—working at the table on her balcony in the dead of winter without freezing to death was one of the joys of living in Arizona—and typed a reply.

Hey, Chicken Chet, What do I think? I think you should have the fire department on speed dial.

She hit the backspace key until the reply disappeared one letter at a time. The question would not be featured in this week's "Hey, Helen!" column, no matter how tempted she was to answer it. She opened the next email in her inbox.

Hey, Helen!

The lady in the next cubicle wears the same perfume as my ex-wife. How do I ask her to stop wearing it without sounding demanding? —Getting a Noseful

Hey, Noseful, You can't avoid sounding demanding while actually being demanding. Stop it.

Again, the backspace got a workout. Helen wasn't usually this snarky, but she'd had a long day. First, the comments section for her last column had turned into a bloodbath, and she, like an idiot, had actually read the carnage. Then, her computer had decided to install an update in the middle of the day, locking her out for over an hour. When she had finally logged back on, the ad bar on her browser had been filled with click-bait links to articles she knew were getting more hits than hers. And, to top it all off, Valentine's Day was just around the corner.

She was not a fan of Valentine's Day. Her objections weren't the usual garden-variety, "It's too much pressure to have someone in your life," or, "Why is there no day celebrating being single?" objections. She simply thought it was ridiculous to guilt trip people into buying things to prove how much they loved their special someone, and then jack up the prices on the exact things required as evidence of devotion on that one day a year.

Yet for a full month before every February 14th, Valentine's Day dilemmas and drama consumed her inbox. Add to that the fact that her Valentine's Day themed columns got more traction than any of the others, and she couldn't get out of writing about it, though she had originally kept it to just one of her weekly columns. Last year she had made the mistake of answering Valentine's Day specific questions for the *two* weeks leading up to the holiday. Both posts had gone viral. This year, the papers that carried her column wanted three weeks of Valentine's content. *Three.*

Hey, Helen!

What she wouldn't give to chew out Chicken Chet instead. But he didn't have bills to pay; at least not *her* bills. For the next few weeks, making a living meant focusing on the emails about the one day a year when the depth of a person's feelings could be proven beyond a doubt.

She opened one with the subject "Valentine's Day dilemma" and hoped for the best.

> Hey, Helen!
> *I am training for a marathon. I run every morning and every night. The marathon is really important to me. My girlfriend is supportive and encourages me. Except, she says I have to skip my nightly run on Valentine's Day. I told her I can just run after we get back from whatever we end up doing, and she got mad. Am I so wrong to think that my goals shouldn't have to come in second to Valentine's Day? —Love on the Run*

She could make that one work for the column. "V-Day junk" sat just below that one in her inbox.

> Hey, Helen!
> *Every year for Valentine's Day I go all out, but my wife is always disappointed. This year, should I add one of those cards that plays music to the cheese and sausage gift basket? Women like that junk, right? —Cheese Louie*

Cheese Louie? The guy was going to have to come up with a different fake name, but his question was right on target. She just needed one more.

Neil, who lived next door and shared a divided balcony with her, looked up from his textbook. "How's the column coming?"

"Better than studying for an accounting final."

"Hey, don't talk smack about accelerated depreciation."

Helen eyed the next email in the queue. "What do you think of 'Valentine's Day Fruit Basket'? Does that sound promising?"

"Are you shopping or reading submissions?"

She opened the email. "I am not buying myself a fruit basket for Valentine's Day."

"Fair enough." He closed his book and settled his attention on her. "What does 'Fruit Basket' have to say?"

Neil had been a lifeline the past year. He joked with her over the more ridiculous questions she received. He offered insights when she wasn't completely sure how to answer some of the things she was asked. They often ordered pizza and hung out while she worked to make her deadlines and he studied for tests and did assignments.

Hey, Helen! I asked my girlfriend if she wanted a fruit basket for Valentine's Day. She said she didn't need a fruit basket, she already had one. Then she threw me out. So, fruit basket? Yes or no? —Not a Fruit Basket

Helen rubbed at her face. "Surely some of these questions answer themselves."

"Then that's a *no* on the fruit basket?" Neil asked.

She eyed him doubtfully. "You sent the email?"

"No." He pulled a face that was confident to a ridiculous extreme. "I am an expert at Valentine's gift giving. Beef jerky, for example, is always a safe choice."

"I think Cheese Louie would agree with you." She closed her laptop. "Seriously, do these people think I'm a personal shopper?"

"Who is Cheese Louie?"

A personal shopper? That idea actually had merit. "That could make a good column, I think."

"Cheese Louie?"

"Rather than go through all of these emails, since I know most of them are questions about gifts on Valentine's Day, I could just do a 'Hey, Helen! Guide to Valentine's Day Gift Giving.' It's the right balance of click-bait and actually helpful advice for it to get some traction without me having to sell my soul to the page-view gods."

Valentine's gifts weren't really her thing, but she knew enough about the holiday to give good advice. Her trademark tone was no-nonsense, with a thin layer of snark. This topic would lend itself to that.

"I kinda like it." She tapped her fingers on her closed laptop. "Uh, Helen?"

She looked at Neil over the balcony divider. "Yeah?"

"Who is Cheese Louie?"

She quickly explained, then returned to her column idea. "I could write about stuff to get that special someone."

"Better yet." He got out of his rickety lawn chair and crossed the balcony. "Do a 'what *not* to get that special someone.'"

"Oh! I love it." Her mind was spinning a thousand miles per hour. "I could ask friends about really bad Valentine's gifts they've gotten. I'm sure they all have stories."

He leaned on the low, transparent dividing wall. "I think everyone has a bad Valentine's Day story."

"Do you?"

He just laughed. "Hundreds."

She grinned. "Write me a letter."

"What?"

She sometimes forgot to verbalize the thoughts that led her from one part of a conversation into another. "For my column. You should write me a letter about your hundreds of bad Valentine's Days."

He leaned his forearms on the balcony wall. "What about the 'what not to buy on Valentine's Day' idea?"

"I can still do that one. I have three columns to write."

His gaze narrowed. "And one of them is going to be 'Neil MacKay's Valentine's Day Blooper Reel'?"

She hadn't really thought of it that way. "I guess that would be pretty weird for you, huh?"

"A little, yeah." He turned back toward his patio table and textbook, but stopped before he'd stepped away. He turned back enough to look at her again. "Actually, I do have a Valentine's Day question."

"Really?" Hope bubbled. "Great! What is it?"

He just shook his head. "I'm going to write you a 'Hey, Helen!' See if you can pick my letter out."

She assumed her most confident posture, allowing her expression to turn smug. "Challenge accepted."

Neil sat at his computer, staring at the "Hey, Helen!" submission page and realizing he was an idiot. He'd meant his "I'll send you a letter" comment as a joke; Helen appreciated humor. But his only actual Valentine's Day dilemma involved her, and that made writing to her about it . . . uncomfortable.

Hey, Helen! I think you're amazing, and I've been in love with you for almost a year. Remember me? I'm the one behind the accounting book.

He couldn't write that to her, but he also couldn't keep being a coward.

Hey, Helen! I have a secret crush—

No. What was he, an eight-year-old girl?

Hey, Helen! I'm afraid to tell my neighbor how I feel about her. Because I turn into an idiot when I talk about this kind of stuff. And I'm kind of afraid of her.

Hey, Helen!

Which wasn't precisely true. He wasn't afraid of Helen, just of losing her friendship. There was no recovering from, "I know we're friends, but I want to be more than that," followed by a, "No, thanks."

Hey, Helen! I want to tell someone how I feel about her, and I think Valentine's Day would be a good day to do it. How do I—

Something less direct.

Hey, Helen! I want to tell someone how I feel about her, but I don't want to ruin our friendship by making it awkward. Valentine's Day is coming up, and that would be a good time to show her. Is there any good way to do it?

Better.

It asked his actual question, while still fitting the theme she was working on. Would that make it totally obvious, though, that the letter was from him? He knew what topic she'd picked, and she knew he knew.

He needed a decoy.

Neil signed the first question "Dude With a Dilemma." She usually changed the fake name, anyway. He hit the submit button, then refreshed the page and started typing.

Hey, Helen! What's the best Valentine's Day gift for a person who thinks Valentine's Day is kind of stupid? —My Neighbor Thinks Valentine's Day is Stupid

There. She would know that was from him, since the question was obviously about *her*, and she wouldn't guess that he'd sent the other question. He hoped. She might not answer the first submission in her column, but she talked to him about most of the questions she received. When she brought up Dude with a Dilemma, he'd casually press her for her thoughts.

This might work.

Might.

Two

Helen rang Neil's doorbell a couple of days later, her laptop bag slung over one shoulder, a pizza in her other hand. She'd gathered a bunch of bad Valentine's gift stories from friends and colleagues and was ready to knock out her first column.

He opened the door, then eyed her bag and pizza box. "You're writing tonight?"

She nodded. "Do you mind helping again?"

He motioned her inside.

She couldn't remember when she'd started running ideas past him, but he was a great sounding board, and he didn't mind her dropping by unannounced. Pizza and writing had become a regular pastime of theirs, even though he wasn't a writer. He was just really fun to hang out with, and smart. His advice was usually pretty good, and it never hurt to get a different perspective on the questions she was asked.

She set the pizza on the coffee table and dropped onto her usual spot on the couch. "How'd yesterday's test go?"

"Aced it." He sat in his orange armchair, same as always. "I've just got to get through this semester, and I'm done."

"No more telemarketing job." She knew how much he hated his temporary career.

"With my luck, I'll end up working as an accountant for a telemarketing company." He flipped open the pizza box. "But as long as I can pay back my student loans, I'm good."

"That is why some of us wisely didn't go to college." She snatched a slice herself.

She had told Neil many times about her strained relationship with the entire educational system. She wasn't stupid—she knew she wasn't—but school had always made her feel that way. She'd spent her entire childhood with a brain that constantly had dozens of balls in the air that regularly crashed down around her in the form of missing assignments, poor grades, and pathetic test scores, despite working longer hours on her homework than anyone else she knew. School just wasn't for her.

She'd done pretty well for herself without a degree. It wasn't as if she was illiterate, or couldn't keep track of her bank accounts. She was a functioning adult. That had to count for something, right?

Out of the corner of her eye, she caught Neil's smile. "What?"

He shrugged. "You were a million miles away. You do that a lot."

"Sorry." She had heard it before. A lot.

"I wasn't complaining." He moved to the kitchen and pulled a couple of glasses out of a cupboard. "You write your best columns on the days when you're super distracted."

Why did that weird compliment touch her so deeply? Sure, she had some insecurities about her writing, but she didn't need constant validation. And she was a little embarrassed about her flighty brain, but she didn't need people to tell her she was okay even if she had days, a lot of them, when she couldn't focus on anything for very long. And, yet, his bit of praise felt like a lifeline.

"Thanks for always helping me with the columns," she said.

He set a glass of water on the coffee table in front of her. "You don't really need my help, but it's fun."

"I don't need your help?" She scoffed at that nonsense. "Do you remember the letter from Super Sinus?"

His laugh started low and quiet but quickly grew. "You almost told him to buy stock in facial tissues."

"But you, rightly, told me to suggest he see an ear, nose, and throat doctor. And when he wrote back to tell me that he'd had a surgery that fixed pretty much everything, you didn't even gloat."

Neil retook his seat. "I'm great like that."

His sense of humor had taken a little getting used to. It was dry and usually really subtle, but once she'd learned to recognize it, she liked it.

His phone chimed. He pulled it out of his pocket and eyed the screen. "Mom and Dad must be fighting again."

His parents texted him when they were arguing, each complaining about the other and insisting he take sides. It happened all the time.

"Which one texted you first this time?"

"Mom," he said without looking up from his screen. His thumbs moved quickly.

"The usual response?"

He nodded. "'Sorry. I'm sure you'll work it out.' It'll make her mad—it always does—but I'm not getting in the middle of it."

His phone chimed again. He stayed bent over his screen. "Ah, Dad. Right on time."

"Let me guess. You're typing, 'Sorry. I'm sure you'll work it out,'" she said as his thumbs tapped against the glass screen again.

"I can't write exactly the same thing to both of them," he said. "Dad's getting 'Sounds tough. You'll figure it out.'"

She nodded her approval. "You have become an expert at this."

"Unfortunately." He set his phone on the coffee table. "So, what do we have for the column tonight?"

Neil didn't usually like to talk about his parents' problems. Helen had learned to let him change the topic as abruptly as he wanted.

"The 'what not to buy on Valentine's Day' column. I've

collected some hilarious stories." She popped open her laptop with one hand, holding her pizza slice in the other. "So, it won't be the traditional question-answer-question-answer format. You don't think that'll be a problem, do you?"

He shook his head. "Just open it by saying that you get a lot of questions about Valentine's presents, so instead of answering them all individually, you're just going to cover the whole topic."

"I like it." She made a quick note to include an intro with this particular column. "Then I'm thinking I'll put in 'What Not to Buy on Valentine's Day' then dot-dot-dot, and I'll just list them. If they're funny enough, they won't even need an explanation."

He nodded. "It would probably be funnier if the readers know that the list is based on actual Valentine's Day gifts."

"I thought so, too."

Neil's phone chimed again. "Sorry," he said as he picked it up. He read whatever had arrived, but didn't respond. He just set it back down again. "Keep going."

"Are you sure? If you need to put out a fire—"

"I'm not their firefighter anymore." He slouched a little lower. "What else've you got for the column?"

"I'm thinking I start with food and work my way toward power tools."

"Power tools?" Neil laughed, which was a good sign—not just for the column, but for him as well. His parents' constant fighting and their insistence on pulling him into it had taken a visible toll on him over the year she'd known him. But today he seemed to be dealing pretty well with it. "Did someone actually have a power tools for Valentine's story?"

"Yup. I worked with her back when I was doing data entry. A boyfriend gave her an electric screwdriver for Valentine's Day. Didn't go over well."

"Why would he think she wanted an electric screwdriver?" Neil, as usual, hit on the heart of the problem first thing.

"That's actually the single underlying problem with these gifts: not understanding what matters to the other person. Some people buy really unusual things, like electric screwdrivers, for people who couldn't possibly want them. Others bought generic Valentine's stuff for someone who wanted something more personal."

His brow pulled in thought. "So the issue is not knowing the person you're giving the gift to well enough."

She pointed her pizza slice at him. "Exactly."

"So you have the electric screwdriver for someone who is, apparently, not a big fan of home improvement," Neil said. "What else?"

"A guy gave his girlfriend a first-person shooter video game, because he knew she wouldn't actually want it and would give it back to him."

To his credit, Neil looked shocked. He really was a good guy. Why was he single? She'd heard about dates he'd been on, but nothing ever seemed to come of them. Maybe because his parents constantly interrupted him with inappropriately detailed play-by-plays of their unending arguments.

He ignored the most recent chime of an incoming text message. His jaw tightened, but he didn't budge.

"I think I'll start with a story from a guy friend of mine," Helen said. "For Valentine's Day he was once given a little shepherdess figurine and never could figure out why his girlfriend thought he would want something like that."

"What guy doesn't?" Neil said with his trademark dry wit.

"I'm so relieved, because I got you a shepherdess figurine."

He fist pumped and mouthed, "Yes!"

She scrolled through her column notes. "I'm debating between the guy who got a set of sequined throw-pillows, and the one who gave his vegetarian girlfriend a subscription to the Steak of the Month Club."

"Steak of the Month Club," Neil voted. "Drives home the 'take a minute to think about *who* you are giving the gift to' point perfectly."

True enough. "I'm trying to decide which generic gifts to mention: helium balloons, heart-shaped box of chocolates, or those teddy-bear-inside-a-balloon things that people on street corners sell off the backs of their trucks?"

Neil grinned, just as she'd hoped he would. "On street corners." And then he was laughing again.

"Right? If you're in a serious relationship with someone you know puts a lot of stock in Valentine's Day, and you buy a present that screams, 'I bought this at the intersection on my way home,' you probably won't get the reaction you're hoping for."

"What about flowers?" Neil asked. "They're a pretty generic gift, but I think most women love them."

"Most do." She quickly highlighted "teddy bear balloon" in her notes. "Personally, I think they're a little ridiculous."

"Why?"

The earnestness of his tone drew her gaze to him. He looked almost worried. Was he planning to buy flowers for someone on Valentine's Day? She couldn't think of anyone he'd mentioned a lot lately. And she saw him on his balcony pretty much every night.

"Most women like flowers on Valentine's Day," she reassured him.

"Why don't you?" He leaned forward, watching her closely.

She slumped against the back of the couch. "The cost of flowers on February 15th is like a quarter of what it is on February 14th. It's just crazy that shops charge so much more on the one day when guys are pretty much required to buy something from them." She shrugged. "The practical side of me can't get on board with that."

"Hmm." Either he was re-evaluating his own feelings about

Valentine's Day price gouging, or he was contemplating how weird she was.

"Come on. You gotta admit it's a pretty sweet arrangement for flower sellers."

"I guess so." He didn't seem convinced. "But maybe that's one reason flowers are such a big deal on Valentine's Day, because it's a bigger sacrifice than usual."

"Maybe." She still didn't like it. "Isn't that kind of like saying, 'I will measure the depth of your love by how much money you spend on me'? That's kinda sick."

"Hmm."

"Is that a, 'Helen is pretty smart. No wonder she has her own advice column,' hmm. Or a, 'How do I get this chick out of my apartment? I think she might be a weird-o,' hmm?"

He grabbed another slice of pizza. "Why can't it be both?"

"You know, for an accountant, you're pretty funny."

As the evening went on, they joked their way through her column idea. To the flood of texts he continued to receive, he gave only a few generic responses. By the time the pizza grew cold, she was ready to write, and he, more likely than not, was ready to have himself legally declared an orphan.

He pulled out his accounting homework, as usual, and they both got to work. She was comfortable around Neil in a way she wasn't with very many people. He didn't get on her case when her thoughts jumped all over the place, or complain that she was too jittery. She couldn't remember the last person who'd been so patient with that aspect of her personality.

Fate had been kind of a jerk to her over the years. But she thanked it regularly for bringing him to the apartment next door. She wasn't as lonely as she'd been before he'd become her neighbor. She had someone to talk to and laugh with, someone who liked spending time with her and didn't grow frustrated with her quirks and her constantly distracted mind. His friendship was arguably one of the best things in her life. She didn't know what she'd do without him.

Three

Maybe Valentine's Day wasn't the best timing for confessing his feelings for Helen.

She, Neil had discovered, had very specific ideas about the holiday. She wasn't a fan of boxes of chocolates, because they were a fall-back for guys who couldn't think of anything more personal. She objected to flowers on a supply-demand economics basis. Anything bought on a roadside, last-minute, was out of the question. Non-traditional gifts only worked if they were really personal and fitting.

That was a lot of pressure.

He'd spent the few days since their pizza-and-writing party trying to decide how to move forward. He wasn't super good at words, so he'd figured if he picked the perfect Valentine's Day gift, it would communicate his feelings for her in a way he couldn't. But if he was just going to mess this up after all the time they'd spent talking about how to pick a meaningful gift, then he'd probably be better off not trying.

She was currently working on her balcony again. Neil tried to focus on his accounting homework, but his thoughts kept returning to her. Did she think of him at all in the way he thought about her? If there was nothing on her end but friendship, would he ruin everything by confessing his true feelings?

But I can't keep doing this either. Wanting something deeper and never even trying for it was out of the question.

Helen snapped her laptop closed and dropped her head onto it. "I quit," she said. "Writing columns is for idiots."

"Do you like being a columnist?" he asked.

"Not at the moment."

He pushed his patio chair up to the balcony divider. "I mean, overall. Do you like it? Or would you rather be doing something else?"

She lifted her head enough to look at him. "I like to write."

"That's not really the question I asked."

She sat up again, and then slumped lower in the folding chair. "With this job, I can write and I can pay my bills. There aren't many other options where I could do both."

"Again," he said, "not my question."

She sighed and stood, crossing to the divider. She set her forearms on it, leaning forward enough for her shoulders and head to be on his side of the balcony, coming close enough to him for her perfume to fill the air around him. He did his best impression of someone who wasn't secretly in love with her—a person who had no clue about his feelings. She wasn't being flirtatious or trying to send any kind of romantic message. He knew that.

"I've always wanted to write books," she said. "But that doesn't come with a steady paycheck. You're an accountant; you know how that would work out."

"I'm not an accountant, yet," he reminded her.

"And I'm not a novelist. At all."

Interesting. "Why not?"

She eyed him with more than a hint of annoyance. "I told you. I need an income."

"I work at the telemarketing company in the mornings so I can have an income while I work toward being an accountant." He held her doubtful gaze with a confident one of his own. "Why not keep writing the column *while* you work toward becoming a novelist?"

"I wouldn't know where to start." A heartbreaking tinge of fearful hope touched her words.

"How about starting with, 'It was a dark and stormy night'?"

She laughed a little. "I do know enough to know *that* would be a really bad beginning."

"So come up with something better."

She straightened. "I don't think I'd be any good at it. Look at how difficult it is for me to write a single column. A whole book would probably kill me."

Neil took a risk—a big one—and slipped his hand around hers. "You're a good writer, but you're not happy. It's time you reached for something bigger."

She held fast to him. "What if I'm no good at it? What if it doesn't work out?"

"What if it does?"

She didn't answer immediately. She was pondering the idea, but she didn't appear to be any more convinced than before.

"Helen." He stood, sitting on the dividing wall. "If someone wrote you a 'Hey, Helen!' saying they wanted to be a novelist, that they were a good writer with experience and a job that gave them the flexibility to try their hand at writing a book, but they were afraid to try because there was the possibility of failure, what would your advice be?"

Her gaze shifted away. "I'd probably tell them to quit being a baby and just do it."

"Helen?"

"Yeah?" She looked back at him warily.

"Quit being a baby and just do it."

She laughed immediately, and he joined in.

The time he spent with her always included a great deal of hilarity. He appreciated that about her. His parents had almost never enjoyed each other's company. He'd spent most of his childhood promising himself that someday he'd find someone who was happy and cheerful, despite how hard life could be sometimes. Helen was all that and more. How could he not have fallen for her?

"I'll think about the book thing," she said. "In the meantime, I have a day job, and I don't know how to answer the Valentine's Day marathon runner without sounding too snarky. A little snarky, but not *too* snarky."

"What are you going to tell him?"

She shrugged. "His girlfriend has a point: on a special occasion she ought to be able to have his undivided attention. But it isn't like he's saying he wants to run *instead* of going on a date with her."

Fair enough. "But didn't he say that his goals shouldn't come in second to Valentine's Day?"

"That wording is what I keep getting stuck on, too. She's saying, 'Hey. This day is important to me. This day and your efforts to make it meaningful are a reflection of your dedication to our relationship.' And he's saying, 'Running doesn't come in second to that.'"

"Maybe he doesn't realize what she's saying?"

Helen stepped back from the dividing wall. "So that's how I answer: focus on what she's saying, and that he's likely not hearing her."

"I think that probably gets in the way of a lot of relationships: not hearing what someone's actually saying." His parents, for example, hardly ever said to each other what they said to him. That, he'd discovered, was 90% of their problem.

"And sometimes a person doesn't say what they actually mean," Helen added.

Which hit a little too close to home, and the things he was trying to convince himself to tell *her*. "Relationships are tricky."

"Which," she said with a mischievous smile, "is why I have job security."

And why I have no idea what I'm going to do.

Helen's head snapped upward, her eyes focused on his sliding glass door. She did exactly that every time something snatched her attention. She jumped from one thing to the next with more energy than he could ever imagine having.

"I think I heard your doorbell," she said.

"Really?" He hadn't.

"I've told you a million times, I have the hearing of a bat." It was probably more that she never tuned anything out. She was hyper aware of pretty much everything.

"Well," he said, "if I ever need to travel entirely by sonar . . ." He gave her double finger-guns.

She swatted him away. "Go answer your door."

Finding his dad there was a shock. His parents had only visited a couple of times in the thirteen months he'd lived in this apartment, and they'd always arrived together, however unhappy they'd typically been in each other's company.

"Hey," was all Neil could think to say.

"Can I stay here?" Dad asked. "Your mom changed the locks."

Neil held back a string of words that probably would have made Mom lock him out, too. He couldn't turn his dad away, but letting the man stay meant being pulled into the middle of yet another argument, one that was apparently even worse than usual.

He stepped back so his dad could come inside. A quick "thanks" was all Neil got before his dad dropped onto the sofa and grabbed the remote. No explanation. No estimate of how long he'd be there. No apology for the inconvenience.

Neil ought to have stopped expecting either of his parents to take responsibility for the mess they'd made of their own lives, as well as his, but somehow he kept hoping. It was tough being the only adult in the family, especially when that had been the case since he'd been in elementary school.

"Make yourself at home," he said

Dad must not have heard the dryness of his tone. He answered with an, "Okay," then started flipping through channels.

"I'll just be on the balcony, studying."

"Are you still in school?"

Honestly, his parents paid no attention to him at all.

"It's my last semester," he said. "Then I'll have my degree and can start a career."

Dad's channel surfing settled on a baseball game. "Land yourself a good job, and you can find a nicer place."

Yup. And not tell either of you my new address.

When he stepped outside again, Helen was typing fast and furious on the other side of the balcony. He dropped into his chair and grabbed his textbook, not wanting to interrupt her when she was on a roll.

But she spoke right away, surprising him. "Who was it? The super finally coming to fix your garbage disposal?"

"Nope." He flipped a page. "It's my dad."

"Really? That's weird."

"Oh, it gets weirder." He looked over at her. "Mom locked him out, so he's staying here." Neil gave a half-hearted "raise the roof" and an unenthusiastic, "Hooray."

"Has your mom texted about it yet?"

He hadn't thought about that. He knew it was only a matter of time. "You aren't friends with any criminals who'd like to come steal my phone, are you? Because I would not put up a fight."

"That doesn't change the fact that your dad is right inside, and you'll have to listen to him all night."

Neil dropped his head in defeat. "I would rather be working an extra telemarketing shift. At least I wouldn't be stuck here with him all night."

"So tell him you're having dinner with a friend," she said.

"That might work. He'll probably still text me all night long complaining. Mom will be doing that anyway."

Helen closed her laptop. "Tell them you have a date. Then when you don't respond to texts, they'll assume you're distracted by your romantic evening." She said the last two words with such an exaggeratedly flirtatious tone that he couldn't help laughing.

"How am I going to find a date on such short notice?"

She shrugged a little; smiled a little. "Ask nicely?"

Quick as that, his heart was lodged in his throat. A date. With Helen. He'd imagined asking her out a million times. Now he had the perfect opportunity. It would be a fake date, he knew that. And he knew she'd only offered so he could get away from his parents. But it was still a date.

"Helen, would you like to have dinner with me?"

She pretended to ponder it. "That depends. Is this a date?"

He played along, matching her exaggerated tone. "A very romantic date. So romantic I will be unable to answer my phone or read a single text the whole time."

"Perfect." She slipped her laptop under her arm. "I'll expect you to pick me up as soon as humanly possible."

"See you in a minute." He stepped inside his apartment once she disappeared inside hers.

"Do you have anything to eat?" Dad asked.

"There's stuff in the fridge. Help yourself. I'm headed out."

Dad sat up a little straighter and eyed him. "Where are you going? I just got here."

"Sorry," Neil said, even though he wasn't in the least. "I didn't know you were coming, and I already had plans."

"You can't change them?"

"It's a date," he said. "A *first* date. I'm not gonna break it."

Dad stood up, shock darkening his expression. "You're seeing someone? I didn't know that."

"A *first* date," he repeated. "I'm not seeing her, yet, but I'd like to be. Being late would probably hurt my chances."

For a minute Dad didn't seem to know what to say. Neil

waited, bracing himself for some kind of argument. But then Dad sat down again. "Have fun."

That was it? *Have fun*? Neil grabbed his jacket and pulled the door open. If he left fast enough, Dad wouldn't have time to change his mind.

"See you," he said as he pulled the door shut behind him.

Four

HELEN HADN'T EVEN had time to grab her stuff before Neil knocked. She opened the door, gave him the "just a second" signal, and snatched her coat from the closet.

"Did he give you any trouble?" she asked.

"Not once I told him this was a date."

She pulled on her coat. "I said he wouldn't."

"That's why they call you 'Hey, Helen.'" He waited while she closed and locked her door, and then walked at her side down the hallway. "Where should we go?"

"The Indian place down the street? It's not too cold out. We could even walk."

He nodded. Nothing was said between them as they made their way down the complex's exterior stairs. The corners of Neil's mouth pulled down, and his forehead pinched in lines of frustration. His parents wore him down; she'd seen it countless times. When those two were weighing on him, not even a fake date was likely to lift his spirits.

She threaded her arm through his as they stepped out onto the sidewalk. That earned her a questioning look.

"I'm on a date," she said, making her tone overly serious. "A little arm snuggling seems called for."

"Plus it's kind of chilly." He sounded a little less burdened.

"I like the date reasoning better." And, oddly enough, she found she meant it. Being on a date with a guy she had been friends with and a neighbor to for months and months ought to have been a little awkward, but it wasn't. Not at all, actually.

In fact, this was going better than her dates usually did, and she was only two minutes in. They were comfortable with each other. There was none of the weirdness of wondering what the other person thought, or if they'd be impressed or repulsed, or if they'd turn out to be a creep.

"Your mind's jumping around again, huh?" He always seemed to find that amusing, not in a mocking way, but as if he actually liked that about her.

"Of course it is." She wrapped her arm more snuggly around his.

"You don't have to put on a convincing show," he said. "It's not like my parents can see us or anything."

"I know. I just—" An unexpected and totally uncharacteristic bashfulness swept over her. "I just like holding your arm."

He gave her a smile different from his usual. It held an unexpected softness, without being sappy. She had no idea what to make of it.

An abrupt change of topic seemed in order. "My editor really liked the 'What Not to Buy' column. She thinks it'll get a lot of traction."

"It's a good topic, good timing, and you're a good writer."

Where had Neil been back when she'd first started working for a tiny, no account website and couldn't convince anyone including herself that she could write worth anything?

"My editor wants the next column to be a traditional question-and-answer format. But the one that'll run on Valentine's Day, she thinks should be more of a think piece, more insightful, less snark."

"Snark is your trademark, though."

She sighed. "Yup. So I either go against her advice and write my usual, or I try writing something really different from what I've written before. Neither choice is particularly appealing."

Hey, Helen!

They stepped inside the restaurant. It always smelled amazing. This had been a good choice. They were shown to a quiet corner and a table with a lit candle and a sprig of flowers. This fake date certainly had the look of a real one.

They had only just been seated when Neil's phone announced the arrival of a text. He didn't even glance at it.

"That is some impressive self-control," she said.

"I'm on a date. I'm very good at dates."

The server arrived to take their drink order.

"Ice water for me," Helen said.

"And a bowl of lime wedges," Neil added.

He remembered that? Ages ago, she had told him she liked lime in her water.

Once the server left with their order, she said, "You remembered."

"I told you. I'm very good at dates."

As the evening continued, she discovered how right he was. Their conversation was varied and fun. He asked interesting questions and genuinely listened to her answers. They joked around a lot, though they also touched on more serious topics. Even though they'd known each other for quite a while and had spent nearly every evening together, there were still new things to discover about him. And he found things to ask about that she hadn't shared before.

"Do you know yet which questions you're going to answer in your next column?" he asked after the kheer pista arrived to end out the meal.

"Marathon Runner," she answered between bites. "One I got from a woman who's single and wants to know how to make the day less miserable, and another one from a guy who doesn't know how to tell the woman he has feelings for that he has feelings for her."

"Really?" His keen interest was a good sign.

"It's a good assortment: single, potential relationship, and struggling relationship."

"And you know what you're going to say to—to all of them?"

She nodded. "More or less. Though, heaven knows I'll be at your house with pizza tomorrow night, running ideas by you."

He winced. "Dad might still be there."

That was a bit of a predicament. "Maybe you can come to my place instead." She felt weirdly nervous the moment the invitation left her lips. She shook it off and adopted a light tone. "Tell your dad it's another date."

He hesitated. "I don't really want to lie to him."

"So don't lie." First nervousness, now a lump in her throat. Fake dates apparently messed with a person's emotions.

He spoke between bites. "Tell him I'm hanging out with my neighbor?" Neil's gaze narrowed on her. "Or do you mean making it another date?"

She shrugged to hide her sudden nervousness. "Couldn't hurt."

"I suppose not." That wasn't the most enthusiastic response.

Though she'd made the offer to help him out of a difficult situation, his lack of excitement . . . hurt. She was having a good time on their "date." Wasn't he? It was weird how much she hoped he was. Helen didn't know quite what to make of it.

"Or I could go to your place," she offered, "even with your dad there. He'll probably leave you alone if you have company. I'm game for whichever option would work best for you."

Neil considered it, before saying, "Surprise me."

And that was the rub.

Everything about this was beginning to surprise her.

Five

THE NEXT AFTERNOON, Helen approached Neil's door with a pizza in hand. As far as she knew, his dad was still there. If so, she was happy to serve as a buffer. If not, so much the better. She'd have another night of Neil's company.

She'd thought a lot about their "date" the night before, trying to sort out why it had flustered her. In the end, there'd only been one logical conclusion: she liked him in a way she hadn't expected. How far that "liking" went, she didn't know. Truth be told, she wasn't sure she wanted to find out. She'd answered too many letters from people whose friendships had been ruined by this kind of thing.

She shook off the thought and knocked, hoping his dad didn't answer. The door opened. Fate, as it turned out, was still kind of a jerk.

A man who looked a lot like Neil, only older, eyed her a moment, then turned back toward the apartment and called out, "Pizza's here."

"I didn't order pizza," Neil's voice called back.

His dad faced her again. "Sorry. Wrong place."

He started to close the door. She quickly called out, "Neil, it's Helen."

Apparently her knowledge of his son's name was enough to make Mr. MacKay at least hesitate before closing the door on her. Neil appeared in the next moment.

"Hey," he said. "I wasn't sure if you'd be coming by or not."

She tried to look nonchalant about the whole thing. "Well, I didn't get asked on another date, so I figured this was my best option."

"Is this who you were on your date with?" his dad asked. "The pizza delivery girl?"

"Yup." Neil grinned as he waved her inside. "What do we have tonight?"

"Pepperoni, with a side of work and studying."

"Sounds good to me." He moved to the kitchen to grab cups, same as every other pizza night.

His dad watched her with confused curiosity. "You're the one he had the date with?"

"Is that so shocking?" She kept the question casual but meant every word; Mr. MacKay looked genuinely surprised.

"I just assumed he'd go out with someone less . . ."

Oh, that didn't bode well. "Less *what*?"

"Dad." Neil's sharp tone didn't deflect either of them.

"It's just that I think—" His dad didn't seem uncomfortable, so much as unsure of the best way to say exactly what he was thinking. She kept him in her pointed and unflinching gaze. "You seem out of his league, to be honest."

She had not been expecting that. Neil's eyes pulled wide and unblinking. He, apparently, had been caught by surprise as well.

For the briefest of moments, she felt flattered. But then she was hit full force with the reality of what his dad had implied. Nothing about Helen shouted, "great catch." When he'd thought she was the pizza delivery girl, he'd dismissed her out of hand. Saying someone he'd blown off so quickly was out of his son's league was not a compliment to her, so much as an insult to Neil.

"I think we're exactly in each other's league," she tossed back, setting the pizza on the coffee table and making herself at home on the couch. She turned her head enough to talk to Neil, who was walking over from the kitchen. "I don't need much feedback tonight, so you can dive right into your studying, and I'll just start typing."

"Sounds like a plan." Neil handed her a glass then sat, not in his usual chair—his dad had taken that one—but next to her on the couch. "Do you mind?" he asked, scooting a little closer.

Mind? Not at all.

Her gaze caught his dad's, and she saw unmistakable disapproval there, though for which one of them she couldn't say. So she settled in more comfortably against Neil and eyed his dad with a look of challenge. He was a visitor in his son's home. He didn't get to decide whether or not she was welcome.

The show of confidence did the trick. Mr. MacKay snatched up the remote and began flipping through channels.

Helen grabbed a slice of pizza. "You can have some, too, Mr. MacKay, if you want."

"Thanks." But he didn't reach for any. He gave every indication of sulking.

Helen set her pizza on the plate Neil had brought along with her glass. She leaned a little closer and, lowering her voice, said, "He doesn't seem very happy that I'm here."

"He's not happy about anything."

"Because he's on the outs with your mom?"

"Because he's not a happy person." Neil shifted a little, settling closer to her.

Was he simply searching for a more comfortable position, or did he want to close the gap between them for more . . . *personal* reasons? Her stomach flipped about as her mind attempted to sort out the possibilities.

Get it together, Helen. You're gonna make this weird.

He popped open his accounting textbook. "Maybe I should let Dad read a chapter or two of this baby. That'd cheer up anybody."

"Sure," she said. "Nothing like benefit-cost ratios to brighten a person's day."

Neil looked impressed. "You've been paying attention."

She did her best impression of his over-blown show of arrogance from the night before. "You're not the only one who's good on a date."

"That was pretty nice last night, huh?" He made the observation, really casually, like it wasn't a big deal one way or the other.

Her immediate response, though, wasn't so content. She'd been thinking about those few hours every minute since their dinner out, and she couldn't make sense of it. *Couldn't* wasn't the right word. She *wouldn't*. She wouldn't allow herself to think about it too deeply. Neil was her best friend. She wasn't going to risk losing that friendship over feelings she wasn't entirely sure of herself.

"So, when's your next—" She made the mistake of meeting his eye. He gave her a look of quiet amusement that proved charming in a way Neil had never been charming before.

What is happening?

She forced her mind to refocus, something she seldom managed without a great deal of effort. "When's your next test?"

"In a couple of weeks," he said, grabbing some pizza. "Then it's the final."

School. Keep talking to him about school. "Are you nervous?"

"Not really. I know this stuff forward and backward."

"Doing accounting backwards seems like a bad idea. But I'm no expert."

"You do give good advice, though," he said.

"Speaking of which." She opened her computer, snagged her neglected dinner, and settled in.

"Write like the wind, Helen."

Over the top of her screen, she spotted his dad watching the both of them, his brows pulled so tight they almost touched, his mouth turned down in a perfect frown.

She gave him an innocent look. "Did you want some pizza?"

His dad stood up, antsy and clearly uncomfortable. "I'm gonna go for a walk or something."

Neil turned a page in his book. "Have fun."

Helen didn't look up again from her computer, though she was tempted. After a minute, the door closed.

"I don't know how you managed that," Neil said, "but thank you. I have not had a minute to myself since he arrived."

A minute to himself. He wanted to be alone. That was a splash of cold water. "Should I go?"

"Of course not. I'm not going to eat this pizza all by myself, and I'm not sharing with my dad."

Dry humor. Familiar footing. "Your mom would probably approve of letting him go hungry."

"She'd think I was taking her side." He closed his book again, his gaze on the closed door.

"Do you think your folks will get back together this time?"

"I don't know." He leaned his head back against the top of the couch. "I want them to be happy. I also want them to leave me alone. Probably not going to get either."

She touched his arm. "I'm sorry."

"Family is complicated, right?"

"Very." She didn't see or hear from her family often. That was a complication in and of itself. She laid her head against his shoulder. He didn't object.

Helen closed her eyes, refusing to think too deeply about her shifting feelings. Leaning against him for a drawn-out moment was all the indulgence she would allow. Maybe she was a coward, but until she saw something—anything—from him that told her he felt at all the same pull, she simply couldn't risk it.

Six

HELEN WAS DIFFERENT over that next week. Neil wasn't sure what had brought on the change, but he wasn't complaining. When they were together, she sat closer to him than she used to, even leaned against him now and then. Her smile had changed to something warmer, more personal. If it turned out to all be an act put on to dupe his dad...

"You're out of cereal." Apparently, that was his dad's version of "good morning."

"I'd bet Mom has plenty at home," Neil said. "She also buys the chips you like and keeps the right amount of red meat in the fridge." All things Dad had complained about. "You would probably be happier there."

"I'll go back when your mom quits being so demanding." Dad grabbed a box of crackers out of the cupboard. "She has to be right about everything."

I should have just kept my mouth shut.

Dad shoved his hand inside the box. "Do you have any idea what that's like, living with someone who has to have everything their way all the time?"

"I'm starting to," Neil mumbled.

"It's not just your mother. That Helen is the same way."

That Helen?

"She comes here and sits wherever she wants. Eats our food. Tells me I have to turn the TV down like she lives here."

Neil was actually starting to feel a little sorry for his mom, though he knew she was every bit as unreasonable.

"You do remember that *you* don't actually live here, right? Helen has been coming by regularly since I moved in. She is allowed to sit wherever she wants, because I am okay with that. I *do* live here. It's my place and my food and my TV."

"Are you throwing me out?" Dad demanded.

Was it really so much to ask that his parents be grown-ups? Sometimes Neil felt like he was refereeing a middle-school playground brawl.

"You're my dad, and I love you. And I love Mom. I hate that you guys fight all the time, but I hate even more that you pull me into it every single time." Neil grabbed his coat. "If you aren't even going to try to make this right between the two of you, then it's time you found your own place."

"You're throwing me out?" Dad at least sounded a little less defensive.

"I'm saying you have to fix this, one way or the other. And that's not going to happen if you stay here." Neil pulled the door closed behind him.

He stood in the hallway for a long moment. *I just threw my dad out of my house.* He knew he was being reasonable, and he'd done the right thing. Why did he feel so guilty about it?

Maybe another letter to "Hey, Helen" was in order. Something along the lines of...

Hey, Helen! My parents make my life miserable, so I told my dad he couldn't live at my place anymore. On a scale of 1-10, how bad of a son am I? Like 15? 20?

No. He really had done what needed to be done. And he'd eventually figure out how to be okay with that.

The morning passed slowly. Only a couple of his calls resulted in sales, but that ratio wasn't too bad in the telemarketing world. And in only a few more weeks, he'd be done with it and could deal exclusively with fun stuff like balance sheets and payroll deductions. He'd have his apartment back by then, he hoped. And maybe he'd even have Helen as a more permanent and personal part of his life.

While he waited for class to start, he pulled up her latest Valentine's column on his phone—it had just gone live. This was the one where he knew she'd answered, among others, the question she didn't know was from him. But what had she said?

He skimmed past the marathon runner question, settling on the familiar words he'd sent only a few short weeks earlier.

Hey, Helen! I want to tell someone how I feel about her, but I don't want to ruin our friendship by making it awkward. Valentine's Day is coming up, and that would be a good time to show her. Is there any good way to do it? —Dude with a Dilemma

Dear Dude. I get this question a lot, and it's a hard one to answer. Admitting to a friend that you have deeper feelings than what has become comfortable between you two is always a risk. Always. When we have something good in our life, it's natural and normal to not want to risk losing it. Sometimes, though, protecting the status-quo means losing something. Losing a chance, an opportunity, hope, love. At least seeing if there is something there is usually a risk worth taking. You don't have to set the house on fire to find out if there's a flame. Test the waters. Move forward by degrees. Until you know for sure, you'll always wonder, and that will cast a shadow on what you have now.

Take the risk, she was saying. Move forward by degrees. See if there's something more.

He was almost certain there was more than just friendship between them, though how much more he couldn't say.

Hey, Helen!

The question hung in the back of his mind all through class and during his trip home. He found himself walking quickly past Helen's door, his mind still spinning, not ready yet to talk with her.

When he stepped inside, his dad wasn't there. That, he knew, was no guarantee that Dad was gone for good. He'd been staying there for a week, and Neil never knew when the man would be around. He might have just gone out for cereal or to a movie or something.

Neil did a quick search and didn't find a note or text or anything explaining his father's whereabouts. The mystery would resolve itself eventually. If there was one thing Neil knew about his parents, they weren't likely to exclude him from any drama.

The question of Helen was harder to sort out.

The email alert on his phone buzzed. He opened the mail app. The return address, helen@heyhelen.com, instantly set him on edge. A message from her official account. That was weird. Had she figured out that Dude With a Dilemma was actually him?

He read the message, every muscle in his body tense.

"Dear 'My Neighbor Thinks Valentine's Day is Stupid'." He breathed a sigh of relief. She was responding to his decoy question. "I don't usually answer questions directly, but I thought this one warranted it. And I hope it isn't creepy that I happen to know your email address."

Question submissions didn't ask for an email. She was writing to him on purpose because she knew he'd sent that one in.

"I have it on good authority that your neighbor doesn't have such a low opinion of Valentine's Day. She just isn't a big fan of the usual approach: generic gifts or the pressure to do the perfect thing on that one day. Perhaps she's just a hipster at heart. Pizza and hanging out on the couch are more her style. Just so you know."

Just so you know. She was telling him that she liked hanging out with him, and that on a day when people express their deeper feelings, she was in favor of being with him, even if it wasn't in a way most people would think was romantic.

He didn't know for sure that she was saying she had deeper feelings, but it was still encouraging.

Seven

IN THE YEAR and a bit since Neil had moved next door, Helen had never climbed over the dividing wall between their balconies. But sitting outside, hearing raised voices echoing out of his apartment, she decided it was time she did just that. There really wasn't time to go out and get a pizza and make her usual entrance.

She slipped over and stepped up to the edge of his sliding glass door, peering inside. He was there, standing a bit away from a man and a woman—the man Helen recognized as Neil's dad—involved in a heated exchange. His dad had left a couple of days earlier. What had brought him back? And why was his mom—she assumed the woman was his mom—there now?

Neil was closer to the patio door than the other two. She lightly knocked on the glass with her knuckle. He glanced in her direction. After a quick double-take, he pulled the door open.

"What are you doing out here?"

"I came to see if you were okay. I could hear them fighting."

He pushed out a tense breath. "I was afraid of that. The whole complex has probably heard them."

Helen eyed his parents, still going at it. They hadn't even noticed her arrival. "I thought your dad had left."

"Apparently he told Mom he'd been staying here. She decided that meant I had taken his side in whatever they're fighting about this time, and she came over to 'set the record straight.'"

"And he came to . . ."

Neil shrugged. "Make his case? I don't know. They were already fighting when they arrived. I haven't been able to make much sense of it."

His parents made her so angry. Did they not realize how they were hurting their son? Did they just not care?

"Do you think there's a nice way to tell them to leave me alone?" Neil's weary gaze returned to his parents.

"I think you've been trying the 'nice' way all your life," she said. "Looks to me like you've hit crisis mode, and it's time to be firm."

"They're my parents," he said. "I don't—They're my parents."

She touched his arm. "I know. You don't want to hurt them, even if they're hurting you."

"Maybe I should just move and not tell them where I went."

Move? That was not happening. "Or maybe you should ask 'Hey, Helen!' what to do. She's good in a crisis."

He raised an eyebrow in inquiry.

"I got this." She slipped past him and directly toward his parents.

She forced her way between them and kept moving. Their arguing paused as both watched her cross the room. She stopped at the front door, then turned and faced them fully.

"Good evening," she said calmly. "I was intrigued by your shouting. Clearly you have a lot of problems—*a lot* of problems—in fact, by now this entire apartment complex realizes that you do. Your son has been patient and loving and considerate, traits he clearly didn't learn at home. If you insist on going at each other like a couple of schoolyard bullies, you're welcome to do so in the privacy of your own home. Just don't drag Neil into it anymore. Parents who care about their children don't do that." She pulled the door open. "Your son deserves to have his home back."

"What?" his dad snapped.

"Who are you?" his mom demanded.

"Someone who cares too much about Neil to watch the two of you continue to hurt him. You have a home of your own. You can take this slugfest there."

They both turned to Neil, apparently expecting him to take their side. While the show of unity might have been encouraging under other circumstances, it was nothing short of frustrating just then. He was expected to do their bidding, no matter how much they mistreated him.

Helen didn't say a word. She kept her expression as neutral as she could manage. He had to be the one to decide how to move forward; she had simply introduced the possibility of putting an end to their manipulation.

"I love you both," he said to his parents. "I always will. But I have been your referee for too long. I spent my childhood as the rope in your tug-of-war, and I'm done. You need to go home, and you need to figure this out without pulling me into it. That's not how love in a family is supposed to work."

"Neil?" His mom sounded shocked, even a little wounded.

Please stay strong, Neil. They have to stop doing this to you.

"Go home." He spoke firm but soft. "Figure this out between the two of you."

His mom slammed her fists onto her hips. "Your dad turned you against me, didn't he?"

"I did nothing of the sort."

Quick as that, the shouting started again. How had Neil endured this growing up?

Helen spotted a purse on the coffee table. Beside it was a set of keys. Neil kept his keys on a hook by the door.

She picked up the keys and, catching Neil's eye, said, "Your dad's?"

He nodded.

She grabbed the purse as well, knowing it was most likely his mom's. She let out the shrillest whistle she could produce, grabbing the war-mongers' attention once more. With an overly sweet smile, she showed them the items she held.

Their eyes pulled wide.

With all the ability of a former softball player, she pitched the keys as far down the hallway as she could.

"What the—" Mr. MacKay took off in a run, chasing his keys.

Helen met Mrs. MacKay's glare with an unflinching one of her own. "Anything in here that wouldn't survive a similar flight down the hall?"

"You wouldn't."

Neil jumped in. "At this point, I might. Take it and go, Mom. After all these years, I deserve a little peace in my life."

His mom looked back at him. "Don't I deserve peace? I don't have any with that man."

"I know." Neil's tone was more weariness than agreement. "Maybe eventually you'll figure it all out."

She didn't say anymore. Stepping to the door, she took her purse from Helen's hand, but not without a narrow-eyed look of disapproval.

The moment his mom stepped into the hall, Helen shut the door and locked it. She turned to Neil, intending to share a moment of triumph or at least relief. But the pain in his expression pierced her through.

His shoulders dropped with a heavy sigh. "I know that needed to be done—I can't keep letting them do this—but I hate tossing them out like that."

No words of advice or reassurance sprang to mind. Helen simply moved to where he stood and slipped her arms around him. He returned the embrace, silently clinging to her.

"Love is complicated and complex," she said, "because people are complicated and complex. We know that it can be painful, so we treasure it that much more when it is kind and strong and beautiful. I am sorry that it stings now, but I hope you realize that it doesn't always hurt. That it doesn't have to."

"I know," he whispered.

She leaned against him once more, and he held her as the minutes ticked by. Neither of them spoke. Neither of them pulled away.

After a while she asked one of the many questions swirling around in her mind. "And you're not really going to move away, are you?"

"No," he said. "I will probably stop answering my door, though."

"Then I guess I'll just have to make a habit of climbing onto your balcony."

His chuckle lightened her heart, while his arms wrapped around her kept her pulse pounding. "That was the closest thing to a superhero rescue I've ever seen: Hey, Helen! courageously scales wall to restore peace to the land."

Too many men would have felt threatened by a woman "coming to the rescue." She was glad he wasn't one of them. "If *I* ever need a superhero, I hope you'll scale that wall as well."

"It's a deal."

Eight

"Test the water. Take the risk. Move forward by degrees." Neil silently repeated Helen's advice as he sat, once again, on his balcony watching her across the divider.

She had embraced him the night she'd thrown his parents out. And she'd stayed in his arms for quite a while afterward. That was more than promising. It was his turn to make the next move.

I hope you'll scale that wall as well. He knew she hadn't meant it literally, but that was how he was taking it.

His accounting book pushed aside, Neil rose from his usual spot and crossed to the dividing wall. He slung a leg over, then the next.

Helen looked up from her computer and smiled. "I get the feeling neither of us is going to use the front door anymore."

"I've come on a rescue mission," he said.

She closed her laptop. "You have?"

He nodded. "I heard a rumor that you're not a big fan of Valentine's Day."

She frowned deeply in an overblown look of contemplation. "I am pretty sure I cleared up that rumor already."

"Did you?" He sat on the edge of the patio table, facing her.

"I sent an email to the person who started it. His name was 'My Neighbor Hates Valentine's Day' or something like that."

Neil shook his head. "The names people are giving their kids these days. It's getting out of hand."

She had an amazing smile. It made her eyes twinkle and her whole face light up. "What does your rescue mission have to do with my opinions about February 14th?"

"According to my sources, you would prefer to spend the holiday hanging out and eating pizza."

Her smile drooped a little. "Kind of pathetic, huh?"

"No. Teddy bears bought on the side of the road: that's pathetic."

"Don't get me started. I could write a whole column about that." She leaned her head against her upturned hand, her elbow propped on the table. "Pizza, though. That's a great idea."

He nodded firmly and stood once more. "Pizza it is."

"Are you asking me over for Valentine's Day?" Was that hope he heard in her voice?

"I am, if you're interested." *Please be interested.*

She glanced down, and when she looked at him again there was something different in her eyes than he'd seen before, a warmth, an eagerness. "I'm interested."

His heart jumped to his throat. Somehow he managed to say, "Alright. Seven o'clock?"

She nodded.

"I'll see you then." And, because he didn't know what else to do, he hopped the wall again, grabbed his book, and retreated into his apartment.

Helen was coming for Valentine's Day. She was "interested." All he had to do was not blow it.

Nine

HELEN HAD ALWAYS been pretty chill about Valentine's Day. Sure, she had some strong opinions on the gift options and the pricing structure, but the day itself wasn't a big deal. Yet sitting in her living room on February 14th, watching the clock on her phone count down to 7:00, knowing Neil was waiting for her next door, this Valentine's Day had her totally on edge.

He'd been flirtatious when he'd extended the invitation. There'd been the smallest hint of something more than mere friendship in the way he'd interacted with her before that, too, from cozying up beside her on the couch to holding her in his arms the night of his parents' yelling match. She didn't want to lose that. Truth be told, she wanted even more of it.

She didn't know if she was glad he'd chosen to do exactly what she'd said she preferred on Valentine's Day, or if she was disappointed that he hadn't even suggested something more.

7:00 arrived. *Here I go.*

She gave herself a quick mirror check, something she didn't usually do on her way to Neil's. At his door, she paused for a quick, self-directed pep talk, took a deep breath, and knocked.

He answered, dressed in a nice button-up shirt and slacks. Maybe this was at least kind of a big deal to him. That was promising. Unless he'd had a job interview or something. That was probably it. She knew he was looking for work, now that he was almost done with his degree.

"Hey," she said, as if everything were as casual as ever.

"Hey." It was the same word, but not said in the same way.

At the very tender tone of his voice, warmth spread deep inside her. She stepped across the threshold and immediately stopped, eying the transformation with surprise. The table, tucked into the corner of the kitchen area, had been set with nice plates and napkins and a cluster of lit candles. Soft music played from somewhere. This was not pizza-and-chill-as-usual.

"I know you're not really big into Valentine's Day," he said, "but this seemed like a good compromise. Still pizza, still at my place, but with a little something more."

She looked up at him, desperate to know what he meant by "something more", but too nervous to actually ask.

"I have something for you," he said.

"Other than the pizza?" *Other than your friendship?*

He took her hand—she resisted the very strong urge to clutch it in desperation—and led her to the kitchen. He grabbed a bag from the counter and held it out to her. "I know you have very specific requirements in Valentine's Day gifs. I did read the gift-giving column, you know."

She took the bag, but didn't look inside. "I didn't mean the column as a hint."

"I know. It was a welcome challenge, and I think I've done pretty well."

Her pulse pounded in her neck. He'd taken the "Giving Gifts to That Special Someone" column as a challenge. And had a gift for her as a result. What had he chosen? Was she reading too much into this?

She peered inside the gift bag and pushed away the tissue paper. "A book?" She pulled it out. "*How to Write the Great American Novel.*"

He stepped closer. "You want to write a novel, and I want you to know that I believe in you. I'll be right there with you while you reach for that dream, if that's what you want. I just don't want you to give up on yourself."

Of all the thoughts swirling around in her mind, the only thing she managed to verbalize was, "A book."

"Hey, at least it wasn't a teddy bear from the street corner." Under his teasing tone was a note of wariness. He thought she didn't like it.

"I don't mean *this* book." She met his gaze and held it. "A book of my own. You're giving me a book of my own."

"A dream of your own," he clarified. "And I want to be part of it."

Every thought halted. Even her lungs ceased to function. It could be a gift from one friend to another. But—she tried to breathe through the thought—it could also be something much more.

"I read what you wrote in last week's column," he said, "about testing the waters and finding out if friends can be more than that."

She swallowed against the lump in her throat. "You read that?"

"I wrote it, Helen. I wrote that question."

"But . . ." She stumbled a moment. "No. You wrote the one about the neighbor and the stupid Valentine's Day?"

"I wrote that one, too, but as a decoy." He watched her closely, uncertainty heavy in his expression. "I—I had hoped you would answer 'Dude With a Dilemma' without guessing he was me."

"Then, you—" She couldn't say it out loud.

"You are the greatest friend I've ever had." He slid his hand softly down her arm. "But I want us to be more than that. I want to be a part of your whole life and your plans and your dreams."

"You do?"

"I do." He threaded his fingers through hers. "I love you, Helen. I have loved you for a very long time."

Love. Excitement and disbelief bubbled inside her. Neil loved her. He loved her.

"And you didn't even buy me a teddy bear in a balloon?"

He slipped an arm around her waist. "There's still time. If I go now, I could probably find a guy with a truck full."

"I'd rather you didn't."

He pulled her the rest of the way to him. "You don't want me to go get you a last-minute gift?"

"I don't want you to leave."

"Then don't you worry, Helen Blakely. I'm not going anywhere."

Hey, Reader.

Valentine's Day. Again. For some of you, the return of this day means flowers, chocolates, gifts of love and affection. For others, it means disappointment and frustration. For a few, this day shines a spotlight on a table set for one.

Sometimes life is the worst.

The past three years I've heard from a lot of you struggling through moments when life hits its lowest point. Issues with family, with friends, with co-workers. Issues with your past, your present, your future. While those problems and worries and struggles have been as different as the people who write to me about them, there's been a common thread, one that seems fitting to discuss on this day in particular.

Love.

Not just love in the romantic sense, but in matters of friendship, family, and basic human kindness. A kindness we should extend to ourselves, as well as those around us. Sometimes the problems I hear are about people wanting to give love, but not knowing how. Sometimes, it's people who desperately need to know they're loved, but they can't find anyone willing to offer it. Sometimes, the world is simply too cold and uncaring, and life too terribly unfair.

This Valentine's Day, accept a challenge from "Hey, Helen!" Spread the love. Be a little kinder, a little more generous, a little more forgiving, a little more loving. Let the day mean something beyond gifts and greeting cards and the expected words of adoration.

Let it mean love.

—Helen

Sarah M. Eden is the author of multiple historical romances, including the two-time Whitney Award Winner *Longing for Home* and Whitney Award finalists *Seeking Persephone* and *Courting Miss Lancaster*. Combining her obsession with history and affinity for tender love stories, Sarah loves crafting witty characters and heartfelt romances. She has twice served as the Master of Ceremonies for the LDStorymakers Writers Conference and acted as the Writer in Residence at the Northwest Writers Retreat. Sarah is represented by Pam van Hylckama Vlieg at D4EO Literary Agency.

Visit Sarah on-line:
Twitter: @SarahMEden
Facebook: Author Sarah M. Eden
Website: SarahMEden.com

Dear Timeless Romance Anthology Reader,

Thank you for reading *Valentine's Day Collection*. We hoped you loved the sweet romance novellas! Heather B. Moore, Annette Lyon, and Sarah M. Eden have been indie publishing this series since 2012 through the Mirror Press imprint. For each anthology, we carefully select three guest authors. Our goal is to offer a way for our readers to discover new, favorite authors by reading these romance novellas written exclusively for our anthologies . . . all for one great price.

If you enjoyed this anthology, please consider leaving a review. Reviews and word-of-mouth is what helps us continue this fun project. For updates and notifications of sales and giveaways, please visit our Facebook page: Timeless Romance Anthologies, or sign up for our monthly newsletter on our blog: TimelessRomanceAnthologies.blogspot.com

Also, if you're interested in becoming a regular reviewer of the anthologies and would like access to advance copies, please email Heather Moore: heather@hbmoore.com

Thank you!
The Timeless Romance Authors

More Timeless Romance Anthologies

Check out our Timeless Regency Collections!

www.ingramcontent.com/pod-product-compliance
Lightning Source LLC
LaVergne TN
LVHW021758060526
838201LV00058B/3144